Advance Praise

"*Thickafog* is insightful and beautifully written. There were so many things I liked about the novel, including the description of the island and how up-to-date the author is about all sorts of things."

— Jane Smiley, Pulitzer Prize-winning author

"*Crime and Punishment* meets *Demon Copperhead* in this fast-paced philosophical novel that had me guessing until the final pages. Is the narrator reliable? Is he truly capable of patricide? And, if so, does the father have it coming? The author's inventive use of first-person narration with omniscient point of view added to the overall mystery."

— Anna Blauveldt, author of *The Leavetaking* and *Awakening*

"*Thickafog* invited me into a community on an island off the coast of Maine, made me glad to have discovered it and, having gotten to know it and the personalities who live there, made me sad finally to leave it. Using the device of a murder mystery and set on that isolated island, which becomes a character itself, the novel does what all good mysteries should do: it reveals the humanity of its characters, with all their failures and triumphs, hatreds and redeeming love, and above all the ways a community can test and nurture and connect us to each other."

> — Wayne Karlin, author of eight novels including *A Wolf by the Ears* and *Marble Mountain*

"*Thickafog* is as much a psychological novel as a mystery, and so much of narrator Jon's voice sings. The author has skillfully created a believable world, a sense of place, with characters who are fully dimensional, as well as a suspenseful plot well-orchestrated."

> — Joyce Kornblatt, author of *The Reason for Wings* and *Mother Tongue*

THICKAFOG

An Archer Island Mystery

by Caleb Mason

Other Books by Caleb Mason

Non-Fiction

The Isles of Shoals Remembered (1992)

Fiction

(written under the pen name Don Trowden)

Normal Family (2012)

No One Ran to the Altar (2016)

All the Lies We Live (2017)

Young Again, co-authored with Valerie McKee (2022)

THICKAFOG

An Archer Island Mystery

by Caleb Mason

Copyright © Caleb Mason, 2025

All rights reserved under International and Pan-American Copyright Conventions. Published by Publerati.

This book is a work of fiction. Names, characters, businesses, organizations, places, events, and incidents are either the product of the author's imagination or are used fictitiously. Any resemblance to actual persons, living or dead, events, or locales is entirely coincidental, except where indicated by the author.

Trade Paperback ISBN: 979-8-9866178-4-8
Ebook ISBN: 979-8-9866178-5-5

Cover design by William Oleszczuk

The cover photo was taken by the author from the granite ledge on Vinalhaven island that planted the seeds for this novel.

A portion of all Publerati book sales is donated to Worldreader to help spread literacy around the globe.

"A work of art does not answer questions, it provokes them; and its essential meaning is in the tension between the contradictory answers."

— Leonard Bernstein

"So much of life, it seems to me, is determined by pure randomness."

— Sidney Poitier

"It's not the clear-sighted who rule the world. Great achievements are accomplished in a blessed, warm fog."

— Joseph Conrad

Dedicated to islanders everywhere who build unique communities of love and hope.

And to Teddy Brookings

Chapter One
August 2023

Bobby Davis's final Facebook post was "It's a great day to be alive," his words accompanied by a photograph taken from the granite shelf high above Swan's Cove, the sunrise lighting the fishing fleet below. It was a beautiful photo taken on a crisp late-August morning, the feel of autumn in the air. Jonny Morton could make out his lobster boat *Cheryl Anne* in the photo as he powered out to sea for the day, happy the fog had lifted that morning following a week of damp weather. Yes, indeed, it was a beautiful day to be alive, Jonny smiled at his teenage daughter who was guiding a string of lobster traps off the stern. Little did he know Bobby's body would be found the next morning in the brush below that same ledge by neighborhood children searching for a baseball. When Jonny heard the news at the bar, all he could do was shake his head and feel sympathy for me. When Ingrid's son Kevin heard the news, he muttered under his breath "Good riddance."

Bobby was my father, and Ingrid had been his last girlfriend—the love of his life, or so he told me the week before he died. At the time of this revelation, I was incapable of responding as I now wish I had, due to the fact we had not been emotionally open with each other since my childhood. I wish I

1

could have said how happy I was for him. Instead, as I sat in stunned silence thinking about all the women he had loved, including two wives and several affairs, I was like a computer with a full hard drive, incapable of taking in any additional data involving my old man. Afterall, he had only known Ingrid for nine months.

They met at the market shortly after I moved my father from an assisted living facility in Florida to Archer Island off the coast of Maine. Bobby had been kicked out of Woodridge Homes for unacceptable behaviors, rumors circulating he had upset a lady of some means with his unwelcome advances. When it came to my father and women, there was no good way to separate fact from fiction, so who knew for certain what had happened. I had my suspicions. At age eighty-five, he had outlived his savings and was broke. He was ineligible for Medicaid because he was functioning at a higher level than state-funded residential living facilities required. His mind was still sharp and he was able to pass the activities of daily living test; he could bathe himself, get dressed, walk without falling. As his only surviving child, I had little choice but to move him in with me on this remote island, ten miles out to sea and only reachable by ferry. The ferries didn't run past 3:15 in the winter, which meant coming and going was difficult, especially on stormy days when some or all boats were cancelled. Not the best arrangement for an elderly person, given the limited medical services on the island, but it was the only remaining option. My sister Edith had died fifteen years ago in a car accident, and my brother Jonas had committed suicide. So, Bobby was all mine.

Ingrid Backlund was her name, and although reclusive, she could be found on occasion at the town library reading a new poetry collection, or at the Saturday morning flea market buying dahlias and daisies. Years ago, she had hired me to build a shed at her grand John Calvin Stevens home overlooking Hopkins Cove. One sees almost everyone on an island of 1,200 inhabitants, and Ingrid was difficult to miss, her eyes an unusual greenish-gray color like the quarried granite of the island. When a gust of wind would send strands of silver hair across her face, my father would remark that she looked like an Icelandic knit sweater. Her freckles had melded into age spots, adding a weathered gravitas to her Nordic beauty, a beauty that had broken the hearts of two previous husbands, or so my father told me. He liked to joke that she was descended from Viking warrior queens, and she would usually laugh at this.

The old man had taken the ferry out to live with me eight years after the death of his second wife, who was not my mother. He was happier to see me than I had anticipated, following his assisted living captivity, for which he blamed me. I was the responsible adult who had to enforce the tough love required to keep him there against his will. It seems none of us is good at objectively evaluating our situation in life, and my father was no exception. Following a fall in the shower and an extended stay in rehab, he no longer could live alone in his condo in Sarasota, so I had to find him a suitable place. He hated Woodridge Homes from the start, missed his freedom and privacy, and tried to escape more than once. He was what they call an elopement risk, and it was a huge relief when he begrudgingly settled in after six months. But when his money ran out, he had to leave. Money. Bad behavior. Probably a bit of both.

My island home is perched high above a former quarry, facing southeast and looking out over the main harbor with panoramic vistas best viewed from my wrap-around porch. I bought the home thirty years ago from a summer family that no longer could make the long trip from North Carolina to ten miles off the coast of Maine. For several years their house sat vacant, the roof leaking and shingle siding facing the ocean mostly turned to dust. Many of the windows were broken and covered with blue tarps that the locals put up to keep their children from getting hurt playing inside. There are many neglected old homes out here, mostly summer homes that pass down through generations until they arrive at a young generation not interested or able to tackle the expenses of maintaining an island home. I went to the Town Hall one snowy January morning and found the property owner's name and phone number. No taxes had been paid in five years so the town was eager to settle this matter with the heirs. I called the owners who were happy to unload the place at what I felt was a fair price, and now decades later, with the many updates I've made, the house is worth a lot of money given its prime location.

Most mornings, weather permitting, I would sit on the

wrap-around porch overlooking the harbor and sip my hot coffee, enjoying the sounds of lobster boats humming out to sea. On mornings "thickafog," (a favorite expression of the locals), the blast of the ferry's horn in the harbor would send seagulls scattering. It was exactly the life I wanted. Quiet. Removed from mainland stresses. Not at all like life now.

With five bedrooms and me living alone, I had plenty of space for my father. But let's not pretend I was eager to have him living with me. Bobby had been a shitty father and not a good husband to my mother or stepmother, nor to the other lovers who found him devilishly handsome, but almost always unable to commit. I had modelled much of my adulthood on *not* being like him, his usefulness as a negative role model only carrying me so far as I made mistakes similar to his, especially my battles with drinking, with all the starting and stopping, which I now think was my unfortunate inheritance, but as I've learned lately, apparently from my mother's side and not his.

But, in fairness, his brief time with Ingrid was different from previous relationships, particularly in the way he cared for her as her memory faded. Either he changed on his own or more likely she changed him through the power of their love. What I believe now that Bobby is dead, is that his last girlfriend was indeed the love of his life. I find it sad that neither my mother nor stepmother were true loves, apparently just "suitable matches," as my sister used to say. But not suitable enough to last long. How might my life have turned out otherwise had Ingrid been my mother? Would I have grown up in a loving home with two parents there for me, unlike what happened? But I have no reason to complain. Life is hard on everyone.

As I think back across this year of upheaval and tragic events, I find myself stuck on an endless carousel of belief and disbelief. Is there some divine force guiding our lives and the circumstances that shape us? Some genius writer and orchestrator constantly testing and challenging us to realize that bad fortune will eventually shape us in positive ways? Understanding only attainable in our final scenes? Here on earth as in heaven? Or is everything just a series of random events strung haphazardly together?

Chapter Two
November 2022

Ingrid Backlund, born at the end of the Great Depression and before the start of the Second World War, was the granddaughter of a Swedish stonecutter who had emigrated to quarry granite back in the nineteenth century. Ingrid had attended the small public school, with ten children per grade, and left the island for an extended period just once in her life, to attend Wellesley College. She is the only island resident ever to be accepted by Wellesley. "She's a true one of a kind," my father said after his first few weeks getting to know her. "Smartest woman I've known, and not just in the ways of books, but in the more important ways of nature, music, and intuition."

Ingrid saw Bobby for the first time at the small market in town on a late-November day, nine months before he would meet his untimely demise in August. Bobby stood out among the others at the market, clearly not one of the lingering summer residents nor one of the locals—this elderly gentleman dressed in a tweed blazer with elbow patches, pink button-down shirt with plaid tie, and forest green woolen pants. No one wore neckties on the island unless there was a funeral, and Ingrid was always among the first to know when someone was airlifted for medical care or, worse, had died. There were no funerals now, thank goodness. This new man in town looked lost as he scanned his shopping list, staring blankly at the shelf in front of him. The aisles were narrow and Ingrid did not want to disturb him, so waited patiently until he moved on, which he did not.

"Do you need help finding something?" she finally asked.

He looked up through watery blue eyes, silver hair tucked beneath a black woolen hat. "Yes, I suppose I do. I'm new in town and unfamiliar with this market. My son has asked me to get sardines in lemon and oil, but all I see are these ones packed in oil."

She ducked her head to search in the open space on the middle shelf. "It could be they have been pushed to the rear. Or more probably they are out of stock. I heard yesterday's freight truck couldn't make it over due to rough seas."

"I thought the shelves looked bare. Is there no other market in town?"

"This is it. One learns to make do with what we can get out here, which I understand is not the case on the mainland."

"I see. Well sardines in oil it will have to be then."

She said: "Truth be told, this market has an exceptional selection given it is so small. The owners go out of their way to get pretty much anything customers ask for. Some people have food sent over from Hannaford Supermarkets, but it's not really necessary."

"That's good to hear," he said. "I noticed the wine and cheese selection is excellent."

She smiled and he smiled back. "Who might your son be?" she asked.

"Jonathan Davis. Do you know him?"

She laughed a disproportionately boisterous laugh for such a simple declaration. "After a lifetime of living out here there aren't many people I don't know. I've hired your son to do small fix-it jobs for me. He's an excellent carpenter."

"Thanks, I like to think he's a good boy. He's taken me in to live with him after I was kicked out of assisted living in Florida. I feel badly imposing upon Jon, but doubt I'll be around for long."

"Going somewhere?" she asked.

"Aren't we all?"

"Ah, I see. I'm a bit slow on the uptake these days." She glanced off into the distance out through the gray towards the waterfront, where seagulls perched atop carved granite pillars facing the ocean. There were only a handful of cars in the parking lot across the street. She turned back to him. "My name's Ingrid Backlund, welcome to the island. Getting kicked out of assisted living, there must be a story there," she reached out to shake his hand and held on longer than normal, rubbing her thumb along the top of his hand.

He introduced himself. "Robert Davis, a pleasure to meet you. Friends call me Bobby."

She smiled a vacant smile. "Robert. A lovely name. I'm Ingrid."

"Yes, I know."

"You do?" She looked puzzled. "Have we met before?" He realized she must suffer from cognitive impairment, and knew from experience to let it go.

"Oh, just call me a great mystic."

"Isn't that something," she touched his forearm, patting him affectionately. "What a beautiful sportcoat, how I love the feel of real wool." He didn't stop her as he gazed into her greenish-gray eyes, noticing how happy touching him seemed to make her.

"Do you live alone?" he asked. The forwardness of his question caused Ingrid to take a step back.

"God, no! I've got the birds and flowers, my poetry books . . . the sea, the wind."

"No man, then?"

"Certainly not. Who needs them? I value my freedom too much to be held back by a needy man. Been there. Done that."

He laughed.

She continued. "I mean . . . don't get me wrong, men come in handy when you need the snow shoveled or a heavy box lifted."

"Ah, I see. We make good pack mules."

"Oh, stop."

"Well, that's certainly the way you make it sound. I suppose that doesn't bode well for me, as I can't lift much of anything anymore."

There was a vivacious charm about this woman that captivated Robert. She possessed a warmth that radiated from her eyes, spreading across her face like an advancing sunrise. Warmth and wisdom were the words that came to mind, as he stood awkwardly with her, neither speaking, neither moving on. In an effort to make small talk, Robert filled the silence with: "It must be difficult being deprived of so much on an island like this. Don't you miss Starbucks? Target? The movies, the theatre?"

"I do at times," she said, "but that's partly the point of living here."

"I don't follow."

"It's precisely because we don't have everything available to us *all the time* that we truly appreciate those mainland activities when we visit family and friends over there. But while on the island, as you will come to learn, it's the simple pleasures that bring us back to our true selves. Life here is real in ways I cannot fully explain. We have no shopping malls, no gated communities. How I abhor the very idea of those segregated enclaves. We live among each other and look out for one another. Rich next to poor. Summer resident next to year-round. The children run free, the way I did as I child. It's the authenticity of island life that is so appealing. There is nothing fake about life here and so much of mainland living seems contrived, artificial, unnecessary."

Robert took this in as the memory of the chocolate croissant at the French bakery back in his childhood neighborhood

11

came to mind. He wasn't at all sure he would be able to live in such an isolated place, deprived of so many of life's pleasures. It was as if she could read his mind as she said: "You'll see. It takes some time for newcomers to settle in to the slow life here but give it time and I bet you'll come to love it. Especially our summers, when the low-floating fog whispers its way into the summer sunshine, seagulls and wild roses everywhere."

A man with a scarred face raced around the corner. "There you are," his look combined annoyance with relief. "Don't go wandering off like that, Mom."

"Kevin, I'd like you to meet someone. He's new to the island." There was an awkward pause while Robert waited for her to introduce him by name. When it became obvious this was not going to happen, he broke the silence. "I'm Robert, nice to meet you, Kevin."

Kevin looked warily at the old man, a lifelong distrust of people *from away* evident in his expression. He reeked of marijuana and kept twitching his head to the right and sniffling in a compulsive paranoid way. Bobby figured Kevin must be at least six-foot-four, a muscular man like other multi-generational lobstermen who work long hours. Kevin ignored him, clearly unimpressed, and took his mother by the arm. "C'mon, let's get this ovah with. I ain't got all fuckin' day to waste at this stupid stow-ah."

Ingrid looked down, embarrassed by her son's language. Kevin nudged her toward a long line at the only cash register, the high school checkout girl off restocking shelves instead of tending to customers. Robert chuckled in the realization this was evidently what happened when there was no competition, capitalism broken on an island of limited options. Eventually a purple-haired girl with a nose ring—a wry smile overspreading her pimply face—returned to the register and took her sweet time sliding the items through the scanner. Robert stood in line with his tin of sardines, directly behind Kevin, who lost his temper and threw their few items off to the side yelling: "What the hell is wrong with you Crystal! For fuck's sake, let's get outta he-ah, Mom. We don't need any of this shit anyhow. I'll shop at Hannafids when I'm ovah there on Friday and get some actual edible food." Ingrid shot Robert a resigned smile as she hurried to catch up to her son, who was already outside. Robert watched them through the pane glass window, while Crystal muttered under her breath *asshole* and maintained her indifferent snail's pace as her captives waited patiently.

Chapter Three
August 2023

I was asleep when my cell phone rang. I ignored the call, assuming it was a spammer. I had been dreaming about my mother but could not recall the details as I heard the ping of a voicemail. Like Pavlov's dog, the sound brought me back into partial consciousness, and I checked to see who it was. "Hello Jon, this is Walt Wentworth. Call me back as soon as you get this. I'm afraid there's been an accident involving your father."

I sat up on the sofa and rubbed my hand through my hair. The dream had exhausted me. I had been searching for my mother, but when I called to her no words came out. She was in a sunny kitchen with a man I didn't recognize. She was a young woman. They were laughing and having a good time. I was in the dark— I think it was raining on me even though I was inside, perhaps in a crib, details of the dream slipping away into my subconscious. I don't know, but this recurring dream was apparently trying to tell me something important. I felt oddly outside myself, still not convinced I was awake. I returned Walt's call and he picked up on the first ring.

"Jon, I have some terrible news. Boys playing baseball in the quarry this morning found Bobby's body. It looks like he might have jumped to his death."

"Shit," I mumbled.

"Can you get down here before the police arrive?"

"I'll be down in a few."

I had passed out the night before and was wearing the same shorts and T-shirt I had been wearing for three straight days. My clothes needed to be washed, smelling of cigarette smoke from the bar. I stumbled to the bathroom and splashed water on my face. My eyes were bloodshot and I needed a shower, but there was no time for that. I returned to the living room and picked up the beer cans strewn about the floor, depositing them in the returnables bag hanging from the hook in the entryway. The fog had rolled in last night and was unlikely to break until midday. I walked out front past the honking of the neighbor's chickens—*twhack, twhack, twhack*—they seemed to be mocking me as I climbed into my Chevy Silverado to make the short drive down the hill to the quarry pit, where I saw Walt and a small crowd of curious onlookers gathering.

"Jon, over here," Walt waved to me as I stepped from the pickup.

"Sorry . . . it took me a while to get here. I was asleep when you called."

Walt placed his right hand on my shoulder. "Hey, Jon. It looks like he jumped. Was Bobby depressed?"

I hesitated for a moment. "I suppose he was. Can't say I'm completely surprised. He and Kevin got into a heated argument yesterday, and Kevin threatened to kill him if he ever came near his mother again. You know what a hothead Kevin can be, always up for a fight."

"Hmm . . . that's not good." Walt was one of two EMTs on the island, as well as a lobsterman and volunteer fireman. A good man I had known since high school. He glanced off through the fog and said: "The medical examiner and state police are coming over in the Coast Guard cruiser. They should be here soon. Timmy Tetreault is on his way over from Dunbar Island. In fact, I can hear that knucklehead coming now."

I knew Timmy Tetreault. Most everyone on the island did. He had grown up here, living with his mother. His parents had divorced back when Timmy was in elementary school and his father now lived on the mainland where he was a bigwig with the state police. Timmy was a good kid but a bit slow, with some sort of learning disability that made him the butt of jokes in high school. It was always difficult to find someone willing to relocate to the island to serve as island police. The position had been vacant for eighteen months before Timmy finally passed his state tests and agreed to be based on Dunbar Island, just a short motor boat ride away across from Archer Island. Everyone knew he would not have gotten the job without the influence of his father.

Timmy sped to the scene with his siren blaring, a sound not often heard out here, and unnecessary for this situation. His police cruiser skidded in front of us. A pudgy boy with a bowl haircut approached through the thick fog. "Hey, Mr. Wentworth, what do we have here?"

"Hey, Timmy. Not sure but it looks like a possible suicide," Walt said. "I'm afraid it's Jon's dad."

Timmy glanced down at his feet and mumbled, "Sorry, Mr. Davis."

Walt continued: "I waited for you to get here before doing anything other than call Jon and the mainland authorities, who are on their way."

"Let's have a look," Timmy led Walt to where my father's body lay in the dust of the quarry floor.

I saw Becky Barton standing in the small crowd off to the side, tears in her eyes as she walked over to hug me. "Jon, I'm so sorry. We grew to truly enjoy Bobby. How could this be happening?"

"I don't know. Maybe he slipped and fell. But he was depressed yesterday, so who knows? I told him to stop coming to the overlook but he loves the panoramic views of the harbor and islands. There's no way to tell that stubborn man much of anything these days." I heard myself use the present tense, as if Bobby were still alive.

Becky said: "Geez, wouldn't have been able to see much of anything in that pea soup fog last night."

"I know, but he liked going for walks and listening to the fog horns."

Bobby had been on the island for just nine months, yet in his own gregarious way had become popular with many locals who got a kick out of his sense of humor. He had moved in with

Ingrid over the winter and taken care of her as she increasingly lost her independence.

Becky's husband Hank stood staring at the ground, not sure what to say. "Let me know if there's anything we can do to help. Anything at all."

"Thanks, man."

I watched as Timmy and Walt stooped over my father's body. Timmy rolled him onto his side so he could see the back of his skull. A trickle of blood oozed out and he got up and rushed off to the side of the brush where he threw up. Walt rolled Bobby onto his back so the wound was hidden.

"That's one nasty wound," Timmy returned to the scene, wiping the sleeve of his beige police uniform across his mouth.

"Sure you're up for this, kid?" Walt asked in a teasing tone, enjoying seeing this boy he had known for years attempting to become a man. He figured this was the first serious situation he had encountered. Walt had dealt with many injuries over the years and had pretty much seen it all. The worst of these was when his good friend Jamus Warren washed ashore dead after getting tangled up in his fishing lines.

Timmy didn't much like Walt's superior tone and overcompensated by attempting to take control of the scene instead of waiting for the state authorities to arrive. He searched for signs of blood in the adjacent brush. Not finding anything, he asked me to go with him up to the cliff to look around. I rode in his cruiser up to the overlook where we searched the area surrounding the granite shelf but saw nothing unusual. By the time we got down the hill to my father's body, the medical examiner and state police officer had arrived from the mainland. They had cordoned off the area with yellow crime scene tape.

The state cop was perched over the body with the medical examiner. He turned to look back at me. "Are you his son?"

"I am."

"Would you mind coming over here to positively ID him?"

I ducked beneath the yellow tape and approached my father's body lying there spreadeagled on his back, surrounded by thick brush and tossed-off granite boulders from what had once been a prosperous quarry.

"That's him," I gazed at the old man lying there with a blissful look on his face, lips curled up into a hint of a smile. His eyes were shut. I could make out the blood oozing from the back of his skull. Even though the old man had been mostly dead to me for many years, seeing him *actually dead* left an empty pit in my stomach. Bobby was gone. Forever. Gone.

The state cop called out to Tetreault. "Do I know you?"

"No sir. I just started covering the island last month. Tim Tetreault, sir."

"Were you the first one on the scene?"

"No, Walt was."

Walt walked over. "Hi, I'm Walt Wentworth, the island's lead EMT."

The state cop looked annoyed. "What's the story with all these footprints I see around the body?"

"Those are ours," Tetreault said.

"What the hell are you doing walking around without protective gloves and shoe coverings? For Chrissakes, just stand off to the side while we handle this."

The medical examiner was a skinny man, holding a black valise, and looked more like a Bible salesman than a medical examiner. "Look he-huh," he turned to the state cop. "There's a pretty good wound on the back of his head that I guess could have come from his fall, but maybe not. Why don't you look around while I snap some photos and get him bagged up."

The officer investigated the surrounding brush. He and the medical examiner wore special crime scene gear to avoid leaving marks of their own. The officer returned: "I don't see any signs of blood on these boulders, which judging from the head wound could have caused that kind of gash if he lost his balance and fell. Or jumped."

The medical examiner rose from his kneeling position on the quarry floor. "I'd like everyone to let us get the body bagged up and over to Oceanside for an autopsy. Back away, folks."

They zipped up my father into the body bag and loaded him into the ambulance for transport to the harbor, where the Coast Guard cruiser was docked. The medical examiner went onboard with the body while the officer stayed back, asking Walt and me to show him how to get up to the ledge. We walked in silence from the harbor up High Street and left onto Hilltop Road, then down to the overlook. Timmy Tetreault and a small group of locals followed us to the ledge.

"Let me look around up here," the state cop gestured for us to stand back. He was an officious older man with a buzzcut who had most likely been on the police force for decades. The ground was wet from the fog, a pervasive gray enveloping us that made it difficult to tell where the ledge ended and the steep cliff began. The officer slipped and stumbled on the ledge.

Tetreault came over to give him a hand. As the cop was lifting himself up, he pointed to the granite shelf he was standing on and said: "Looks like there's blood all over the place right here."

I walked close enough to see. "Nah, that's not blood. That's graffiti from the neighborhood kids who play up here. It's just red spray paint. I've seen them out here doing it."

The officer bent down for a closer look at the ledge. "Hmm . . . I see what you mean. Looks like Annie loves Stanley."

"Yup, two neighborhood kids I see playing over here a lot."

"You live nearby?" he asked.

"I do. In that shingled house right over there."

"Did you see anything unusual last night?"

"Nope."

Walt chimed in. "It was thickafog last night, couldn't rightly see your own hand in front of your face."

The cop nodded and turned back to Jon. "Was your father living with you?"

"No . . . mostly with Ingrid Backlund."

"Who's she?"

"Friend of his. Friend of mine, too. Nice lady."

"So . . . your father must have been with you last night if he jumped from here, right?"

I paused, trying to piece together the events of the previous night. I had been drunk. "Yes, he came over in the evening and then went back to Ingrid's. Or so I thought."

"Where does she live?"

"Way up island, about twenty minutes from here."

"When did you last see your father?"

"Around five or six o'clock, I think."

"How'd he seem?"

"Upset."

"Why?"

"Ingrid's son Kevin didn't like my father living with her and confronted him about it yesterday afternoon. Kevin has been a douchebag to my father. He's always been a douchebag."

The cop looked cold, shivering in the dampness. "Okay, I need you all to step back so Tetreault and I can take a look around without you breathing down our necks." The two cops spread out, tromping through the thick brush off to the side of the ledge. Tetreault stepped down in front of the ledge, careful not to slip. A few minutes later he emerged holding something he had wrapped in clear plastic. I was too far away to see what it was but it looked like a stone.

He showed what he had found to the other cop. "Do you think this looks like red paint?"

"Nah, looks like blood to me," he placed the stone in a sealed crime bag. "We need to get this down to the boat quickly so the medical examiner can dust for prints."

They turned to leave.

I hung back with Walt.

"Who in God's name would want to kill your father?" Walt asked.

I stood there kicking small stones at my feet. "I think I can take a pretty good guess."

Chapter Four
November & December 2022

I was fixing supper when Bobby came back from the market with the can of sardines. He was in high spirits, after successfully driving the short distance to town on his own. My father's license had been revoked in Florida the year before last, but I agreed to let him drive on the island given it is so easy to get around. Bobby had been living with me for just a few days and we were getting accustomed to having each other underfoot. I had just stoked the old pot belly woodstove in the center of my open floorplan downstairs when he walked through the door.

"Successful trip?" I asked.

"More than," he was animated. "I met this lovely lady at the market who helped me find these sardines. Sorry they aren't exactly what you asked for, but I hope they'll do."

I took the can from my father and added the sardines to the spaghetti sauce I was preparing. I added capers and black olives, and turned the heat down low since we'd be eating later. "Settle in, Dad. Enjoy the fire."

"Could I inconvenience you for a glass of wine?" he pulled up an old needlepointed chair I found at the bargain barn last year. The needlework was of a puffin, a bright and cheerful chair I was happy to add to the mishmash of old furniture in my house.

"No inconvenience at all. What would you like?"

"A cabernet if you have some."

I had stopped drinking four years ago in an effort to clean up my act to appease my girlfriend of the time, who made me choose between her and drinking. But being sober was not enough to keep her here, as she moved to Virginia to take a medical assistant's job in Richmond. I missed her very much but was grateful she helped me stop drinking.

"I have this bottle of Zinfandel. Will that do?"

"Sure."

I poured him a glass and helped myself to a non-alcoholic beer. We sat together in front of the fire listening to the crackling wood and occasional moaning of the metal as the temperature rose inside the stove.

"This is very nice," Bobby heaved a sigh.

"Tell me about this lovely lady you say you met in town."

"Her name is Ingrid Backlund and she told me you've done some work for her."

"I have. She's known locally as the Island Queen, one of the old-timers who pass along forgotten island history. I believe she is third or fourth generation, not sure."

"I'd love to get to know her better. Do you think that can be arranged somehow? Maybe a party?"

I felt irritation rising in the pit of my stomach. "Don't you think you're a bit old to be chasing women?"

He looked startled. "No . . . not at all. I'm not chasing women, as you say. Just looking for companionship and some fun. Growing old isn't a walk in the park."

I had been around this track with my old man many times in the past but decided to let it go this time. "Well, there is a church supper next Thursday. It's a fundraiser for work to be done to the church's granite steps. I doubt she'll be there, though. From what I gather, she's mostly living up at her house with help from her granddaughter Susan."

"That's too bad. So, she doesn't get out much? I can relate to that. I'm so relieved to be free of that old folks' home in Florida."

"It wasn't an old folks' home. It was a very nice assisted living facility with plenty of activities and socialization. It took a lot of work on my part to find a suitable place for you after your rehab stint. That place was good for you." It irritated me that my father never thanked me for anything, how he simply took what I had to give as if I had nothing better to do with my time or money.

"Good for me . . . sure . . . whatever you say."

"If you don't mind me asking, what exactly did you do to get thrown out?" This had been nagging at me for weeks and no honest answer had been forthcoming from the assisted living facility, undoubtedly for legal reasons, or from my father, who seemed to be simultaneously relieved and embarrassed.

He took a sip from his wine glass and said: "I tried to break out with a woman friend."

"You and your woman friends."

"What can I say. They like me and I like them."

"Isn't eighty-five a little late for hooking up?"

He laughed. "It's not hooking up. Her name was Doris Epstein and we had many common interests, including the old music, which we listened to whenever possible. She was from Illinois and had been a professor at the university there. A real smart bridge player, too."

"So . . . how did you get caught?"

"Once they didn't know where we were, they had to call the police. It's their legal responsibility. We were picked up at a blues club in Sarasota, about a mile from the facility. Then they took us to the hospital for psych evaluations, also apparently a requirement."

"Jesus," I got up to add another log to the top-loading stove.

"They released us under the care of the facility with promises not to run off again. In truth, I suspect this happens more than we know. The staff at the facility keeps it quiet, so we settled back in, but then were informed we had to find a new place with tighter restrictions. You know, the ones where you must be let out by staff. Locked doors."

"I guess that's when they phoned me," I took a belt of my non-alcoholic beer.

"And . . . now here I am!" he exclaimed. "And happy to be here with you, Jon."

I found myself unable to reciprocate the sentiment. There was a knock at the door and I got up to see who it was. My good friend Freddy Ames was standing there holding a six-pack of Bud Light. "Hey, bub, come on in."

"Hope I'm not interrupting," he saw my father sitting in front of the fire.

"Not at all. Glad you stopped by. Want me to put those in the fridge?"

Freddy knew I was a recovering alcoholic but tended to forget given all the hard drinking common to the island. Island drinking was as routine as breathing air. It starts young, with high school boys drinking and speeding in pickup trucks, leaving tire marks along the winding island roads like animals marking territory. I handed him a can of Bud Light and put the rest in the refrigerator.

"Thanks, Jon. This must be your father."

Bobby got up slowly from his chair, wobbled slightly, and shook Freddy's hand. "Nice to meet you," he said and then sat back down. Always the gentleman, I thought, rising when someone enters a room. Especially a lady. As far as I could tell, no one did that anymore.

Freddy pulled up a chair to join us. "How long have you been on the island, sir?"

"Please, call me Bobby. Just since Thursday."

"Well, you've come at a good time what with the holidays and all. The town knows how to do up the lights real good and there are fun activities. After that, once we get into January, the entire place is dead. Just the bar stays open and even that closes for the entire month of March."

"Sounds like I better make some friends," Bobby said. The old man had led an active social life, traveling for business as a sales executive, and I'm sure had many opportunities to be unfaithful. What I remember most from my childhood is being home with my mother and siblings, Bobby off somewhere unknown. I felt at times like my mother was a single parent, which she was for the most part.

"Might you know Ingrid Backlund?" Bobby asked.

"Sure. We're related. Most everyone on the island is."

"How so?"

"Through Ingrid's sister, Jen, who died many years ago. Jen's daughter Alice died from a quick hittin' cancer ten years ago, or thereabouts. Alice was too young, a real shame. Left behind three boys. Worked at the fisherman's co-op handlin' the finances."

"I'm sorry to hear that," Bobby said. "Did she die on the island?"

"She did, in part thanks to my friend Donna Littlejohn. Donna works at the ferry terminal and was a lifesaver gettin' Alice over and back for all her chemo appointments so Alice could spend her final days with family here."

"I imagine working at the ferry is a tough job."

"Understatement," Freddy laughed. "Pay is not great for one thing. Difficult to hire crew nowadays, which means many boats get cancelled. Other islands are always taking the new boat that was built for us. You've got summer people pissed at you for how difficult it is gettin' a line number off the island in July and August, and then in the winter you've got the locals pissed at you because the last boat goes at 3:15, which makes it hard gettin' back from doctor's appointments. The locals pretty much think the ferry captain is a wuss, not able to pilot the ferry in the dark, when the older generation did it no trouble. But Donna is good at her job. A nice lady who deals with a lot of bullshit best as anyone can. Doesn't take guff from no one."

Bobby sipped his drink. "So . . . do you see much of Ingrid?"

I didn't like where this was heading, as the last thing I wanted was for my father to get involved with another woman. My mother, his first wife, was far away in El Segundo, California, and I only saw her once or twice a year. My stepmother had relocated to Texas, before dying from sudden cardiac arrest at the age of fifty-five, and had avoided Bobby after she divorced him, returning his unopened Christmas cards until he finally stopped sending them. My old man had been unfaithful to both wives, with many affairs, which as he grew older with less of a filter he insisted on telling me about, something that made me very uncomfortable. For one thing, I could never be certain if he was telling the truth or living in an increasingly delusional world of self-aggrandizement.

Freddy drained his beer and I offered him another, which he gladly accepted.

Bobby continued. "I met Ingrid at the market just now. What a lovely lady."

"Yup," Freddy pulled open the tab of the beer can, making a distinctive sound my muscle memory associated with drinking to excess.

My father persisted in the way a man short on time is apt to do. "I'm hoping I can see her again. Got any ideas on how to make that happen?"

"Dad, please, let it go. You're too old for any more romance."

"Being old doesn't mean I can't have lady friends."

Freddy saw I was eager to put an end to this and tried to help. "Well, here's the thing, Bobby. Ingrid hasn't told many people this, but she was recently diagnosed with vascular dementia, and her son Kevin is waiting for an opening at the Eldercare Center. She's living all alone in that rambling house of hers up island, and can't be doing that for much longer."

My father swept this aside. "I gather she has some memory issues. Who doesn't at our age?"

"True," Freddy laughed, glancing at me. "I'm struggling with it a bit myself these days. I suppose she'll be at the tree lighting ceremony on Saturday. I doubt she'd miss that for the world as Ingrid likes to go with her granddaughter and great-grandkids."

And so that became the plan. The Christmas tree lighting on the first Saturday in December always brings out a large crowd of locals, and I agreed to take Bobby. Snow was falling as we drove up Main Street, Christmas lights festooned around power poles, storefront windows alight as the few merchants were open, counting on holiday sales to get them through the winter. I parked in front of the old Carnegie library across the way. We walked toward the bandstand in the town common, where families with small children had already gathered around the tall spruce tree. Children were running around with dayglo lights in one hand and hot chocolate drinks in the other. The local choir was singing Christmas carols on the bandstand. The manger was aglow in front of the tree, baby Jesus with mother Mary.

My father spotted Ingrid at the edge of the crowd with a couple and two small children. They were standing next to the old oxen-drawn galamander, used back in the day for hauling large granite stones to the waterfront and onto ships heading for New York.

"Ingrid, it's so nice to see you again," Bobby approached. She paused for several seconds and then remembered him from the market.

"Ah, it's you. The handsome man kicked out of assisted living."

He held her outstretched hand while the woman with Ingrid waited to be introduced. Ingrid paused, searching for his name but was unable to retrieve it. She withdrew her hand from Bobby's and said: "Please forgive me, I'm terrible at remembering names. Handsome faces, on the other hand, I never forget."

"That makes two of us," my father said cheerily, feeling more confident there was a spark between them. "It's Robert but friends call me Bobby. And who might these two adorable children be?"

"Svea and Logan, my great-grandchildren. This is their mother—my granddaughter Susan, and her husband Travis."

"Nice to meet you," Susan extended her mittened hand. Her eyes were the same greenish-gray as her grandmother's. Travis slipped away to chat with a friend.

"And you as well," Bobby replied.

"It's good to see you again, Ingrid," I said. "Are you still living in your beautiful home?"

"I am, thanks to Susan who has been keeping an eye out for me, along with my son Kevin."

Susan seized this opportunity to restate what had been top of mind for several months. "You really should not be living in that big house anymore, Grandma. Kevin is right. You're bound to take a tumble down that long staircase and we all know what that will lead to. I wish you'd agree to move into the Eldercare Center where your friends Barb and Janice are eager to see you.

33

You'd be much happier there, as opposed to living isolated halfway up the island."

Ingrid dismissed this. "I'm fine, thanks all the same, and want to live where I belong in the home your great-grandfather built. All my books and treasures are there. My memories." She turned toward Bobby and touched him on the forearm of his gray woolen overcoat. "My grandfather was one of the first Swedish stonecutters on this island. You might not know this, but our pink granite was highly valued by architects working in New York, Philadelphia, and elsewhere, and those were boom times for the island. Well before lobstering became the primary industry. He was a tall strong man and I have great memories of him when I was a little girl. He would sit in front of the Stowell Granite Company smoking his pipe, which gave off the most memorable smell."

"How delightful," Bobby smiled.

"He would just sit there and smoke his pipe," she repeated.

"He knows that, Grandma. You just said it," Susan looked off impatiently as her children joined a group of friends waiting for the tree lighting to commence.

Ingrid continued undeterred. "My grandfather and father ended up buying the company with a group of investors out of Philadelphia, and then with time, were able to buy them out."

Bobby gazed down the hill toward town where he saw a couple emerge from the bar, backlit by a street lamp casting long yellowish shadows through the lightly falling snow. They were arguing, the man pushing the woman away, she shoving him back so hard that he stumbled off the curb and onto the street. They looked drunk. There were other young people in front of the bar drinking and smoking. The woman charged off for her Ford pickup truck cursing over her shoulder as she jumped in and sped off. The truck raced up the hill where all the people were assembled awaiting the tree lighting. She sped by, dangerously fast with so many children running around.

Susan yelled after her: "Slow the fuck down, Hayley!"

The woman flipped her the bird as she sped by, tossing an empty beer can out the window.

"What was that all about?" Bobby asked.

Susan's face flushed with anger as she waved to her children to move closer. "That bitch needs to leave the island and stay the hell away. She's always coming and going bringing drugs with her. Just when I think she's gone for good she shows up again and shacks up with some lowlife she's found on the mainland. She got my friend Riley hooked on Oxy and now he's a hot mess, living on the mainland up north trying to get sober."

"Are there a lot of drugs out here?" Bobby asked.

"More than there should be," Susan replied. "Mostly transients. Bad apples. Not at all representative of our loving and supportive community. They bring that crap over here and get our vulnerable ones addicted. It's especially bad now with fentanyl mixed in with Oxy and heroin."

I knew all about this. There were drugs everywhere in America and the island was no exception. The difference was you truly noticed every single person who ventured out to the island, given the population is so low. Archer Island is a microcosm of the larger world; we have good people and bad people. Good people who mess up and do bad things on occasion. On the mainland, they easily get lost within the larger population, but out here every person is conspicuous. I should know. Back when I was drinking heavily, I did dumb things, like smash my pickup into the neighborhood mailboxes after a night of hard drinking. I was blind drunk and blacked out in my truck unaware of the damage I had done until I saw it the next morning. But there were no serious consequences. No police report. Locals don't report locals is the unspoken law. Oh, the neighbors knew and were angry at me as they repaired their mailboxes and I pretended to be innocent despite the dent on my pickup's bumper. This was around the first time I cleaned up my act. And, as you know, that wasn't the last time. To be honest, which I'm working on being more often, I was also concerned that I could become addicted to OxyContin. I had hurt my back after falling from a ladder at a job site, and the doctor prescribed this new miracle drug that promised to take away my pain, which it did, only to replace it with a worse kind of pain, an addictive pain that threatened to ruin my life and relationships. So, I stopped cold turkey before I got too deep into it, and now with all we know about that evil drug, realize I am one of the fortunate ones.

But the fact that drug and alcohol abuse is so visible out here is probably a good thing. The island is a self-contained community where everyone needs to help everyone to get through the year. Trumpers help Bidenites, and vice versa. Non-believers help Bible thumpers. Don't get me wrong . . . we can hate each other on social media and when not in person, but once people get together in the flesh, they are much more decent than when online. The people who need help on the island can get it. There are plenty of fundraising events—church suppers, yard sales, online groups. Some people clean up after finding God. Others clean up after they've lost everything and barely survive a drug overdose. It's a mixed bag, but a small bag where everybody is seen.

A wave of voices arose from behind us as the tree lighting countdown began. "Ten, nine, eight . . ." the crowd shouted in unison, and then the large spruce tree blazed with its many-colored lights. The crowd let out a roar of approval. Bobby saw Ingrid's face lit by the reflection of the Christmas lights. He thought in that moment she looked as happy as any person could possibly look. Perhaps she was thinking of long-gone years, maybe back when she was a little girl holding onto her father's mittened hand, sipping her hot chocolate. Excited about what gifts awaited beneath the tree at home. She looked so contented to him, and he walked over and put his hand on her shoulder, startling her back to the present. Ingrid didn't object as she turned to face him.

Bobby smiled. "This is just magnificent. It's like going back in time, what with all the children running about freely, the caroling. What a magical place."

"It is," she replied.

I was ready to go home but Bobby and Ingrid wanted the evening to continue, so we walked the short distance to Susan's in-town home for hot rum and cider. Her home on Cove Street had been owned by Ingrid's father when he first took over as president of the Stowell Granite Company, before he bought the house where Ingrid now lived. Susan's home was a prime example of Second Empire architecture with its slate mansard roof. The black wrought iron fence out front had many of its original finial spikes. The old fence has been well taken care of over the years, with some recent replacement posts. Granite had been used in every imaginable way in the yard—from benches to birdbaths to four granite pillars that stood ten-feet high and supported climbing clematis and roses in the summer.

We walked up the granite steps onto a fine old porch, and entered the house through heavy oak doors. I shook the snow from my parka and left my boots in the entryway. As I took a seat in front of the fireplace, I was disappointed to see that Ingrid's son Kevin was there. Back in high school, Kevin enjoyed bullying me. Once he slit all four tires on my truck for unknown reasons. I think I made the mistake of talking to his girlfriend at the senior dance. Kevin had been dealing drugs on the island since high school, mostly marijuana, but then I heard also OxyContin. He didn't look well as I watched him fidget in the doorway between the living room and kitchen.

38

"Hey Kevin," I greeted him.

"What's up, Jon?"

"Nothing much. Just been to the tree lighting with my father."

"Lucky you," there was a large dose of sarcasm in his voice. "That's your fathah?" Kevin looked over his shoulder where he saw his mother and Bobby in the kitchen making rum and cider drinks.

"Yes."

"What brings him he-huh? The holidays?"

"No . . . he's moving in with me."

"Hmm."

I felt uneasy being alone with him. He was one scary looking man, with a pock-marked face damaged from teenage bad acne, made worse by two knife scars on his right cheek. He had lifeless black eyes that were too close together. His arms and neck were covered in tattoos, including a scorpion that extended from his neck up across his bumpy bald skull. Kevin was in the habit of standing closer than was normal, his chest and jaw protruding in a combative stance, as if you had done something to offend him. His head was shaped like an anvil, long and flat on top, tapering down into a protruding jaw. I felt badly for Ingrid having such a bad egg for a son. How this came to be was a mystery, although some of the oldtimers who knew his father said he was just like him. I hardly ever saw Kevin's father who mostly kept to himself earning a living as a lobsterman.

39

Bobby and Ingrid came in from the kitchen with their drinks and sat on the sofa directly across from Kevin and me. Susan and her husband Travis were upstairs putting Svea and Logan to bed.

Ingrid addressed Kevin: "I wish you had joined us. It was such a magical evening what with the snow. You used to love it as a boy."

Kevin shifted in his armchair. "I know, I probably shoulda went but my back's been killin' me and I didn't want to stand for that long."

"Did you take an ibuprofen?"

"Thanks. I'm all set."

"I wish you had joined us, Kevin. It was such a magical evening what with the snow." There was an awkward silence as Bobby looked at me wondering if Ingrid had just repeated herself. I nodded. Kevin, probably accustomed to this from his mother, let it go.

Ingrid could see I was not drinking and correctly surmised I was working on staying sober. "Would you like a ginger ale, Jon?"

"Thanks, I'm good."

"This rum and cider is excellent," Bobby said.

"Old family recipe," Ingrid smiled. "Wasn't that just a gorgeous evening? How I love the caroling."

"Yes, that was a lot of fun," Bobby said.

"Jon here tells me you've moved in with him," Kevin

scratched his forearm. "No place else to go?"

"Afraid not."

"Hmm. That's tough." Kevin didn't like the way his mother was looking at Bobby. He could tell she liked him and the last thing he needed was a man complicating his already challenging situation with his mother. Kevin had been looking after her for the past five years, once it became clear she was having memory issues. During the pandemic she needed extra attention, especially since she was unable to remember to wear a mask at the market, which most locals did given the Medical Center would be unable to handle a Covid outbreak. Even though she was well-known and beloved on the island, the pandemic created such a wave of fear and controversy over masking and vaccines, that Ingrid received many a disapproving glance as she waltzed around town without her mask. The challenges of the pandemic advanced her cognitive impairment more rapidly than would have most likely otherwise occurred. Especially the social isolation. Susan and Kevin had split the responsibilities of looking after her until the pandemic finally lessened in severity and life returned to normal. Nowadays, it was Susan who spent the most time helping her.

Susan came downstairs and then brought out a plate from the kitchen of cheese and crackers, which she set in front of Bobby. "How long will you be staying with Jon?" she asked.

Bobby spread some goat cheese on a Carr's water cracker. "For the foreseeable future, if Jon will have me. I'm not sure where else to go."

"You have no home?" Susan looked surprised.

"I had to sell it when I went into assisted living. That place took everything I had."

"Where was this?"

"Sarasota."

Kevin leaned forward in his seat. "Why did you leave they-ah?"

"Long story," Bobby said.

"We ain't goin' nowheres."

"Well . . . I just didn't like it there. Felt like a prisoner. I was in much better shape than most of the other people, who were on walkers and generally not in good shape. I like to walk. I like physical activity."

"I can certainly understand that," Ingrid said. "Kevin and Susan want me to go to the Eldercare Center but I refuse. The thought of being cooped up with all those old biddies . . ."

Susan exhaled and gazed at Kevin, who shrugged. Ingrid continued. "I'm happy you're here, Robert. It's nice to get new blood out here for the full year. There are lots of interesting summer people, but once they leave, the island becomes a bit . . . bleak."

Kevin laughed. "Good riddance I say. The summah jehks are so fuckin' obnoxious."

"Oh, stop that!" Ingrid snapped. "The summer people give the island much of its appeal. Not to mention money. Last I heard they pay the lion's share of our taxes and don't even use our school or other services. Don't talk that way."

"Well, think what you want, but I'm always happy to see them go. Just a bunch of entitled jehks who expect to get whatevah they want whenevah they want it. People who always get what they want bug the shit outta me."

"No one *always* gets what they want, as you say. That's a huge oversimplification. Anyway, I don't want to discuss it," she put an end to the topic. We sat in silence for several awkward moments, which I took as an opportunity to try and end the evening. "Let's go home, Dad. I'm tired and need to be up early to help fix Jimmy's storm door."

We stood to go and Bobby asked: "How will Ingrid get home?"

"I can take her," Kevin said.

"Nonsense," Bobby replied. "Let us drive her home. It can't be that far out of our way."

"Actually . . ." I started to explain it was twenty minutes up island in the pitch black and snow, but let it go.

The look on Kevin's face made it clear he would rather not drive his mother home. Susan disappeared upstairs to check on the children.

"We'd love to drive Ingrid home," my father offered. "Right Jon?"

I had no choice. "Sure. But let's get going before it gets too late."

43

Chapter Five

December 2022

I hadn't been to Ingrid's house in more than five years and was surprised when we arrived to see how this beautiful old home had fallen into disrepair. One of the second-floor wooden shutters was dangling from a tenuous support, and several of the front porch Ionic pillars had been replaced with temporary pressure-treated beams. At 6,500 square feet, even in the best of times the exterior wooden shingles were in various stages of warping, but now the entire home needed to be re-sided. As we climbed the wooden steps onto the grand porch, with its panoramic views of the ocean, two of the floorboards had rotted through, requiring careful navigation on our way to the four French doors leading into the living room. In the corner of the living room, I could make out the wicker porch furniture covered in tarps along the same wall as Ingrid's grand piano. It was damp and chilly inside and Ingrid asked if I would make a fire in the large fieldstone fireplace.

"What a magnificent place this is," Bobby followed Ingrid across the living room toward the kitchen, staring at the open space above. I knew the house well since I had done several small jobs for Ingrid. A somewhat unusual example of John Calvin Stevens's architecture, the open living room design was the centerpiece of a vaulted space with no ceiling other than the top floor roof, so the eye was pulled upward upon entering the room, similar to the grand entryway of a nineteenth-century museum. A sweeping stairway with finely carved newel posts led up to the second floor, which had a circular passageway that reminded me of the running tracks in old gymnasiums of my youth. About eight feet wide, this passageway encircled the complete upstairs exterior walls, with large multi-paned windows letting in plenty of light. There were built-in window seats every ten feet with needlepointed pillows, some done by Ingrid, others by her mother. The newel posts used on the stairway were continued around the center circle so viewers could look over the railing at the living room. The bottom three feet of the circular exterior wall, which wrapped around the entire space, was shelving for the thousands of old books. Six bedrooms could be accessed off the circular hallway, three of which opened onto exterior porches with ocean views. It was an unusual design that was elegant and unpretentious. Many new money people come out to the island and build ugly monstrosities lacking the fine workmanship and architectural design of these old homes, mostly built by Boston families at the turn of the nineteenth century.

I lit the fire and warmed my hands, listening to the voices of my father and Ingrid in the distant kitchen. Once again, my life seemed to be off course, and by now I had learned not to fight events I could not control, and to make the best of the situation. Ordinarily I would have been home asleep, resting before my morning work. But somehow my father always had a way of leading me astray, into doing things I didn't want to do, and I felt a growing resentment as I listened to his laughter echoing around the house. He had always been the life of every party, an extravert, whereas I was happiest by myself. My mind slipped off into how I could find an acceptable living situation for him, one that would give me back my freedom, as living together for the rest of his life was simply not something I could tolerate. I heard their voices grow louder as they came into the living room carrying drinks.

"Here, Jon, have a brandy to warm you up," he passed me a crystal brandy glass.

"I'm not drinking, remember?"

"Silly me, why of course. Here, I'll drink it."

"Would you like me to get you some apple cider?" Ingrid offered.

"No thanks. We really should be getting home, Dad."

"We just got here," he sat in one of the yellow and blue floral chairs off to the side of the fire. "Ingrid, you have so many books! When do you find the time to read them all?"

She laughed. "Good lord, there is no way I could ever read all these books. Most have been in this house for over a hundred years. But I try to pick away at some of the ones I think are most unusual."

"For instance?" he asked.

"Well, I've been *very, very* slowly making my way through my father's four-volume set on Abraham Lincoln, written by Carl Sandburg. Sandburg was quite the man, winning two

Pulitzer Prizes for poetry and another for this history of Lincoln titled *The War Years*."

"Are these them?" my father reached for an old blue volume with no dustjacket on the end table.

"That's the final volume and I'm almost done. It's been over three thousand pages in total so I'm eager to move onto something else, but the writing is just so good I'm not sure it will be easy to move onto another author."

"What have you learned?" I asked.

"Too much to say, but it is remarkable how much our present times are like the Civil War period. As divided as we are now, the stakes were much higher then, and if not for the cool-headed Lincoln, I doubt the Republic would exist as we know it today. And the remarkable achievement of Sandburg is the voluminous amount of source material he uses for almost everything that happened. At times it bogs down, or possibly we modern readers are lazier than our forebears. I'm reading the part where Lincoln's dreams seem to portend his assassination, and he and his wife are debating whether our lives are all fated or whether we control our destinies. Lincoln felt there was a divine force dictating our fates, but that we also had to exercise free will for our fates to play out. His wife, quite to the contrary, was not a fatalist. At any rate, it makes for fascinating reading. And it is eerie learning about the premonition nightmares he had shortly before he was shot."

"Do you read fiction, too?" my father asked.

She hesitated before answering, taking a sip of her brandy. "I will not kid you . . . I love fiction very much but with my memory loss I'm finding I cannot follow a novel anymore. With a novel you need to remember what a certain character did before, or who they are, and I find I get hopelessly lost."

"I'm sorry to hear that," Bobby said.

"Oh, don't be sorry for me. I've led a full and wonderful life. I just wish there was some medicine for this dreaded illness."

"Maybe in time there will be," I offered. My words sounded hollow to me, similar to how I felt when friends told me there might be some future cure for genetic alcoholism.

"These Sandburg volumes were my father's. I can see him sitting on the porch during summer intently making his way through each one. We were not to interrupt his reading time. Now that I'm reading these books, I understand why. These were published in the 1930s. Closer to the time period than now, which I usually like in my histories. He asked me upon his deathbed to not get rid of any of his books, but to keep them for future generations."

"Was he a scholar?" Bobby asked.

"No, not in the traditional academic sense. I'm the first in our family to go to college. My father was always working at the quarry business, but managed to make time to expand his own understanding of our world. He was especially interested in history and biography."

"Where did you go to college?" Bobby asked.

48

She hesitated, looking embarrassed. "Wellesley."

"Wow, no need to be ashamed of that!" Bobby exclaimed.

"I know, I know. Inside I'm very proud of myself but education is not all that appreciated these days, especially by some of the locals. I get it, I truly do. We need college-educated people and we need trade school people. We shouldn't judge one over the other. It takes a village."

"Still, getting into Wellesley back when you did, that must have been extraordinary."

"Not really," she blushed. "I'm sure they were looking to diversify their student body and I was most certainly the only hick from a remote island." She laughed.

"I'm sure you were not a hick, as you say." Bobby set down his glass. "Where's the head? I need to go."

"Just before the kitchen, on the left," she pointed.

Bobby got up to use the bathroom and stopped at the grand piano on his way back. "Do you play?" he asked Ingrid.

"Occasionally," she turned to glance at him over her shoulder.

"I always wanted to learn," Bobby ran his fingers along the keyboard and then stopped.

Ingrid got up and walked over to the piano. She pulled out sheet music—Bach's "Adagio in D Minor." She got herself comfortably situated on the piano bench. "I can still play this piece, one of the first I learned as a young girl. I don't need the music but let me prop it up here just in case my brain lets me down." She played the piece beautifully and I felt tears well in my eyes at the pathos of the music, which came from that soulful place where all the best of humanity is shared as we must face our mortality. The work of a true genius. When she was done, she sat on the bench with head bowed, her mouth turned down into a tragic expression.

"You play so well," Bobby walked over and put his hand on her shoulder.

She sighed. "Isn't it something that I can play that piece with no trouble at all, yet cannot for the life of me recall where I put my eyeglasses. The part of the brain that controls musical performance must be remarkably deep within."

"Listen, Dad. We really need to be getting home."

My father didn't want to leave but Ingrid rose from the piano bench signaling she was ready to call it a night. "Thanks for driving me home, Jon. You're a kind man."

"No problem."

"Might I see you again?" Bobby asked.

Ingrid paused before answering: "Sure, that would be nice."

"When would be a good time for you?" he asked.

"Let me check my calendar," Ingrid walked over to the antique desk to look at her large monthly desk calendar. Bobby followed her.

"Looks like you have a busy schedule," he remarked upon seeing all the writing and phone numbers scrawled across the calendar for the month of December.

Ingrid stared blankly at the calendar before flipping the sheet to the month of January. "Kevin bought me this calendar to help keep all my doctor's appointments straight. It's nice having a full month to look at on one sheet of paper. I use my iPhone calendar, too, but that can confuse me."

"I completely understand," Bobby stood by as she stared vacantly at the month of January.

"It's nice to have a full month to look at on one sheet of paper," Ingrid repeated herself.

Bobby let it go. "I should get one of those for myself."

"Good grief, can you believe it's already going to be 2023?" Ingrid turned to look at him, her mouth sunk into an unflattering frown, the left side of her face drooping.

Bobby replied: "I know, I sometimes write the year 1975 on checks. Or my birth year."

Ingrid rubbed her forehead as if in pain. "It looks like I have a library board meeting on January 5th and will be staying in town with Susan, so maybe we could have dinner at the bar that evening? An early dinner before it gets rowdy."

I was concerned at the way Ingrid was rubbing her forehead, and asked: "Would you like me to get you an aspirin?"

"Yes, if you don't mind. They are in the medicine cabinet in the bathroom," she sat down.

I returned with an aspirin and a glass of water, noticing how pale Ingrid looked. "Here, take this."

She swallowed the pill and kept her eyes closed for nearly a minute as my father and I looked on with concern. She opened her eyes and said: "Much better, thank you."

Bobby asked: "Do you get headaches often?"

"I do. My doctor says I have had a few TIAs. Do you know what those are?"

"Yes," Bobby replied. "Small mini-strokes."

"Sometimes my vision gets a bit squirrely," Ingrid drank the full glass of water. "But these episodes always pass. At any rate, sorry about that." Ingrid got up and walked back to the calendar. "I keep track of everything on this large calendar that Kevin got me. Let's see when we could meet for dinner. I have a library meeting on that . . ." She stopped abruptly.

Bobby walked over and held her by the elbow to steady her.

Ingrid looked down at the calendar and saw she had already written in the date of the library board meeting for them to have dinner. Bobby could see her confusion as he said: "Excellent, then, we're on for January 5th. May I have your phone number so we can connect?"

Ingrid stood there looking out of sorts, frightened. "I just have the landline here, but am on Facebook if you want to message me."

"Perfect," he said.

I was concerned about leaving her in this shaky condition for the night, so we waited five minutes until she seemed to be doing somewhat better. We bid our goodbyes and headed out into the darkness for the snowy drive home.

Chapter Six
April & May 2023

I imagine at this point of the story you are curious to understand how it is I was sober when my father first arrived on the island and was drinking again by the time he was found at the bottom of the cliff. I can easily assign the blame for my relapse to others, including my father. The winters out here are long and lonely, and I ended up revisiting my old friend, the bottle, as strains brought on by my father increased. The arrival of Shane Vachon didn't help either. Kevin had been hassling me to keep my father away from his mother, and the sum of all this stressed me out to the point I once again sought comfort with drinking. But during my most recent stint at rehab, I was reminded that no one is to blame for our failings other than ourselves. I was the weak one who succumbed to the pressures. I *am* the weak one.

It was in late-winter that I relapsed. My father had just moved in with Ingrid, although he spent the occasional night with me, typically after they had quarreled and she asked him to leave. Or Kevin insisted he go. Theirs was a complicated relationship made that much worse by her memory loss and resulting confusion. She loved him but also mistrusted him. Some of this was due to her increasing paranoia as she started sundowning in the afternoons, becoming a bit crazy. There was nothing new about women mistrusting Bobby, as this had been the pattern with his previous wives. I had grown weary of this emotionally fraught landscape and was relieved when spring arrived and I found a carpentry job working outdoors, something purposeful I could lose myself in daily. Short on funds after a long winter with just two small jobs, hope seemed to arrive with Shane Vachon, a contractor from the mainland who had been hired to build a new summer house for a wealthy entrepreneur from California. I met Shane at the island's hardware store on a chilly late-April morning. I overheard him in conversation with the store manager Kenny Bickford.

"How often do you get lumber delivered out here?" the man ahead of me in line asked.

Kenny answered: "Usually once a week. We can special order most anything you need. What brings you to the island?"

"I'm building a summer home. It's a big project. Can you recommend any people out here to help?"

Kenny smiled. "Jon, right there behind you, would be a good choice."

The skinny man, who was missing some lower front teeth and had an unhealthy-looking sallow complexion, turned to see who was behind him. "You a builder?"

"I am. Mostly finished carpentry work, but I can do most anything. What are you looking for?"

"Someone who lives out here who knows what he's doing. I've got a mainland job dragging on in Bass Harbor, and need to get this new one started soon, as the owner has offered a 15% bonus for finishing by the end of the year."

"Who's the owner?" I asked.

"Doubt you know him. I think he's only been here once and that was to close on two acres up at Douglas Point. Some tech bigwig from Silicon Valley who invented a cash app he sold to Bank of America. Rohan Patel is his name."

"Nope, can't say I do. That's a beautiful location, though. Not going to be any properties left for the locals the way outsiders have been driving up prices out here."

"I know. It's true for the entire state."

"How far along are you with the project?"

"I haven't been back to the site since the land was cleared and the foundation poured in November."

"Don't be surprised if there was a lot of tree damage over the winter. That land faces northeast and we had some big snowstorms."

"Crap, I hope not. I don't want to bring that crew back over again. They were wicked expensive."

"We've got some fellas who would clear it if you let them keep the trees for firewood."

"Good to know."

"Well . . . I would be interested in joining your crew. What's the pay?"

"Standard hourly rate. $25 an hour."

"I don't know. I get paid $75 an hour for finished work and that will be starting up soon when the summer folks return. So . . . I think maybe not."

The man looked pissed off, compulsively scratching his forearm. Something about him rubbed me the wrong way but I still had monthly hospital bills to pay down from my accident two years ago, so instead of moving on I stood there waiting for a reply.

"What if I pay you $40 an hour for framing and then once I see your workmanship, $75 for the interior trim and other finished work. The architect is using high-end German cabinets and countertops, but there will be interior trim work, and I'm not happy with the guy on my crew who has been handling that."

"That'll do," I shook his hand. "Jon Davis. And you are?"

"Shane Vachon."

The work was rewarding and I quickly proved myself to Shane, who ended up giving me more responsibility than I wanted. He was absent more than any head contractor I had known, which was fine by me. I was in charge when he had to return to the mainland to check on other projects. The hours were long and we worked seven days a week. When on the island, Shane lived in an old RV he parked in the town's parking lot, which pissed off locals in need of parking spaces for launching their boats and going to the market. His RV took up four spaces in the small lot that only had around thirty, parked along the far railing where many lobstermen staged their traps for pick up from the dock. I was one of the only locals who knew who Shane was and why he was on the island. He mostly kept to himself, although the two times I went to call on him at his RV he wouldn't let me in, which struck me as odd. Everything was running smoothly until Shane hired Kevin to join our crew. I wish he had consulted with me first, as I could have set him straight about Kevin and his many problems. Only later would I come to understand why he hired Kevin and by then it was too late.

But like so many things in life, there was good that came along with the bad, in this case in the form of Charlie Walsh. I was eating breakfast before work one foggy May morning, when my neighbor Dale Hildings stopped by with a ragged looking teenage boy in tow.

"Mornin', Jon. Hope I'm not disturbin' you."

"Not at all, come on in Dale."

Dale had moved into his mother's house down the road from me after she was sent away to a nursing home. Her house was little more than a shack, with one bedroom upstairs and a tiny kitchen and living room combo. I liked his mother and helped her as much as I could as she attempted to stay in her home. I had repaired some rotten window sills and patched the roof where it was leaking directly over her bed. I had mowed her lawn and fed her cat. I hadn't heard how she was doing or if she was even alive, so was eager to get the latest news from her son.

"Have a seat," I pulled up two chairs. The boy with Dale was not someone I had seen on the island before.

"Jon, this is Charlie Walsh. He's staying with me and has done well at Oceanside trade school in their carpentry program. I was wonderin' if you might be able to hire him on that project of yours, just for the summah. I'm out straight haulin' now and would like to keep the boy busy."

"Hey, Charlie, nice to meet you," I extended my hand, which he shook with eyes averted downward. I figured he must be around sixteen years old, and looked far too dispirited for someone his age. "What kind of skills do you have?"

"I'm real good with buildin' stuff. I helped make a shed at school and the teacher said it was one of the best he'd ever seen."

"Do you have your own tools?"

"Nah. Not really."

Dale said: "I've got some tools he can borrow. The kid's a quick learner and hard worker. You'd be doing me and him a big favor, Jon."

"Mr. Davis, do you have a bathroom I could use?" Charlie asked.

"Sure, just off the entryway."

While Charlie was in the bathroom, Dale filled me in. "The kid's just had shit luck his whole life. Father ran off when he was four and his mother got picked up in Oceanside last month with fentanyl in the car. She's been raisin' the boy on her own ovah in Warrenboro, workin' at Walmart. She's a repeat drug offender . . . someone I used to date before she got too far gone and I left. It's a shame because I know she tried real hahd to be a good mom to Charlie, but the drugs just took ovah her brain the way they do. I agreed to take him in with me while the court looks for any relatives he might have. It's just a temporary deal, most likely."

"That poor kid."

"I know. And raising a teenager ain't sumthin I know nuthin about, other than he needs to stay busy and earn some spendin' money this summah to help give him some sense of pride and self-worth. He's a good kid . . . just dealt a bad hand. I'm out at 5:30 in the mornin' to haul, but back by mid-afternoon most days, so could come get him after you finish up for the day. Just weekends for now until school is out for him."

"Good lord, Dale. You're one helluva kind soul. Not sure I would have done the same under the circumstances. I mean, he's not even your flesh and blood."

"Well, maybe I am an okay human being, afterall," he smiled. "I just think there are times when we're challenged to do the right thing and I've always been someone who just naturally steps up. Too big a haht, my mother always said. Hell, the boy needed help. The boy *needs* help. There's just not enough kindness in this world what with all our political squabblin' and hatred of people we don't even know. What evah happened to the notion of a lovin' community?"

"I hear you, Dale. It's sad to see."

"Used to be one helped anyone who needed it. No questions asked. Nuthin expected in return. Just bein' a decent person."

"Yup. So . . . he's enrolled at the school?"

"Just started last week. I think it's been rough on him, with no friends and all. Plus, I'm not sure how much schoolin' he's already missed. He's smart and all, but maybe not book smart."

"How's he getting to school if you're out to haul? The bus?"

"Unfortunately, the school still can't find a bus driver. But I ain't been goin' out every day yet. Just stahtin' to get some traps set, paintin' buoys, the normal spring prep before the season shifts into high gear. What with the price of bait and fuel, I doubt I'll be headin' out much until the end of June. On days I can drop Charlie at school, I do. Other days he walks."

"Dale, I'd like to help, but I've got my father living with me and just don't think I can take this kid under my wing right now. I'm sorry."

"I understand. I thought it was worth a try. I'll figure something out."

I felt guilty. Here was Dale being so generous and I was thinking about myself. "If you need me to drop him at school on days you can't, I can take him. The school year will be done in mid-June."

"Thanks, Jon. That'd be a huge help."

We sat in silence waiting for Charlie to come back. My conscience was bothering me as I sat there smiling sheepishly at Dale, who was probably judging me, and not in a favorable light.

I sighed. "Tell you what, Dale. Seeing that tomorrow is Saturday and we're working at the job site with a limited crew, I can take him with me and get a sense of how he does."

"That wud be great, Jon. I'm headin' out in the mornin' and don't like him sittin' around all by himself playing video games. I'd bring him with me but he gets seasick and it's supposed to be blowin' pretty good outta the north tomorrow, so it'll be choppy."

"Okay, drop him by tomorrow morning and I'll give him a trial run. I need to check with the boss, first. If there are any issues, I'll let you know. Otherwise just bring him by."

"You're a godsend, Jon."

Charlie returned from the bathroom, his oily black hair falling freely about his face. I noticed he had large brown eyes and a holy trinity of pimples on his face—one on the forehead, one on each cheek. His baggy shorts were slung low revealing the elastic band of his red boxer shorts.

Dale spoke: "I've got good news, Charlie. Mr. Davis is gunna let you apprentice with him tomorrow on a big job he's got goin'. He's gunna give you a trial run and if you do good, you might be able to stay on for the summah and have some spendin' money. Just do what he says and learn as much as you can. He's a great carpenter who knows a lot. This is a solid opportunity for you, son."

Charlie looked up from sad hound dog eyes. "Thanks Mr. Davis. I'll do my best."

"Tell me, Dale, what's the latest news on your mother?"

"She's still kickin'. Gunna be ninety-two next month. I'm just glad to get her off the island into a safe place."

"That's good to hear. I won't kid you, I worried about her when she was here and started wandering off at night. Especially over the winter."

"I know, I know. We all did. And I appreciate the work you did on her house for no pay. Well . . . let's be off Charlie. Thanks, again, Jon. I'll drop him by tomorrow morning."

And so it began. The good that comes from the bad. Dale dropped Charlie by my house at 5:30 that Saturday morning, and after realizing he had not eaten breakfast, I made us scrambled eggs and bacon and then we drove to the job site at the northern tip of the island. Driving in my pickup with Charlie brought back memories of when I was a teenager apprenticing with Lars Jost, an ornery man who put up with my many rookie mistakes, most memorably the time he trusted me to put roofing shingles on a small shed, only to check on me and see I had put two rows on upside down. Old man Jost was known to have a temper and a drinking problem, but I'll never forget what he said to me, words I've carried inside for the rest of my life. "Even God makes mistakes, Jon," said with a wry smile overspreading his face. I wasn't sure if he was referring to my shingling or my birth. He was that kind of taciturn difficult-to-read old salt.

Charlie sat in uncomfortable silence as we drove to work that first morning, and I sensed he was confused and angry about his lot in life. Who wouldn't be? I did my best to draw him out and provide some escape from his many problems.

"How's school?" I asked.

"Okay, I guess."

"Made any friends?"

"Nah, not really."

"Give it time. Most of the kids out here have been together all their lives and are not used to someone new showing up for high school."

"Yeah, I guess so."

"I can relate to what you're going through. I moved out here when I was ten with my mom, who met a lobsterman after she split from my father. She was out here in the summer on vacation and fell in love. Man, how I hated school and living here back then. Felt like I'd been dropped off in a zombie movie. There was nothing to do. No place to go. It sucked."

"Right," he replied.

I realized my situation was nowhere near as bad as his. But there was something about being with Charlie that brought those old days back to me—how numb I was after my parents split up and how weird it was having a new father. I think three years passed without me seeing Bobby. I hated leaving my friends and life back home in Danbury, Connecticut and was angry at my mother for remarrying. Those times were tough, but like most kids, I eventually figured things out and grew to love the island and the people who accepted me for who I am.

We sat in silence for a good five minutes as I remembered my teenage years. "Is Mr. Larkin still the biology teacher?"

"Yup."

I laughed. "Larkin used to ride my ass on the baseball field. Didn't think I was trying hard enough. Wasn't disciplined, was what he said. I heard he had been a Marine in a previous life. Was always making me run extra laps after practice to *shape up, boy!* Do you play any sports?"

"Actually, I like baseball."

"Good for you. You should play. Everyone gets to play given there aren't enough kids to field a team some years. Your timing is good as the season just started. I think they lost their first game. I'm sure they would welcome you with open arms."

"Maybe."

"If you do, don't mention you know me to Coach Larkin. And never sass him. Trust me."

Charlie managed a hint of a smile as he continued gazing out the window of the truck, watching the woods speed by. We left the paved roads for dirt ones heading to the farthest reaches of the island. Spring was always slow to arrive in Maine, and even slower out here surrounded as we are by cool ocean waters and daily fog banks coming and going. A good thing about working on the northern tip of the island meant we were likely to see more sun than on the southern coast, where the fog was especially persistent. We arrived at the job site where the sun was shining and Kevin had already arrived.

"Hey, Kevin. This is Charlie. He's going to be job shadowing me today."

"Shane okay that?" he asked.

"Shane knows."

Kevin grunted and returned to where he was sorting the recent delivery of framing lumber into like piles.

"Charlie, you just watch what I do and then once we get you up and running, you can help with the framing. Sound good?"

"Sure, Mr. Davis."

"Please, call me Jon. Mr. Davis sounds like my old man."

Kevin walked over. "And no one would want to be like that old creepah." Kevin was wearing a sleeveless men's muscle shirt, revealing his bulging biceps and patches of hair dotting his shoulders.

Not one to defend my father, I was still put off by Kevin and knew he couldn't be trusted. Ever since he'd been hired, I was parking my truck down the road a good ways, just in case he was still slicing tires for fun. Paranoid, I know, but the man scared me. Kevin was unable to lobster that spring due to his boat being out of the water waiting for a new engine to be installed, something he should have dealt with last fall to avoid missing the prime season. Just my luck. "Leave my old man alone, Kevin. Mind your own damned business."

"Once your old man started hangin' with my muthah, he became my business. Can't you make him disappear?"

"I'm afraid it's not that easy, Kevin. What do you want me to do? He's my father and has no other place to go. Do you think I want him messing up my life now, too?"

He spat off to the side. "I'm tellin' ya, I don't trust that man as far as I can spit into these woods. For fuck's sake, I've got enough goin' on with my muthah without him playin' with her head."

Two Guatemalan day-laborers Shane had found on the mainland arrived, speaking broken English, laughing at some inside joke.

"Miguel, dat woman don't like you. Can't you see?"

"Oh, she gunna like me. It's you she can't stand. Says your breath smells like someteen died inside you."

"You bullshitter. You'll see, I'll win her over."

Shane was on the mainland for the week, so I oversaw herding the various cats into workgroups to begin setting the pressure-treated sill plates atop the concrete walls. The foundation footprint covered 8,600-square-feet, a huge house. I left Kevin to supervise the Guatemalan day workers, and took Charlie with me. It was easy to see how numb Charlie was from recent life events, as he stumbled about the job site like a wounded deer, seeking direction and solid footing to help remove the fog of adolescence.

"I'm sorry, Mr. Davis," he leaned over to pick up the nails that spilled out of the small cardboard box I had handed him.

"It's okay, Charlie. And please, call me Jon."

"Yes, sir," he saw my disappointment with this salutation so quickly followed up, "I mean, Jon."

I bent down to help him gather the nails and saw a tear streaming down his left cheek. I spoke in a hushed voice: "Don't cry, Charlie. It's no big deal." He kept his head bowed, not wanting the others to see him sobbing. We continued sweeping the nails back into the box.

"Life is tough, Charlie. But we just keep on going with faith that better days lie ahead. And I can tell you from my experience that better days will come for you. Hang in there, bud."

He collected himself. "I'm trying to be strong. I'm sorry."

"Don't be sorry. You have nothing to be sorry about. What's happened to you is not about you, it's about your parents and their issues. You're very strong, Charlie. Stronger than anyone your age should have to be."

"What's going to happen to my mother? Is she going to jail?"

"I don't know, but the state never wants to separate children from their parents unless there is no other option. And for now, you've got Dale and me to look after you while things get sorted out with your mother."

"Why does she keep taking those stupid drugs?"

"It's tough, Charlie. Drugs are very addictive. Especially

nowadays."

"But why can't she just stop? Doesn't she see how it messes up her life? My life?"

"I'm sure she feels awful about herself. But listen, I'll find out what's going on with her. In the meantime, try and lose yourself in work, and that'll help you feel better."

Back in town at the end of that first day, I took Charlie for an ice cream cone. He had done a good job and seemed to have enjoyed himself.

"What would you like Charlie? My treat."

"Can I get a mint chocolate chip sugar cone?"

"Sure."

While we waited for our cones, a boy wearing Grunden boots and an Archer Island baseball uniform trudged into the store. "Hey, Charlie. Hello Mr. Davis." It was Walt Wentworth's boy, Luke, wearing eye black smeared beneath his eyes.

"Hey," Charlie looked up.

I offered to buy Luke a cone, which he happily accepted.

We took our cones outside to the picnic table and sat together. The fog was rolling back into town for the night and we could no longer make out the boats in the harbor across the street. "How's baseball going?" I turned to Luke.

"Not too bad. We only have ten players and Austin, our best pitcher, can't play this weekend, so we're probably going to get destroyed."

"Who's Austin?"

"Austin Philbrook."

"Why can't he play?"

"I dunno. I think he got into a fight at school and his grades are borderline."

"You know, Charlie told me he played on the mainland before moving out here. Right, Charlie?"

"Yeah, I guess."

Luke's expression lit up. "I know you! I thought you seemed familiar. You pitched for Ashland last year. You guys whooped us. You're good. Why don't you play for us?"

"I dunno. I just got here and all and am not sure I can make time for baseball. I've got a lot goin' on now."

"C'mon," Luke pleaded. "We could really use you, what with Austin out and all. Come to practice on Monday."

"I don't have my gear."

"You can borrow a glove from me."

I encouraged him: "I can get you some sweats and cleats or whatever else you need at the swap shop for practices. You should do it, Charlie."

So, Charlie joined the baseball team and that cheered him up a bit. He did well and made new friends. He was even popular with the girls, pimples and all. I went to see him pitch against Northland Valley on a mostly sunny Memorial Day weekend, the fog bank just offshore adding a cooling breeze to the warm day. The entire town came out to see the girls' softball team play and then the boys right after them. The athletic director and the English teacher picked up the visiting team at the ferry and brought them to the field in two large vans used for island kids with disabilities. They arrived at the field late-morning and would be returning on the last boat. It was a long way to go to play a baseball game and this was the second and final home game of the season. I hadn't been to the old baseball field in years. As I sat on the sloping hill down the right field line, I was impressed to see what a great pitcher Charlie was. Many of the visiting team parents were sitting near me and I could overhear them talking about how beautiful the island was and what a supportive community we had. The Archer Island boys were excited to be ahead going into the final inning, and Charlie struck out the side to finish off the game. I walked over to intercept him as he headed for the gym.

"Wow, Charlie! You're amazing."

"Thanks. I had my good stuff working today."

A tiny eighth grader who had played right field ran up to Charlie and gave him a high-five. "Way to go, Chuck!" The boy had his uniform shirt untucked and it came down to his knees.

"Thanks," Charlie managed a smile.

A woman I hadn't noticed on the island before approached. "How to go!" she hugged the boy who had greeted Charlie. "Great game, Connor."

She introduced herself. "I'm Linda, Connor's mom."

"Hi, I'm Jon."

"Are you the star pitcher's father?"

"No, just looking after him."

"Well, that was quite the game he pitched."

Charlie wandered off with Connor as I chatted with his mother.

"Don't believe I've seen you around before, Linda. Are you new to the island?"

She smiled broadly. "Technically I'm an islander, as I was born here. But my family moved to the mainland when I was young. I moved back this fall with my kids to take a job at the school. You must be that kind man who is looking after Charlie while his mother's unfortunate situation gets sorted out. I work in the guidance office at the school, so am aware of what's been happening with Charlie."

"It's Dale Hildings who is the kind man. Charlie's living with him. I'm taking the boy under my wing as an apprentice on the Douglas Point project. Honestly, it's been kind of difficult, what with my father moving in with me too."

"Ah, the old sandwich problem. Lots of that going around these years. Raising kids while taking care of elderly parents."

"Yes, that's true. And I value my alone time."

Linda had a cheerful disposition, one that conveyed a positive outlook. She said: "Charlie talks about you when we meet. He says he's excited to have the opportunity to learn from you, to gain new skills. It's sad to see some of these neglected kids. On the one hand, we have many students with doting parents and grandparents, and then we have the handful of kids who are left to fend for themselves."

"I know. It's sad. Are you happy to be back on the island?"

"Honestly . . . yes and no. It's difficult enough being a single parent on the mainland, but at least over there I had my mother nearby to help. Out here, I'm struggling a bit without her around to deal with the last-minute needs that arise, like watching sick kids when I'm at work."

"Sorry to hear that. Where do you live?"

"I'm in the apartments over by the cemetery."

"You've got a nice view there."

She laughed. "I suppose if you consider looking out at gravestones to be a nice view—"

"Oh . . . no. I meant the cove you can see from there."

"I know, I'm just joking around."

"You're lucky to have found a year-round place," I said. "Very little available to rent or buy."

"It's not a bad apartment. The heat's good. Three bedrooms so the kids each have their own room. I don't like sharing the laundry with others, though. Been a long time since I did that. It's one of those old machines that requires quarters, which I never have on hand."

"You're welcome to use mine if you want. I live up the hill from you."

"How sweet of you. I might just take you up on that if

you're sure it's not a bother."

"No bother at all," I said.

"Well, it was very nice to meet you, Jon. I've got to run along and get dinner started for Connor and his sister."

Linda would later tell me while doing laundry at my place that she thought I'd looked a bit like Jesus that day, with my long hair and scraggily beard. That comment led me to get my first haircut in four months, and for her to later tell me she preferred it long. That's me when it comes to women. All the wrong moves.

Chapter Seven
September 2023

Timmy Tetreault's police cruiser pulled out front of my home ten days after Bobby's body was taken to Oceanside for the autopsy. September is my favorite time of year on the island, most summer people departed, the island handed back to locals. The state cop who had been at the quarry site was in the cruiser with Timmy. I met them out front, and we headed for the outside deck where we sat in my weathered Adirondack chairs. I offered them a soda, which they declined.

The state officer took the lead. "I'm sorry to report the autopsy confirmed your father was murdered."

"Shit. Who would do that?"

"That's what we're wondering. How were you two getting along?" the officer cut to the chase.

"Fine, why do you ask?"

"We found your fingerprints on the rock we believe was used to bash in your father's head."

"No way," I sat up straight in my chair.

"Why's that?"

"I mean . . . I would never kill my father. Sure, we quarreled on occasion, but I'm no murderer. There must be another explanation."

75

"We know you've been drinking again," Tetreault chimed in. "Maybe you lost your temper that night?"

"Look, I'm the one who took my father in, who has been taking care of him, has been . . ."

The state cop interjected, shooting Tetreault a look that made it clear he wanted to take the lead. "When we interviewed Ingrid Backlund earlier this week, she said you were upset at your father about something. You had been arguing with him in recent weeks."

"Well . . . I'm not the only one who got angry at my father. Have you questioned her son yet?"

"We have," the state cop said. "Kevin's fingerprints were also on the rock. And there are others not in our database."

"Why are my fingerprints in your database?"

"They're from your drunk driving arrest in Warrenboro five years ago."

I had forgotten about that. "Listen, you gotta believe me. I swear I didn't kill my father. It must be Kevin. He had motive. Isn't he on probation for the job site theft?"

The cop said: "He is. But we think he has an alibi for his whereabouts the night of your father's murder. We're still looking into it." He stood up and walked over to the edge of the deck. He turned to face me and said: "We talked to the owner of the bar yesterday. Betty Jean. She told us you were drunk the night of Bobby's murder. That she had to cut you off and you became belligerent, so your friend drove you home." The cop looked at notes he had scrawled on a small flip-up notepad. "Says it was your friend Freddy Ames who drove you home. Sound 'bout right?"

I had been struggling to recall that night. I remembered being at the bar, and think Freddy Ames and Walt Wentworth were there, too. They pour steep drinks and I had maybe three, possibly four, Seagrams with ginger ale. But until now, I hadn't realized that Freddy drove me home. What I remembered was waking up the next morning to the phone call from Walt.

Tetreault added: "And Ingrid told us your father had been after you to stop drinking, but that you refused to listen. She said the drink was making you say and do crazy things."

The state cop shot Tetreault a look that made it clear he needed to shut up, as he continued flipping through his note pad. "There's something else that's curious. Your father had a sizeable life insurance policy."

"That's news to me."

"And you're the sole beneficiary."

"I had no idea—"

"Well, don't be expecting anything from it because the insurance company won't pay out until you're cleared of his murder. Obviously."

I sat there puzzled by all of this. "I mean, you say there are several fingerprints on the rock? Including Kevin's? How can that be?"

"That's what we're trying to figure out."

"Should I be getting a lawyer?"

Tetreault butted in again: "Truth is, Jon, the fingerprint matches on the rock aren't great. It's tough to get good matches off stone surfaces."

The state cop shot him yet another look that spoke volumes, then said: "Get a lawyer if you want. Entirely up to you. But if I were in your shoes, I probably would. We're working on piecing together the best timetable we can of the night of Bobby's death. We'll be back for questioning, so don't go anywhere."

"I'm not leaving. Haven't been off the island in over a month. Been too busy with the Douglas Point project and figuring out what to do about Charlie Walsh."

The state cop said: "Yes, we know about Charlie. His mother just got handed a five-year sentence for drug trafficking. It's good of you to be helping him. Most everyone we've spoken to in the community speaks very highly of you, Jon. You don't strike me as the murderer type, but we've got to follow wherever the investigation leads."

Tetreault refused to stay out of it as he asked: "You don't suppose Ingrid wanted your father gone, do you?"

The state cop snapped: "Don't be an idiot!"

As I watched Tetreault cower like a wounded dog, I realized he could be onto something. I had witnessed an explosion of anger from Ingrid towards Bobby just three weeks before his death, the force of which caught us both off guard. Her personality was undergoing changes due to the dementia, a savage and sudden meanness being one of the most alarming. "Well . . . if you're wondering if I can see her wanting to knock the old man over the head with a rock in a sudden rage, sure. Except I doubt she is strong enough, don't you think? But she's not been herself these past few months, so who knows. Have you gotten her fingerprints?"

The state cop was taking notes: "Not yet. Tell me, how would you describe their relationship?"

"Tough to say for sure. I think they were in love. But I also know she didn't trust him, with good reason. He might have been using her, I honestly don't know. The old man was smooth."

"Why do you say that?"

"Bobby was not a trustworthy person. My mother refuses to even mention his name to this day."

The cop attempted to catch me off-guard: "You know about the missing credit card?"

"I do. I'm the one who made him give it back to her."

"Do you think he stole it?"

"Wouldn't put it past him, but he swore it was an accident. Truth is, his memory had been slipping lately, too. He told me he put it in his shirt pocket at the dinner they had in January. Claimed it was just an innocent mistake."

The officer folded his arms across his chest. "That all sounds fine and good, except did you know he charged things for himself using her card? That don't seem like an accident to me."

"God, no! I didn't. What did he buy?"

"Fine wine. A Brooks Brothers suit. Tickets for a Caribbean cruise—"

"Crap! I had no idea!"

"Are you sure?"

"Of course, I'm sure. That ol' bastard."

"Well, let me tell you something odd about those Caribbean cruise tickets. He bought two. One for himself. The other in your name."

"What the fuck?"

"You heard me."

"You have to believe me. This is all news to me." My palms were sweaty and I could feel my blood pressure rising. I desperately wanted a drink.

They got up to leave. It was clear they had wanted to see my reaction to this news about the credit card. I could feel them sizing me up. Had my father really stolen her card and gone on a shopping spree? I wouldn't put it past him.

"Just don't go anywhere, Jon. We'll be in touch," the state cop said.

"So . . . I'm a suspect? Do you have anyone else?"

"You are, Jon. But for now, there's not enough evidence to bring you in. Just stay put and we'll get to the bottom of this. But if you run, you'll be in serious trouble. So don't."

"I'm not going anywhere." I immediately started thinking of lawyers I could contact to defend me. Joel Katz was a summer resident friend who lived in Boston, so I'd give him a call.

80

The cop asked: "Mind if we look around a bit?"

"I'm not sure that's a good idea based on what you've just told me."

"Well, we can get a warrant. But that seems like a waste of everyone's time since you've got nothing to hide. Right?"

"I don't think I should talk with you without a lawyer present. So, why don't you come back with a warrant and I'll get myself a lawyer."

"You sure?"

"Yes."

"Okay, we'll be back in a few days so you best get lawyered up quick. I'm sure we'll get to the bottom of this. Someone on this rumor-crazed island knows what happened, I'm certain of that."

They walked away and I went inside and spied on them through the upstairs bedroom curtains, where I could see them talking in Tetreault's police car.

Chapter Eight
January 2023

My father met Ingrid at the bar on a cold January evening as the new year got underway. I had offered to go with him but he wanted to meet her on his own. It was a Friday and a good crowd had come out to play trivia. Older lobstermen huddled at the bar in front of the television watching a Boston Bruins hockey game, and a handful of year-round residents—originally from away—sat in the adjacent dining room. Younger islanders who taught at the school or worked at the Medical Center were laughing and celebrating the end of the work week. The jukebox was playing "We Are the Champions" by Queen. Ingrid led Robert to a table at the back of the dining room so they would be able to hear each other.

"I had no idea this place was such a hot spot," he said as he pulled out her chair.

"Considering it's now the only game in town, I'm not too surprised," she said. "This is good. Now you can catch some local color."

Robert said: "I think it's too crowded here for that poor girl trying to wait on everyone. Let me go to the bar and fetch us drinks. What would you like?"

"A glass of Chardonnay, please."

He nudged his way between two men at the bar who were shouting at the hockey game. After waiting nearly ten minutes, he was able to get the drinks and return to the table. He saw Ingrid talking with an elderly couple on their way out.

The woman talking with Ingrid said: "Can't hear myself think straight in this place tonight. Who *are* all these people?"

Her husband added: "Used to be you might see four or five people he-ah on a Friday night in wintah, but nowadays this place is thick with faces I ain't nevah seen before."

Ingrid shouted over the din: "I know, I don't recognize anyone other than Jill and Raymond over there. Oh, well. Guess it's progress."

The man grunted. "Call it what you will, I'm afraid this place is gunna turn into Nantucket if we don't get things undah control right quick. I heard some fancy summah person from New Yawk is lobbying Town Hall to get a helicoptah pad permit so he can fly into his prop-ah-tee. That ain't gunna happen."

Ingrid introduced Robert. "Meet my new friend Robert Davis. He's visiting his son. Robert, this is Doris and her husband Jimmy."

"Nice to meet ya," Doris said. "Not the best time of ye-ah to be out he-ah."

"Actually, I'm growing to like it. It doesn't feel like America out here," Robert said.

Jimmy leaned in. "What . . . you don't like America?"

"Sure, I like America. I just meant it's nice to be removed

from all the problems of mainland life."

He laughed. "Don't be fooled. We got plenty of problems out he-ah, too. You might feel removed but you can't remove all the stupidity from the politicians. Damned country is going to hell."

His wife's face blushed as she attempted to change the subject. "Ingrid, I haven't seen you at bingo this ye-ah. You've been missed."

"Thanks. I find sitting in those fold-up chairs for four hours just does a number on my back."

"Well, maybe you can join us aftah-woods for coffee and tea."

"Thanks. I find sitting in those fold-up chairs for four hours to be difficult."

Doris glanced at Ingrid. "Yes, we know. You just told us."

Robert shot her a look that said *be kind.*

Jimmy was not done as he faced Robert. "What with all these government regulations on the right whales, new fishin' regulations, climate change hoax, green energy shiffabrains everywhere, the rigged elections, we ain't got no common sense left in this country. Meanwhile, we let all those illegals waltz into the country like its theirs."

Robert looked up in surprise. "What do you have against green energy?"

"Where to staht. Those off-shore windmills are gunna kill our livelihoods. My family has been fishin' out he-ah for five generations. They're takin' our God-given fishin' grounds from us slow but sure. Brandon and his cronies."

"How so?"

"They keep blamin' us for killin' the whales when in fact it's that sonic noise from the deep wat-ah drillin' that's killin' them. Them and cargo ships. It sure as hell ain't us. Stupid politicians don't even know that where we fish is hundreds of miles from where the whales are."

"But I've seen photos of them tangled up in fishin' gear and . . ."

He shot Robert a look so he dropped it.

Doris smiled meekly at Ingrid, who nodded in sympathy. "C'mon, Jimmy, let's leave them alone so they can get some suppah," she grabbed her husband by the arm and they headed out the side door onto the main drag.

Robert was enjoying his Johnny Walker, scouring the menu he'd brought back from the bar. "That was interesting."

"He's not alone with those opinions," Ingrid replied. "There's a lot of hatred towards the government and their regulations. These issues are complex and I don't have any good answers."

"But surely these fishermen understand global warming is a threat to their way of life."

"Some do. But not everyone thinks it's because of fossil fuels."

"Being resistant to change is never smart," Robert said.

"Tell me about it. My father used to talk about the end of the granite quarrying business. 'There is only so much granite to be had,' he'd say. He wondered how the islanders would be able to earn a living. But then a new crop of youngsters invested in fishing vessels and built our thriving lobster industry. But now it could well be that lobstering is also winding down and the next generation will need to figure out something new again. I certainly hope not."

"What will people do if they can't lobster?"

"Probably the same as the steel workers, the mill workers, the small farmers—everyone who ever worked in an industry that didn't survive. Find a new way to earn a living on the island or move."

"That will be so hard on these families who have been lobstering for several generations. What else could they possibly do? I know that Biden has set aside monies to help train workers in green energy and other new tech—"

"Let's not talk about that stuff. Our politics are so divisive nowadays, it's enough to give you a stroke. Tell me more about yourself, Robert."

"Well . . . I was born and raised outside of Philadelphia. Had a good career in pharmaceutical sales, raised three children. You know Jon, of course."

"Where do the others live?"

He glanced out the side window at the dark street, lit by one faded streetlight. "They're both dead."

"Oh, I'm sorry."

"Not easy outliving one's children," he looked down, tears welling in his eyes. "Tell me, is Kevin your only child?"

"I have a daughter, Olivia. Had her with my second husband, Scott. A better husband choice than my first, Earl."

"Where does Olivia live?"

"Boston. She's an art restoration expert who does work for many leading museums."

"How interesting."

"Susan is her daughter. Sue decided to settle out here even though it upset her mother."

"Why?"

"Oh, too far away, for one thing. Plus, the career options are not great. And she was not incorrect, as now she rarely sees her grandkids, Svea and Logan."

"What does Susan do for work?"

"She teaches fourth grade at the school. Waitresses in the summer. She's happy out here and I'm glad she's nearby."

He sipped his drink. "We have something in common then."

"What's that?"

"We've both been married twice before."

"Ah, you too?"

"Yes."

"Where do they live?"

"My second wife passed away from a heart attack in

Texas. Jon's mother Jane lives in California."

"Hmm. Nice and far away," she laughed. "I'm afraid my first husband lives on the island. That makes life tough at times as I cannot avoid him. I don't know what the hell I was thinking when I married him. I was young and stupid. Had no idea he had such a temper."

"How long were you married to him?"

"Eight years. Earl scared me at times. Had a wicked short fuse. I needed to protect Kevin. Called him *lardass* and other humiliating names. Kevin was just four years old," she let out a prolonged sigh. "Can you imagine?"

"And your second husband?"

"A better choice, or so it seemed, but Scott died young of colon cancer."

"Was he also a local?"

"He passed away from colon cancer," she repeated herself. So, he asked again.

"Was Scott a local?"

"Yes. A lobsterman who was a kind stepfather to Kevin and a good role model. But looking back, the damage had already been done to Kevin by his birth father. I've made far too many mistakes in my life."

"Haven't we all," he reached across the table and touched her hand. "What do you recommend on the menu?"

"I'm just going to get a salad as most everything is fried and my stomach can't handle that."

"Hmm, I'm leaning toward the fish and chips."

"That's a good choice. It's haddock. Not fresh. Frozen."

Ingrid managed to get the attention of the young waitress on her way to the kitchen, and ordered their food. They sat sipping cocktails as more people arrived for trivia. Robert was interested in a conversation at the next table between two lobstermen. He had difficulty understanding them given their thick accents and low voices.

The one in a red-and-black flannel shirt spoke in a booming bass: "I've had bettah."

"Me too," replied the other man who was dressed in a T-shirt and shorts, despite the weather.

"How much didja pay for whatchu got?"

"I dunno. 'Bout $25 for one, I think it was."

"Dang, that's highway robbery."

He assumed they were talking about drugs until he heard: "I've got some frozen you could have."

The other man leaned in to hear better. "Is the frozen any good? I like it fresh. With a pineapple salsa I make."

"It's good enuf. Nothin' fresh now, anyways. Have a look at this he-ah," he swiped at his phone until he found what he wanted. "This was Grandma Hilda's recipe. It's the only way to prepare haul-a-butt, fresh or frozen. On the grill in mayo and buttah. Wrapped in tinfoil so you don't overcook it. You should come by Sundee aftah-NOON and I'll give you a good-sized piece. I've got more than I can sell or eat leftovah from spring."

89

Ingrid wondered where Robert had drifted off to. "Hello? Anyone home?"

"Sorry. I was just listening to those two fellas over there. I thought it might be a drug deal but apparently they're just swapping recipes!" He laughed.

Ingrid turned to see who it was. She smiled. "Hey, Luther. How are you?" she called across the way.

"Good, Ingrid. How you holdin' up?"

"Still here," she said, and then turned back to Robert. "So, how are you and Jon getting on?"

"Okay, I think. I'm not sure he's very happy having me with him."

"Why's that?"

"I've made some mistakes myself, Ingrid. With him. We've grown apart and I don't think I can repair the damage done."

"How did Jon end up out here anyway?"

"He moved here with his mother who married a local."

"What's her name?"

"Jane Roberts is her maiden name."

"I remember her," Ingrid's eyes lit up. "She married Owen Swears. Owen's a good man, not sure why she left him, though."

"Jane can be a bit challenging. She was never satisfied with anything I did for her, or at least that's how I saw things back then. She met this Owen character while vacationing on the island,

90

divorced me and got married within two years. Impulsive. Not completely right in the head."

"And Jon?"

"Well, she brought him with her and Jon was confused by it all, the way adolescents understandably are. After Jon finished high school, he got a job with a builder out here. Then, his mother divorced Owen and has lived in New Mexico, Idaho, and is now in California."

"Is she bi-polar?"

"Could be. She's never gotten any help from what I can tell. Doesn't believe in Western medicine. Takes a lot of herbs and natural plants. Don't get me wrong. She's an interesting person. I suppose one would say she's neurotic. Which becomes exhausting, so I spent more time than necessary on the road in my job to avoid her. And she found a new man. As I said, I've made my share of mistakes."

"Haven't we all." Their dinners arrived and Robert was enjoying his haddock and fries when a younger man with short blond hair and a goatee approached the table. He was carrying two glasses of wine, which he set down in front of Ingrid.

"Ingrid," he exclaimed, "it's so great to see you out and about. How ya been?"

"Steven, look at you! You're a grown man."

"I know, hard to believe, isn't it."

Ingrid pulled a chair across the floor from the adjacent table. "This is Robert, he's new to the island."

"Nice to meet you, Robert. I'm Steve Coen."

Ingrid said: "I knew Steven's father when we were kids. I used to babysit for Steven when he was just a wee thing. You were such an adorable little boy, playing with your trucks all the time."

"And now I'm in charge of the public works department. It all adds up, doesn't it."

"You loved playing with your trucks," she repeated herself, and Steven started to say something but stopped, seeing Robert nodding his head.

She laughed. "Sure does all add up. It's so nice to see you, Steven. You didn't need to buy us these drinks."

"Actually, I didn't. Cliff did," he pointed to the bar where an older man doffed his cap at Ingrid. She raised her glass to him mouthing the words *thank you.*

Robert turned to see the man at the bar and smiled.

Steven asked: "Got any big plans for your birthday?"

"Probably going to spend it with Kevin and Susan."

"How's Kevin? Staying out of trouble I hope?"

"As far as I can tell."

"Well, that's good to hear."

Robert leaned across the table towards Ingrid: "When's your birthday?"

"January 18th. Maybe you can join us for dinner that night?"

"I'd love to," Robert nodded.

"How 'bout I get you some lobstahs from my brother Billy," Steven offered.

"Oh, don't bother."

"No bother."

"Well, if you're sure, that would be a nice treat. Do you like lobster, Robert?"

"Sure do."

Steven got up to leave. "Okay, then. I'll bring you some the morning of the 18th. Should I come out to your house or will you be in-town at Susan's?"

"We'll be at my place. Are you sure that's not too big a pain to bring them all the way out there?"

"Are you kiddin'?" he smiled, revealing a large gap between his two front teeth. "For the Island Queen, nothing's too big a pain. God, it's so good to see you, Ingrid. I won't kid you, I've been worried about you. Didn't see you a-TALL this summah."

"I'm sure I'm not the only local who avoids town in the summer."

"True," he slid his chair back toward the adjacent table. "I thought I was going to blow a gasket in August with all the day-trippahs and crazy folks on bikes thinkin' they owned the roads. Nevah seen it so busy. Ever since the pandemic. Took the family campin' up in Moosehead and it was good to get away. Well . . . I'll leave you to your suppers."

After he was gone Robert shot Ingrid a mischievous grin.

"Island Queen?"

She laughed. "It's sort of an island joke. Began after I came back from college."

"So . . . you're island royalty? Should I bow? Curtsy?"

She laughed even harder this time. "My grandfather did a lot for the island and the oldtimers loved him. Then my father continued the tradition of giving back to the island, so by the time I came along, the family was very well-respected. I've been meaning to dictate to Susan some of the old stories before they're lost forever. Most of my generation has died off out here. I worry too many of the young ones don't know all the wonderful stories. God, we've had some characters over the years. There is a bumper sticker some wag came up with: You've got to be a little off to be on Archer Island."

Robert laughed. "Love that! Maybe I can get one?"

"I think they don't make them anymore, but you can see them on some older island pickups. You know, the ones that can't pass inspection on the mainland, so are kept out here where they can be driven without a sticker. Like the one you drove here in tonight," she gazed out the window at Jon's backup vehicle.

A woman came out from the kitchen to greet Ingrid. "Hey there, Island Queen. How've ya been?"

"Betty Jean! It's so nice to see you. I've been okay. I'd like you to meet Robert Davis. He's Jon's father."

"Well, anyone who's related to Jon is good by me. I adore your son. He's done some work for me up at my camp."

94

"Thanks, that's always nice to hear," Robert replied.

"Robert, this is Betty Jean Ames, the owner of this fine establishment."

"Ah, lucky you!"

"How's your fish and chips?" Betty Jean asked. She was wearing an apron and had a bead of sweat on her top lip.

"Excellent," he said. "It's nice to dine out for a change."

"How long have you been here?"

"Since before Thanksgiving. I'm living with Jon."

"And how was your salad, Ingrid?"

"Very good, thank you."

"We've got some pies for dessert if interested. Key lime, peanut butter chocolate, and one last slice of banana cream."

"Ooh . . . key lime sounds good," Ingrid said. "Want to split a piece, Robert?"

"Love to."

Betty Jean went to fetch a slice of pie and returned in a few minutes, weaving her way through the crowd. "Here you go. I've got to get trivia going, so hopefully I'll see you around, Ingrid. Please say hello to Susan for me. Nice to meet you, Robert."

They finished their meals and enjoyed the slice of pie, which Robert said was as good as anything he had in Florida. The bar was now packed with several tables playing trivia, Betty Jean calling out questions and keeping track of the scores on a white board beside the bar. The young waitress was under pressure to politely get those not playing trivia out of the restaurant, so more tables would open up for those who came to play. She dropped off the check and Robert reached for it, but Ingrid stopped him,

"Let me get this, Robert. Please, you're my guest."

"No, I insist."

"Then, at least let's split it."

He paused and then nodded okay.

They each placed a credit card on the table and told the waitress to split it down the middle. She hurried off to run their cards and returned five minutes later with slips for each to sign. Robert and Ingrid were eager to leave, with the bar now louder than before. A group of four was lurking off to the side waiting to take their seats. Robert reached across the table and put both credit cards in the top front pocket of his flannel shirt. He held Ingrid's bulky parka, helping her get it on, and then grabbed his lambswool coat and hat. They hurried outside into the starry night, relieved to leave the noise behind.

The evening was clear and cold, a sliver of new moon visible above the spruce tree up the hill, the Christmas lights gone. Robert had driven Jon's island-only truck, an old Ford that served as his son's backup vehicle. Lacking an inspection sticker, the pickup could not leave the island, and had Archer Island spraypainted on the driver's door to assure it stayed put. Unsure of how Ingrid would get home, Robert asked:

"How'd you get here, Ingrid?"

"Susan dropped me off."

"Let me give you a lift home."

"I'm just at Susan's around the corner. But how about we take a ride around town and I'll show you some of my old haunts."

"Sounds terrific," Robert opened the passenger door and gave her a hand as she climbed up onto her seat. He came around to the driver's side and struggled to swing his left leg through the door frame. This old truck had been designed for people much shorter than him, and getting in and out of cars had become challenging, what with locked knees and hips in various stages of arthritic decline. Ingrid reached across and helped hoist him up, Robert landing squarely in the seat.

"There we are," he laughed. "God it's cold and windy."

"Does this old jalopy have heat?" she asked.

"Doubt it," he cranked the engine. "Where to, Island Queen?"

"Head up the hill and take a left on Dunbar. That's my childhood neighborhood. And don't forget to wave to cars coming at us."

He headed up the hill, waving energetically to a passing SUV.

Ingrid laughed. "You wave like you're from away."

"How should I wave?"

"Not like a crazy person. Just roll your hand up on the steering wheel and give a graceful wave."

"Like this?" he practiced.

"That's better, but—"

"How about like this?" he tried again.

"You just keep practicing and I'm sure with time you'll look less and less like a goober."

"Goober?"

"Yes, someone who doesn't know what they're doing. A *goober.*"

Robert repeated: "Goober. Wow, I had no idea. You realize if someone waved at a stranger in Florida, they'd likely be shot, or at least flipped the bird."

"Good thing we're not in Florida, then. Turn left up here by the library. This used to be the Millers' home, up on the right," Ingrid shivered, pulling the hood of her parka over her head. "I played hide-and-seek with Mary Miller and her brother Thomas in their backyard. Sadly, Thomas died in Vietnam. Keep going up this street. That big house on the corner, with the rhododendrons out front, belonged to Earl Swenson, who owned the drugstore on Main Street. Looking back, those were boom times out here, with four grocery stores, several restaurants, two bowling alleys, two pool halls, a newspaper store, millinery shops, traveling musical theatre groups, a drugstore, and four or so fraternal orders like the Masons and Odd Fellows."

"I suppose the population was considerably larger back then," Robert said.

"Yes, about twice what it is now." She laughed. "Funny story about one of those pool halls, it was in a small building no longer here that was perched over the rushing tidal pool, so one side of the pool tables had to be raised and lowered depending on how much the building was moving with the tides."

"That must have led to some calls of cheating," Robert laughed.

"No doubt, and probably a fight or two."

"Independent drugstores and newsstands are relics of the past," Robert continued down the dark street. "I miss the old newsstands with magazines and tobacco and newspapers from around the world."

"Much is lost, yet much is gained," Ingrid said. "I can't believe all the technology that has changed our lives for the better. The Internet. The phones. My Pacemaker! Ooh . . . take a right up here and head down to the old ballfield."

The hill sloped down to a field where two sets of bright LED headlamps on pickup trucks lit a skating pond where families had gathered. Two granite benches sat off to the side as young parents wrestled on ice skates for their budding Olympic champions, some in tears, others laughing and singing.

"Pull in here," Ingrid gestured.

He parked the pickup and left the engine running, a trickle of heat battling the cold in the cabin. The sliver of moon cast shadows through the chestnut trees behind the skating pond, their ancient branches all akimbo, damage from winter storms evident, but at least as yet, unable to topple the stately trees. Ingrid looked at them and saw herself, bent but not broken, still here above ground.

"This used to be a baseball field," Ingrid said. "Right here in the middle of town. The crowds were huge and we had a semi-pro league with some very good players. Butch Warren, Cliff Johnson, Billy Philbrook. I had a teenage crush on Billy. He was good enough to be scouted by the Red Sox, but got his arm tangled up in lobster lines one spring, putting an end to those dreams."

"Why did they stop playing baseball in town?" he asked.

"Lots of reasons. It's very swampy here and as the tides rose higher and higher, it made sense to invest in a new field up at the school for the kids. But it's sad, as no one plays baseball out here at all in the summer, which is the best time to play when the weather finally warms up. The better kids leave the island and play on the mainland."

"Well, it's nice at least to see it being used as a skating pond."

"Agreed. And it's good of the town's public works crew, along with a few volunteers, to clear the brush in the fall, so it fills evenly with water for skating. Let's keep driving, this is great fun for me."

"Where to?"

"Let's head to the bridge. I'll show you how to get there."

They drove five minutes to an old iron bridge crossing narrows connecting the main harbor with an inlet where a few homes were in the dark.

"No one's out now," Ingrid said. "Just pull out onto the bridge so we can look back at town. They used to bring granite down these narrows from the quarry. The old bridge could be raised—what's the word? . . . drawbridge—to let the schooners pass. They would continue into the harbor before sailing south."

"Did you work at the family granite business after college?" Robert asked.

"In fact, I did, for a brief time. After Wellesley my father asked me to manage the customer service ladies. Let me tell you, those older women were not happy about having some college-educated know-it-all—who was the president's daughter—telling them how to change what they had been doing for years. I truly was not needed, but my father wanted me to stay on the island and not pursue my passion so kept me under his wing until I married and got pregnant. I stopped working then."

"What passion did you want to pursue?"

"My word. Such a long time ago," she looked pensive. "I became interested in politics during college and my roommate's father was a congressman in D.C. He offered me a job on his campaign staff but I guess in hindsight it was asking too much of an island girl to venture out into the big bad world. So, I declined and returned home."

They sat without speaking and Robert could see the regret in Ingrid's eyes. They looked at the dim lights of the town across the harbor, the ferry lights off in the distance the primary source of light.

"The old coal-fired electric plant used to be over there, where the docks are now," Ingrid pointed. "Before we got the new wind power. And a large herring operation was just past those docks."

Robert released an involuntary shiver, shaking for several moments in the cold. The old Ford's heater could only contribute so much warmth.

"Too cold for you?" Ingrid turned to face him.

"Afraid I'm a Florida boy after all these years," he smiled. His blue eyes were lit by the moon reflecting off the side mirror. Ingrid pulled herself close to him. "Let's sit together so we can stay warm. Snuggle up."

She smelled like lemongrass, possibly perfume, possibly shampoo. She rested her head against his shoulder and they sat in quiet, watching the darkness envelope the tiny town off in the distance, no sounds at all other than their breathing and the occasional gust of wind.

Chapter Nine
January 2023

It was blowing hard out of the northwest when Bobby and I arrived at Ingrid's for her birthday party. A snowstorm had just missed the island, passing out to sea, dragging down frigid Canadian air and howling winds.

"Can you believe it out there?" Bobby was greeted at the door by Susan, who waved us inside and took our coats to the entryway closet.

"Come join us in the living room. Kevin has a fire going," Susan said.

"Hello, boys!" Ingrid rose from her seat in front of the fire to greet us. "It's so good to see you. Thanks for venturing out in this wind."

"Wouldn't miss this for the world," Bobby gave her a peck on the cheek. "I brought you a gift."

"You shouldn't have," she took the hastily wrapped package, which judging from its weight and feel, must be a book.

"Go ahead, open it," Bobby pulled up a wooden chair next to hers.

"Oh, thank you! Mary Oliver, one of my very favorites. And I don't own this one. How thoughtful of you, Robert. I believe you know everyone, possibly with the exception of Doctor Cocroft and his wife, Ellen."

A young man with a brown beard rose to shake Bobby's hand. The doctor had a shock of unruly hair rising from his head like a plume of smoke, giving him an overall unkempt rural doctor look. Bobby thought to himself this guy would never make it in Palm Beach.

"Pleasure to meet you, Robert."

"And you as well, Doctor."

"Please, call me Jeremy. This is my wife, Ellen."

An attractive young woman with stylish red hair cut into side-swept bangs shook Bobby's hand. "Nice to meet you," she said.

Bobby gestured toward me. "This is my son, Jon."

"We know Jon," Jeremy said. "Good to see you again."

"You too."

The lobsters steaming in the kitchen added a pleasing fishy humidity to the otherwise bone-dry house. The windows were all fogged up. I walked into the kitchen where Kevin and Susan were preparing dinner.

"Anything I can do to help?"

Kevin turned to face me. "We've got things under control. Wanna beer?"

"No . . . I'm good."

"I've got some Geary's pale ale."

"I'll just have water."

"Be that way," he removed the lid from the pot of steaming lobsters and pulled on an antenna or two to see if they broke away freely, which they didn't. He placed the lid back on the black steaming pot. Susan shot me a sympathetic glance as she walked to the old porcelain sink and poured me a glass of water.

"These bugs need another five minutes," Kevin was wearing a chef's apron. Kevin's usage of *bugs* for lobsters was one of those quaint island expressions, like thickafog. I returned to the living room and sat next to the doctor, while my father chatted with Ingrid.

I turned to Doctor Cocroft, who had moved out here three years ago with his wife and two young children. It was just as difficult to keep a doctor on the island as it was to keep police, and the doctor's three-year contract would be expiring this year. "How is everything at the Medical Center?"

"Challenging, as always," he looked weary.

"Why's that?"

"We lost Weezy last week. He had a heart attack . . . we got him to the hospital in Oceanside, but he didn't make it. Such a nice old man."

I had noticed that Old Weezy, as he was known, was no longer sitting on the bench out front of the post office, where he could be found most days across the year. Old Weezy was a true one of a kind, a born and bred proud islander who was the most loving human being you will ever meet. He was always among the first to donate what he could to every charity and was equally loved by islanders and summer residents. He had served in Vietnam and was active at the local American Legion. He would be sorely missed by many.

"I'm so sorry to hear that."

"We had an overdose over the holidays. Fortunately, we were able to get Narcan in time to save her life. But we don't have a paramedic out here now, so I've had to ride on the ambulance for the emergencies. The holidays always do a number on people. Overeating. Drinking to excess. Heart attacks and strokes. My job has become a 24/7 on-call situation, not what I signed up for or was promised by the hiring board. I'm on call right now and hope I can have a night in peace."

"Isn't Walt a paramedic?" I asked.

"No, he's an EMT."

"What's the difference?"

"Walt's a great guy, someone I rely on all the time, but he's not a paramedic, who is trained to administer emergency medicines and provide a higher level of care on the ambulance than what he can."

"Are there no funds for a paramedic?"

"There are, but we can't find anyone qualified to take the position out here. It's not an easy job to fill in the best of times even on the mainland, but the pandemic made it that much more difficult."

"If you don't mind me asking, do you still prescribe OxyContin for pain? Or has that stopped?"

"I try not to, but if someone wants it badly enough, they can always find some doctor on the mainland who will prescribe it. OxyContin is just too addictive, so I mostly use Percocet or one of the other older drugs with more data behind them."

"That's good to hear. I was prescribed Oxy when I fell off a ladder, and could not believe how addictive it was."

"I'm sorry to hear that, Jon. Were you able to break free?"

"I was, but only because I went into rehab for my drinking problem. I managed to kick them both while there."

A rush of noise came whooshing down the stairs as Susan brought Svea and Logan from their upstairs bedroom. The children wore pajamas, excited to be spending the night with their great-grandmother. Svea was holding a well-worn teddy bear, while Logan had a copy of *Go Dog Go!* and pleaded with Ingrid to read to him. He plopped down in her lap by the fire. "Please Grammy!"

As she read to him, I was reminded of how my mother loved to read books to me when I was young. A favorite was *Stuart Little*, and I would ask her to read it every night before bed for almost a year straight. Now, gazing at Logan on Ingrid's lap in front of the fire, I felt a sudden pang in my gut. He looked so innocent. All children *are* so innocent, yet life cruelly leads them off course into hardships no one should have to endure. I found myself in that moment missing my mother, feeling resentful that I was here with my father instead of with her. He didn't deserve to be with me. She was the one who had done her best to care for my siblings and me, despite her depression and other psychological challenges. She hung in there with us, doing her best to be a good mother, while Bobby was off "working," undoubtedly shacked up with some nurse he met while peddling Big Pharma drugs. I vowed to call my mother tomorrow and visit her in California soon. It had been too long.

"Kevin, would you be a dear and order me another box of fatwood kindling from L.L. Bean?" Ingrid's voice brought me back to the party. "I'm running low and it seems we're in for a real winter for a change."

"Sure Mom. Where's your purse?"

"Should be hanging from the back of the chair over by the entry door, unless you've gone and moved it on me once again, which I wish you wouldn't do."

Kevin ignored this comment and retrieved her purse, which was hanging from the kitchen doorknob, and riffled through its contents until he found her pink wallet inside. "I ain't seeing your credit card, Mom. Don't tell me you've lost it again. Here, you look."

Kevin rather rudely tossed the heavy purse onto her lap, and returned to the kitchen to check on the lobsters. Ingrid foraged around inside the purse for several minutes while the rest of us talked and observed her off to the side. She would pull out her keys, then her eyeglasses, and then put them back inside only to pull them out again. When it became apparent that she had forgotten what she was looking for and was becoming oddly obsessive, Susan walked over and took her purse. "Let me look for you, Grammy. It's the Capital One card, right?"

"Yes, thanks dear."

"I'm not seeing it. Where else might you have put it?"

"Maybe in my desk drawer. Look there."

Susan walked to the antique desk next to the grand piano. "Not here, either."

By now the search for the credit card had halted all conversation as we could see Ingrid's increasing distress. She was reaching into her pockets and feeling around behind the sofa cushions, which made it clear to the rest of us we needed to help find her card. We got up and wandered around in what was a truly futile undertaking, a building buzz-kill threatening the party. Susan saw this might ruin her grandmother's celebration, and attempted to redirect Ingrid's attention back to Svea and Logan, who sat on the rug in front of the fire.

"Grammy, why don't you read the children *Blueberries for Sal.* Here's a copy," Susan talked to Ingrid as if she were a toddler. I sensed Ingrid was aware of the bossy and condescending tone in Susan's voice and didn't like it one bit.

Susan's redirection almost worked, but then Kevin returned from the kitchen and asked: "When did you last have the card, Mom?"

Ingrid looked up from the children's book in confusion. "I'm not sure. I don't think I've used it since Christmas."

"Think hard. Did you use it to order heating oil?"

She didn't reply. Susan snapped at Kevin: "The oil company has her card on file so she wouldn't need it for that." An implied *you idiot* was conveyed in her tone.

"How about the J. Crew catalog? Or Talbots? Or Garnet Hill? She's always buying the same things ovah and ovah from them," Kevin looked annoyed. "I've had to return two sweaters this month because she already had one."

"Oh, you didn't, did you?" Ingrid looked up, now effectively redirected. "I have one in yellow but wanted the same sweater in red and blue."

"Drop it, Kevin," Susan shot him a look. "Just go back to the kitchen and I'll handle this. Grammy, I'm sure your credit card will turn up. Let's not ruin the party over this now, okay? It's probably in the laundry. Or maybe in the car. We'll find it tomorrow." Susan knelt in front of Ingrid and started reading *Blueberries for Sal* to the children, Ingrid gazing vacantly into the fire.

We enjoyed a good dinner of lobster, corn bread, salad, and a chocolate birthday cake with orange frosting Susan had made for dessert. Bobby was drinking heavily and I found myself looking at him as if gazing into an unwanted mirror—this man who was my father, who had passed along his alcoholic genes to me, but for whom drinking didn't seem all that problematic. He apparently could drink without becoming a raging lunatic, without needing to be sent away to rehab several times. He was seated at the table next to the doctor's young wife, Ellen, and as I watched

Ingrid observing them, I could overhear tidbits of their conversation.

"Don't you think life is deadly dull out here?" Ellen asked my father. "Don't you miss Florida?"

"No, I'm liking it here."

"Well, don't tell my husband, but I wish we could move back to the mainland instead of renewing his contract at the Medical Center. I didn't want to live here in the first place. Our children are not doing well in school and I miss shopping and dining out."

Bobby leaned in and touched her on the elbow. "Surely, a beautiful woman like you must have opportunities for fun out here."

She laughed. "There's no fun to be had out here in the winter. I like the summers when I can play tennis and swim in the quarries."

I thought I heard Bobby whisper: "I was thinking more along the lines of the *indoor sports*. You know, the warm and cuddly ones."

Ellen blushed and didn't seem to mind this old geezer flirting with her. Could be, what with her husband working around the clock, she welcomed any attention she could get. It was obvious she was a bit tipsy herself. They were laughing and bumping shoulders. Kevin sat at the far end of the table staring at Bobby with a growing distrust. But it was Ingrid who had a new expression on her face, one I had never seen. She glowered at

Bobby in a way that made me wonder if, in that moment of her cognitive decline, she knew who this strange man was seated at her table. One thing was for certain. She looked like she wanted to kill him.

Chapter Ten
October 2023

If you've never been the subject of an unwanted hashtag campaign, consider yourself lucky.

By the beginning of October, word had spread around the island that I was the lead suspect in my father's murder. Back in September, islanders I knew, and some I didn't, launched an online social media movement (yes, movement!): #JusticeforJon. Not only was this campaign online, but it could be found around the island on large hand-painted signs. There had been several horrifying national murders of defenseless Black men in the news, so imagine the bewildered looks of leaf-peeping New Yorkers upon seeing these #JusticeforJon signs, cashmere sweaters draped across shoulders, arriving for a day's escape to the island.

As I've made clear to you from the start, I am someone who values my privacy. An introvert. Now there was no place to hide. Miquel spray-painted in orange dayglo a damaged piece of plywood at the Douglas Point job site with the hashtag; Walt painted a granite boulder greeting visitors as they disembarked from the ferry, and Betty Jean started a GoFundMe page to help with legal fees. $6,500 had already been raised. Pickup trucks driven by people I didn't know had #JusticeforJon chalked on their rear windows, many of which were also emblazoned with Go

Brandon bumper stickers. Not exactly the association I was seeking. A sophomore girl I hardly knew hung a hand-painted sheet from the scoreboard for all to see at home soccer games (the visiting parents wondering who this Jon could be, whispering: "They have Black people out here?"). The outrage among my defenders had gone too far, with an occasional bar fight. It was eye-opening to see how worked up people can get when there is some cause to get behind. I attribute this mostly to boredom. Poor Timmy Tetreault, who was simply trying to do his job while operating under the thumb of the state cop, became the butt of jokes. "Dumbass couldn't tie his own shoe till eighth grade." "Timmy Tetreault puts the T in sTTToopid." "Who's his Daddy? The head of the state police! Duh."

Not all public opinion was in my court, with some locals unconvinced of my innocence. Kevin went out of his way to knife me in the back: "Jon hated his father. They wuz fightin' all the time. He had started drinkin' again and you know what a wicked temper that man has when drunk." There were whispers among some island women who knew Ingrid best: "Maybe she bashed the old man over the head after she found him using her credit card? Wouldn't blame her."

A few weeks after Timmy Tetreault and the state cop had questioned me at my home, I saw them parked outside of Shane Vachon's RV in the town parking lot. The state cop, who I later came to learn had a name—Ray Jackman—was knocking on the door of the RV. The townspeople had grown accustomed to seeing a variety of investigators on the island since the death of my father, and every person on Archer Island had a theory. The town was abuzz with rumors, and facts were difficult to come by.

At the market that morning, two summer people I had done jobs for saw me walking down the aisle and abruptly turned and hurried off. The word was out. I was the lead suspect. I was "that Jon, the hashtag fella." A handful of lingering summer people I had thought were my friends now looked at me in a new suspicious way. Farewell parties I would normally have been invited to came and went without me. People in cars who normally waved as I passed now had their hands firmly on the wheel. I found myself keeping track of who no longer waved, adding them to my growing list of people I would refuse to help in the future. For some I was an innocent; for others I was persona non grata.

I had contacted my lawyer friend, Joel Katz, who was there when the cops searched my house with a warrant. I wasn't convinced Joel believed I was innocent but, being a good lawyer, he assured me that didn't matter. Perfect. The police found nothing of interest and headed off following up on other leads. One of those leads I suggested to them was to check on Shane Vachon.

Now, as I walked towards my pickup in the town parking lot, I saw Officer Jackman and Timmy Tetreault pounding on Shane's

RV door. I had become concerned about Shane following the missing materials mystery at the Douglas Point job site. I was pissed off the way he wiggled out of that mess, especially after Kevin was caught and Miquel took the rap, and then Rohan Patel, the homeowner, dropped the charges. Patel wanted his home built and correctly assumed there were no other contractors available. And, as a new wealthy summer resident, didn't want to get off on the wrong foot, preferring to tread lightly so most locals would have no idea who he was. This was the norm for the handful of billionaires with summer homes on the island.

Problems with Shane arose back in June when I was out for ice cream with Charlie Walsh. I was growing to truly enjoy Charlie's company and was happy to see him doing well on the baseball diamond and at the job site. We were passing the ferry terminal one afternoon and I saw Kevin's pickup truck carrying what looked like the expensive German windows we had special ordered for the Patel project. I turned my truck around and pulled into the ferry line next to Kevin's pickup.

"What you got there, bud?" I asked.

Kevin looked surprised to see me. "Nuthin."

"Doesn't look like nothing to me, Kevin. Why do you have three of the windows in the back of your truck?"

He paused, looking nervous and agitated. He reeked of marijuana. "Shane wanted me to bring them ovah to Oceanside so he could show a prospective customer he's got."

"One window isn't enough?"

116

Again, Kevin looked agitated and I suspected he was not just high on marijuana but had also become addicted to OxyContin. I had seen him snorting drugs outside of his mother's one morning after I dropped my father off. I also saw him snorting something in his truck one early morning at the job site. He wasn't pulling his weight on the project and had become a source of constant irritation for me. Shane, for whatever reasons, didn't want to fire him and we were now behind schedule with little hope of earning the early completion bonus. Before I could get a satisfactory answer from Kevin, the ferry worker waved him down the ramp and onto the boat.

"Something's not right, Charlie."

Charlie looked down at his feet and mumbled: "There's something I probably should have told you about last week."

"What's that?"

"One of the day workers—I think it was Miquel—was talking to his pal at the market about stolen materials from the job site. He said when he was over in Oceanside, he saw Kevin unloading some sheetrock into a blue pickup truck waiting at Dunkin' Donuts. And taking cash from the man in the truck."

"Shit, that explains it. I've been matching the delivery slips against the inventory and they aren't right. When I double-checked at the lumber yard to make sure they had shipped the correct quantities, they told me they were correct. To keep an eye on the 'Mexican' day laborers—as they call them. Figures."

The next time Shane was on the island, I went to call on

117

him at his RV to let him know Kevin was stealing. I knocked repeatedly on the door until Shane finally opened up and stood with me out front.

"What's up, Jon," I got the distinct impression I had interrupted him. He closed the door tightly behind him.

"There's something you should know but I don't want you telling Kevin that I'm the one who told you."

"Sure. What is it?"

"I think he's been stealing from the job site."

"Why do you say that?" he wiped his hoodie sleeve across his dripping nose.

"The inventory hasn't been matching up, and I saw him taking some of the German windows over to the mainland."

I expected Shane to be angry but instead he said: "I asked him to do that. I've got a potential customer over there interested in building an energy-efficient home, so thought those might be a good option."

This caught me off guard. Was it possible Kevin had been telling the truth? "Oh, okay. But . . . I don't understand why he had three windows in the bed of his truck."

"Yeah, that was just a mistake on his part. Only needed one." Something about Shane didn't sit right with me. He was such a scrawny little dude, and his sallow complexion and sunken eyes made me think of drug addicts I had met at rehab. It was strange the way he wore long-sleeved hoodies most of the time, even on hot days.

I looked long and hard into his eyes, and he did his best to avoid making eye contact with me.

"Well, Shane, the inventory has also been off for sheetrock. I estimate we've had over three grand of materials go missing."

"Can you show me the slips?"

"I'll bring them tomorrow."

Shane's eyes were searching for a way out like a rat trapped beneath a sewer grate. "You don't suppose the day workers have been stealing?"

"God no, they're concerned about keeping their jobs and work visas. I know they wouldn't do anything that stupid. Kevin, on the other hand—"

"Just bring me the paperwork tomorrow and I'll have a look. In fact, you've got plenty on your plate without managing the inventory, so let me take that over from you. The Bass Harbor job is wrapping up, so I've got more time to help out here."

The next day I brought him the paperwork and nothing happened. After a week had passed, I asked him what he thought, and he said he was still looking into it. Then one day, Miquel didn't show up for work and the other day-laborers told me Shane had fired him for stealing. This really pissed me off. I was furious when I confronted Shane that afternoon at the job site.

"Shane, what the fuck happened with Miquel?"

"Calm down, Jon. That little prick was stealing from us," Shane scratched his forearm.

119

"I'm not buying that for one second. Miquel's a good kid. Hard worker. Honest."

"Well, apparently not."

"You know, Shane, just last week I saw Miquel returning galvanized nails he had in his pocket to the main supply. It was like, ten nails. When I told him not to bother, he insisted."

Kevin approached and spat off to the side. "Told ya, you can't trust those Mexicans."

"They're not Mexicans!" I snapped. "They're from Guatemala. Get a map you idiot."

"Chill, Jon," Shane stood between Kevin and me.

"Whatevah, they're all the same to me," Kevin walked off.

Two more weeks passed and even though I was no longer in charge of inventory, I took photos every day to see if materials were still disappearing. It became clear the stealing had not stopped with Miquel's firing. I no longer trusted Shane or Kevin and decided to contact Rohan Patel directly, which was a risk, but I didn't want to be part of a corrupt project. Now that summer had arrived, I could always find other work if need be. Patel was grateful I had been in touch and asked me to let him handle the situation, that he would keep me out of it, except he needed one small favor. He asked me to install a surveillance camera at the site, one that he could access remotely from California. He would mail one to me with instructions.

One early morning, before others arrived, I attached the

camera to a spruce tree where deliveries were dropped off. Just three days later, Timmy Tetreault pulled up in his cruiser and arrested Kevin, who had been captured on camera loading his pickup with sheetrock, covered with a tarp, and driving off.

"So much for your Mexican theory," I said to Shane as Kevin was taken away.

He didn't reply.

"Maybe you should get Miquel back, seeing he's innocent."

Again, no reply.

Shane had no choice but to fire Kevin. But Patel didn't fire Shane, which I suggested he do, as he wanted to get the house built. Patel didn't press charges against Kevin, who was released on probation. Kevin's boat was now ready to return to the water, so he walked free and returned to lobstering for the summer.

More than walk free, he was having a good old time hanging out with Shane doing drugs. Everyone on the island knew. But no one wanted to mess with Kevin or Shane. At my insistence, after discussing the situation with Patel, Miquel was hired back and there were no more issues with missing inventory.

I sat in my pickup on that early October day, watching as Timmy Tetreault and Officer Jackman stood in front of Shane's RV door. "Open up, Mr. Vachon, this is Officer Jackman. We need to ask you a few questions."

There was no reply so Tetreault walked around behind the

RV and pressed his ear up against the side to see if he heard anything. He whispered to Jackman: "He's in there."

"Vachon, for the last time, open up the door or we'll break it down."

Once again, no reply.

"Timmy," Jackman whispered, "get those people to stand back over there. You keep an eye on the parking lot while I kick in the door."

Tetreault gestured to a few onlookers to move back. He withdrew his gun from the holster and kneeled twenty feet off to the side as Jackman continued. "Okay, Vachon, I'm coming in." He was just about to kick in the door when it flew open and Shane bolted across the parking lot, firing a handgun twice toward where Tetreault was positioned. Tetreault and Jackman chased after him and I followed along in my truck. Shane was a fast runner and made it to the narrow strip of land that connects the parking lot to a residential neighborhood. He ran up behind the Medical Center into the woods and disappeared. I drove around to the side of the hill where the woods opened to a clearing, thinking he might cut through that way, but didn't see Shane. Tetreault and Jackman huffed and puffed beside me, winded from the chase.

"That shocked the shit outta me," Jackman said. "Timmy, go back to your cruiser and call for backup. We might need a chopper, I don't know."

Walt Wentworth and a few other lobstermen ran to the scene. Walt said: "What the hell's he running from?"

"I have a feeling he's got drugs in that RV," I said.

Walt asked: "Do you think he killed your father, Jon?"

"I can't see why," even though it would be nice to redirect attention away from me, the unwitting hashtag hero.

Officer Jackman said: "You're right, Jon. He probably did run off because of drugs, but we need to track that little sucker down. We better get back to the parking lot to make sure no one was hurt from those shots he fired."

Freddy Ames joined us and said: "I wouldn't be so sure he didn't kill Jon's father. That guy has been pissing off the entire town, parking his RV in the lot and ignoring our requests that he move it elsewhere. He's disrespectful of our community. Trust me, you cops are barking up the wrong tree thinking Jon did it. It's never locals. It's always people from away."

"Then how do you explain the fact Jon's prints are on the rock that killed his father?" Jackman asked. He had grown tired of locals always claiming innocence when he knew for a fact there were plenty of them who had gotten into trouble over the years, and many who still would. He had personally locked up more than a few.

"I can't explain it. But there's some reason we just can't see now. I'd bet my life it wasn't Jon. No way in hell he would have murdered his father."

I could hear the police chopper approaching across the harbor and decided I should head back home and let the authorities handle the search for Shane. I could tell Jackman was nervous having all these locals showing up on the scene, worrying a group of vigilantes might take control. It wouldn't be the first time that had happened.

Chapter Eleven

February 2023

One mid-February afternoon, Bobby offered to pay for groceries at the market, an unexpected and uncharacteristic gesture, the first time he had offered since arriving in November. I stood behind him in the checkout line as he slid his card in the reader and watched as the reader kept rejecting the transaction. He rubbed the card on his shirt hoping that would reduce static, but when this failed, I took the card from him and tried myself, and then saw Ingrid's name embossed in silver letters. Eager not to embarrass us both in public, I paid for the groceries with my bank card. Back in the pickup, my mind immediately jumped to the worst possible conclusion, that he had stolen the card from Ingrid. On the one hand this seemed like a stretch, but on the other I simply didn't know. Up until his dying day, Bobby was someone I could not get a good read on. We drove home and unloaded the groceries.

"Dad, that card you were trying to use in the market is not yours. It's Ingrid's."

"What?" He turned to face me with a perplexed look on his face, a look that struck me as genuine.

"See?" I handed it to him.

"I must have mistakenly taken it when we had dinner at the bar in January."

"Well, you need to call her and return it right away. Kevin is bound to think you stole it."

"C'mon, you know I wouldn't steal—"

"Yeah, but Kevin will."

"I'll call her right now. Damn, Jon, I feel badly about this."

Ingrid was surprised when Robert phoned her with the news. He apologized profusely over the phone and insisted on driving the card up to her immediately. I offered to drive him but he wanted to go alone. Ingrid may have become forgetful in recent months, but was still upset about the way he flirted with the doctor's young wife during her birthday dinner. Ever since, she had been ignoring his many messages and phone calls. She only picked up the phone now because she was confused and feeling unwell. Ingrid had mistakenly believed after their January dinner at the bar and subsequent drive around town that their friendship was becoming more than just friendship. Yet how could he possibly be serious about her when he was so insensitive, flirting in front of her at her birthday celebration? She felt ashamed of herself, behaving like a silly school girl, thinking she might actually find love again at her age. She knew better. She was done with men.

Ingrid greeted Robert coolly at the door, blocking him from coming in.

"Hello, Ingrid. I'm *so* sorry about this. I'm afraid my forgetfulness is growing worse. Please . . . may I come in?"

Ingrid held the door so it was open just a few inches, enough to peer through at Robert without allowing him to enter. She said nothing as he continued.

"I must have mistakenly taken your card when we had dinner at the bar. Remember how quickly we got out of there, with the people eager to take our table?"

"Just pass me the card through the door," she said. "And go away."

Robert passed the card to her and she could see tears in his blue eyes, a genuine look of contrition on his face. She exhaled deeply and opened the door so he could enter. Ingrid took his coat and placed it on the sofa in front of the fireplace. They sat side by side without speaking. Robert could tell she was very upset.

"What's the matter Ingrid? Has something happened?"

She turned away from him to face the windows overlooking the ocean and sighed. "I'm not having a good day."

"Please, tell me what's going on. Maybe I can help?"

"No, you are only making matters worse."

That stung. "Would you like me to leave?"

She turned back to him, her expression sunken into a sad frown combining bewilderment with anger. "No, stay."

Robert moved closer to her on the sofa and took her hand in his. "What's the matter Ingrid?"

"I haven't been feeling well. I'm becoming terribly confused. I was just trying to do my pills for the week and don't think I can do them anymore."

127

"I can help if you'd like."

"And now this with the credit card, and your behavior the night of my birthday party—"

"What did I do wrong?"

"Oh, come on now. The way you were flirting with the doctor's wife."

"I'm sorry, I hadn't realized I was."

"Really. Everyone could see it. I thought you liked me?"

"I like you very much Ingrid. I've been so sad that you've been ignoring my messages. I've missed you very much."

She looked at him. "Well, you certainly don't behave like someone who cares for me."

He sighed. "Listen, I'm very sorry. I had too much to drink and should not have behaved that way. I can be a fool at times. I know that."

"You're a terrible flirt. The sort of man I should know better than to let into my heart."

Robert smiled. "Am I in your heart?"

"Listen to me. I sound like a whimpering school girl."

"Well . . . you're in my heart, Ingrid. I'm not sure I've ever felt this way about another woman."

"Oh stop!"

"I'm serious. We had an immediate connection. Who knows what that is. Chemistry they say. Maybe we knew each other in a previous life. I don't know. But there's something between us."

She seemed to be brightening up. "Well, you are not my only problem. A spot has opened up at the Eldercare Center and Kevin is insisting I move in."

"Maybe you'd be happier there? Feel safer knowing there is staff available around the clock."

"Maybe," she gazed around at her beloved home. "I can't bear to leave this place."

"Let's not talk about that now. Have you had lunch?" Robert asked.

"No, I'm not hungry much anymore."

"Let's go into the kitchen and I'll fix us something to eat. You need to eat Ingrid."

Ingrid's pill bottles were open on the kitchen table. Her pill box had three tiers: breakfast, lunch, dinner.

"Would you please help me with these?" Ingrid asked.

"Sure," he sat next to her and read the labels for each of her bottles. He could see she had put too many of her blood pressure pill in each compartment and none of her blood thinner. She sat quietly and watched as he corrected what she had attempted to do.

"There, that looks good," he said. "All these pills are so complicated to deal with."

"And they keep changing the colors and sizes," she said. "As if life isn't hard enough without that."

Robert found some leftover pasta in the refrigerator and microwaved it for them. They sat at the kitchen table, the sunlight

129

slicing through the multipaned window lighting the teacups and tea kettle on the counter. He saw the teacup had on it an etching of Tortola in the British Virgin Islands. "Have you been to Tortola?" he pointed at the cup.

"Yes. You?"

"No, but I'd love to. Please don't tell Jon, but I purchased cruise tickets for next winter for us to go on a cruise together. As a way to thank him for all he's done for me."

"That's very generous of you."

"It's not actually all that expensive. I was pleasantly surprised."

"I took Susan and her kids to Tortola for my 80th birthday. We had a marvelous time. We stayed in a pension on the beach and I watched the children splash and play."

"Sounds divine."

"I've lived a good life, Robert. I've been very fortunate."

"Me too."

"It's important to be grateful for all we have," she said.

"Couldn't agree more."

"But the thought of leaving this home, which I've lived in for so many decades . . . it's just not something I ever envisioned."

They were interrupted by the sound of an approaching vehicle in the driveway. A few moments later, Kevin barged into the house, surprised to see her with Robert.

"Oh, you."

"Nice to see you, too, Kevin," Robert said facetiously.

"Mom, I thought we discussed this."

She looked away.

"I received a text from Capital One that someone on the island tried using your cancelled credit card this morning. I called to check if it was a legit text and it was. Someone at the market."

Bobby said: "I'm afraid that was me, Kevin. I didn't steal the card but mistakenly put it in my pocket when your mother and I dined out in January."

"Really?" he pumped up his chest. "You expect me to believe that?"

Ingrid said: "Yes, it was just an innocent mistake. I now recall how it happened."

"Yet there have been other charges on the card."

"Like what?" Robert asked.

"Like tickets for a fuckin' cruise to the Caribbean, that's what."

"That can't be—"

"Oh, it can be, all right. And also some clothing and wine."

Ingrid could see the perplexed look on Robert's face as she awaited an explanation. He reached into his wallet and pulled out a credit card.

"Good grief, I have the exact same card as Ingrid. See? It's the silver Capital One card. I must have been using hers by mistake thinking it was mine. Here, look. I'll pay back anything I charged mistakenly using her card."

Kevin snatched the card from his hand and saw it was identical to his mother's. "You know what? I don't really give a shit. I don't want you anywhere near my mother. She's movin' into Eldercare next week. You need to stay away from her."

"Kevin!" Ingrid exploded. "Stop! I told you, I don't want to leave here." Her face was beet red and twisted into an angry scowl, a look Robert had not seen before.

"I'm sorry, Mom. But you got to understand, you no longer can make decisions for yourself. You can't think straight."

"I can think straight, how dare you!"

"Trust me, you can't. Your doctor says it's time to go into Eldercare before you hurt yourself. Or burn this place down."

"What does that fool know!"

Kevin exhaled deeply, frustration with this situation that had now dragged on for several years wearing him down. He adopted a less combative tone.

"Maybe if you lived in town with Sue, that would work."

"I don't want to live in town with Sue. I like it here. Why did I have to be stricken with this awful disease? Why me?"

"It happens, Mom. You just turned eighty-five. Be realistic."

"Easy for you to say. I know what you and Olivia are up to. You want my house! Guess what, that's not going to happen. I've been in touch with my lawyer—"

"You what?"

"You heard me. I'm not leaving you or Olivia this house."

"What are you going to do with it then?" Kevin looked crushed.

"That's not for you to know."

Kevin wasn't sure if she was being serious and began to doubt she was, that this was just an idle threat. Still, now he was worried. He would need to find out who she was using for a lawyer and make sure they knew she had dementia. A change in her will certainly could not hold up in court. He was counting on the money he would get when he sold this place, cashing in on what would surely amount to several million dollars.

"It's not safe for you to live alone out here," Kevin continued. "And there is an opening at Eldercare *now* so we should snag it before it goes to someone else."

"I refuse," Ingrid sat with arms folded tightly across her chest. "You can't force me to go against my will."

Robert had been sitting there quietly observing. "I have a suggestion," he said.

Ingrid looked at him with new hope in her eyes.

"I could move in with you," he said.

"Oh, would you, Robert?" Ingrid's eyes lit up.

"Absolutely not," Kevin shot him down.

"Why not?" she asked.

"Because this man can't be trusted as far as I can piss in the wind. No way you're moving in here."

"I wish you would reconsider," Robert said. "Truth is, Jon would appreciate having me out of his hair."

"That ain't my problem."

"I know, but I would be happy to look after Ingrid for you. It would free you and Susan up a bit, given how much you have already done."

"I love the idea," Ingrid was smiling. "It would be so nice to have someone around day and night, someone I like and share common interests with. Come on, Kevin, I want to do this."

"The doctor says you will be needing round the clock nursing help soon. You know, incontinence and—"

"I can handle that," Robert said, even though he wasn't so sure. But it seemed like the right thing to say. "And she's fine now so let's just give it a try."

"Problem is, we'll lose our spot at Eldercare."

"I'm not going there no matter what," Ingrid dug in. "Ask Susan what she thinks. I bet she'll approve of the idea."

Susan's first reaction was not positive, but Logan had been having disciplinary problems at school and Susan needed to focus more of her attention on her children and less on Ingrid, so gave her consent. Everyone seemed happy with the solution, other than Kevin, who now worried his mother would give away the house and everything else she had to this charlatan from away.

Later that week, I helped my father move some of his clothes and personal effects up to Ingrid's, and then went back home and popped open a can of beer, my first drink in several years. A mistake, I know. As always, I thought I could have "just one drink" and then stay on the wagon, the way most normal people can without creating huge problems. But I'm an alcoholic. *My name is Jon and I'm an alcoholic.* How many times had I said those words at AA meetings over the years? I had seen the frequent relapses of others. I knew better, yet could not control my addiction, and began drinking alone once again, something I knew was dangerous.

With my father now at Ingrid's for much of the time, I regained my solitude and was grateful he had come up with what seemed like a win-win situation for all involved. I must admit, I was surprised he had volunteered to help Ingrid to the extent he did. Truth is, now that he's dead and gone, I need to reevaluate my opinion of him. I'm working on that every day.

Chapter Twelve
March 2023

The island is about as dead as any place on earth from March through mid-April, when at last a handful of summer residents can be spotted in the car line heading over from Oceanside. They're eager to check on their homes, to see what damage might have been done by winter storms. They usually find the same things: a few tree limbs down in the yard, Kit Kat and other Halloween candy wrappers blown into shrubs, and occasionally a busted window or two. Inside, there are bound to be acorns stashed under pillows, squirrels having moved in for the winter.

The early March snowstorms, with their wet sticky snow, can do a number on power lines and tree limbs, and we had a blizzard on St. Patrick's Day that year, which caused extensive damage. I helped Walt, Freddy, and some other islanders clean up the mess around town. Once the island roads were clear, I drove up to visit Ingrid and my father to make sure they were okay. I arrived to see the private dirt road to Ingrid's had been plowed, most likely by Kevin. I knocked on the front door and my father let me in.

"Hey, son, good to see you. Come in and warm up."

"Thanks."

"What a storm that was," my father was wearing two fleece-lined flannel shirts over a white undershirt that was pushing layers of loose neck flesh up beneath his chin.

I removed my boots and left them on the doormat by the door. "I'm glad to see you've got power out here. I think we're on the island's backup generator now. Best to only use what appliances you need so there's enough power for Archer Island and also those on Dunbar Island."

"Let me take your parka." He hung my snow-encrusted coat on the coatrack by the front door.

"Ingrid, Jon's here," he called out.

Ingrid was dressed in her pajamas and bathrobe as she entered the foyer. Her long gray hair was tangled, not yet brushed, and I was concerned I might have woken them up.

"It's good to see you, Jon. Please excuse my pajamas. Not going anywhere today given this weather."

"It's nice to see you, too, Ingrid. How have you been?"

"Soldiering on," she said.

"Do you have enough food?"

"We're all set," Bobby said. "We went to the market yesterday."

Ingrid gestured for me to follow them into the living room to sit in front of the fire. The multi-paned windows facing the northeastern side of the house were plastered with a wet, heavy snow. Several overburdened branches of the old spruce tree down by the waterfront threatened to snap. I saw that a snowbank had made a good home nestled into the protected deck corner where the house and deck adjoined. Seagulls circled above the ocean, riled up by the storm, never quite certain when winter was over and spring had arrived. They would need to wait a few more weeks for spring. There was a beautiful stillness outside as feathered storm clouds raced above, leaving a multi-layered patchwork of grays beneath.

Once seated, Bobby asked if I would like a glass of water.

"Actually, if you wouldn't mind, I'd like a beer."

He glanced at me in surprise.

"Are you sure?" Bobby leaned forward, hands folded in front of him.

"I can handle an occasional beer."

Ingrid said: "Oh, Jon. I know how hard you have worked to stay sober. Do you really think that is a good idea?"

Truth was, I knew it was not a good idea, but had gotten back into the groove of daily drinking. Sometimes in the mornings before lunch. I knew from my two previous stints at rehab that drinking before noon was one of the telltale signs of being an alcoholic. But hey! The gods gave us the great gifts of denial and rationalization for good reason, and life on this remote island in winter was bleak enough without an occasional buzz.

"I'm good, I can handle it."

My father returned with a can of Heineken and I took a long gulp, releasing a pleasurable sigh. I had worked up a good thirst while plowing the roads that morning. We sat in silence for a few moments and then Bobby got up to go to the bathroom, leaving me alone with Ingrid.

"You know, he loves you very, very much."

This caught me off guard and I managed a meek smile.

"I realize you men have difficulties sharing your feelings, but I want you to know that Robert is grateful for what you have done for him. And he's very proud of you."

"That's good to hear." I was thinking: *Maybe he could say it directly to me?*

She rubbed her right hand along her cheek, then across her mouth, and sighed. "You're still young, Jon. Young enough to not appreciate how short our time on this earth is."

"Oh, I know it's short."

"Do you?"

"Of course."

"Well, I sincerely doubt that. If you did, you wouldn't push your father away all the time."

"Excuse me?"

"You heard me. Push him away."

"Um . . . I believe I'm the one who took him in to live with me even though he was an absentee father who was always off with some woman." The words came out with more anger than intended.

"We all make mistakes," she looked up in surprise at my outburst.

"Yeah, some more than others."

139

"All I'm saying is you don't want to find yourself full of regrets once your father is gone. Whatever has happened in the past is in the past. It's the *now* that matters . . . what we choose to do with it."

"I know that."

"Do you really want to spend your life living all alone?" she asked.

"Excuse me?"

"You're a good-looking man, Jon. I can't help but ask myself why there is no woman in your life."

"It's not that I haven't tried."

"What became of that sweet woman you were living with? You were together for several years, weren't you?"

"We were. Unfortunately, she left me to take a new job in Virginia."

"I'm sorry. That must have hurt."

"I messed up, I guess."

Ingrid gazed out the window at the whitewashed scenery. "Life goes by in a flash, Jon. We all busy ourselves with unimportant matters when in fact there is only one thing that truly matters, and that is love. To love someone else and to be loved back."

This was making me very uncomfortable.

My father returned and I redirected him: "Would you mind getting me another beer while you're up?"

He shot me a look and then went off to fetch another beer.

The three of us then sat in silence in front of the fire, the green wood not burning very well, an intricate patchwork of black charred squares visible on the surface of the logs. Every time the flame seemed like it would finally bust out into a strong fire, the water in the log's center held it back. *Held it back,* I repeated to myself.

Ingrid got up and walked over to the bookshelves along the far wall, returning with an old dusty volume with several slips of yellowed paper tucked inside the pages.

"What's that?" Bobby asked.

"A book of poems. There is one in here I love. Let me find it."

Oh, great, I thought. Trapped for a poetry reading.

Ingrid seemed to sense what I was thinking as she said: "I know you'll like this one, Jon." She carefully turned the yellowed pages to the poem she had in mind and began reading:

> *The leaves of the oak and the willow shall fade,*
> *Be scattered around and together be laid;*
> *As the young and the old, the low and the high,*
> *Shall crumble to dust and together shall lie . . .*

> *The saint who enjoyed the communion of Heaven,*
> *The sinner who dared to remain unforgiven,*
> *The wise and the foolish, the guilty and just,*
> *Have quietly mingled their bones in the dust . . .*

'Tis the wink of an eye, 'tis the draught of a breath
From the blossom of health to the paleness of death,
From the gilded saloon to the bier and the shroud;
O, why should the spirit of mortal be proud?

We sat in quiet as the words soaked in. I gazed out the window overlooking the ocean as she read the poem, the steel gray sky merging with the cold ocean waters, whitecaps roused in the wind. Across the way I saw the Dunbar Island ferry chugging along for Oceanside with just two cars onboard. So different from the busy summer months.

Robert held Ingrid's right hand. Her hand was bruised, the fingers long and slim and bony. "That was lovely, dear."

"Cuts right to the chase, doesn't it." She set the volume on the end table.

"Whitman?" my father asked.

"No, William Knox. He lived during the early years of the nineteenth century."

I raised myself from my seat. "I think I best be on my way back to town. There's more plowing to be done."

"Thanks for checking on us, Jon," my father got up to accompany me to the door. "Drive safely, son."

"I will. You should keep that fire going in case the power goes out again. There are supposed to be some big winds coming in behind the storm."

"I will, thanks."

"Do you have enough firewood?"

"There's some under the tarp on the deck but I'm afraid it got wet in the blowing snow."

"I'll bring you a load of dry wood later."

Back home later that day, I sat alone in my living room in front of the woodstove polishing off what was probably my sixth can of beer of the day. Not that I was counting. The wind was howling out of the north and I watched the many lobster boats that hadn't been pulled for the winter bobbing on their moorings. I heard a truck pull up and looked out through the curtains to see it was Freddy Ames. He shook the snow off his boots as he let himself in, shivering from the extreme cold air that had plunged down from Canada following the snowstorm.

"Hey, Jon. How was everything up at Ingrid's?"

I had told him when we were out plowing that morning that I was heading up island to check on them. "They seem to be doing well. But I wish she'd not butt into my personal life. Kinda nervy."

"Oh, yeah? Like how?"

"I don't want to talk about it."

Freddy scratched his beard. "Rumor has it Kevin has been upset about Ingrid not leaving him and his half-sister the property."

"Where'd you hear that?"

"It's been going around town. Sounds like Ingrid lost it with Kevin saying she's not leaving the house to him."

"Hmm . . . that's too bad. Can't say I completely blame her, though."

"Why do you say that?"

"Kevin and I have a history going back to high school."

"Oh, yeah. The tires, I remember. That's what you get for talking with his girlfriend . . . what was her name?"

"Peggy Warren."

"Right, I remember her. I think she's living up north now, married with two kids. Anyway, word around town is that Ingrid plans to leave the house to her granddaughter, Susan."

"What about her daughter, Olivia?" I asked.

"Good question. I'm not sure what's up with her."

"Where does she live?"

"Boston, I think. She's married . . . to a woman."

"Well, where Susan is the only one with kids to pass the house down to that probably makes sense. I imagine Ingrid doesn't want it sold after she's gone."

Freddy warmed his hands in front of my potbelly stove. "I'd be pissed if I were Kevin and Olivia. That house and land must be worth a fortune. Sounds like Kevin is looking for a lawyer to do a psychological work-up on his mother so he can have the will thrown out of court."

I pulled back the tab on my can of beer, which made a tinny popping sound.

144

"What you got they-ah, bub?" he noticed the Budweiser empties on the end table.

"Yeah, I'm drinking again."

"When'd you start up?"

"Recently. Would you like one?"

Based on the look on his face I thought he did, but being the good friend he was, he declined. "Truth is, Jon, I came over here hoping you could help me kick the habit. I've been drinking too much and putting on the pounds. My doctor is growing concerned about my heart. Recent physical didn't go so well."

"Sorry to hear that. I don't know, Freddy. I'm enjoying having my house back to myself and these winters are long and tough. I think I can handle the occasional beer without getting into trouble."

He saw right through me, tilting his head down and looking at me as if he expected more. "Doesn't look like an occasional beer from what I see here. It's just a shame, Jon. I know how hard you have worked to stay sober. I'm lucky. I'm not an alcoholic, but—"

"I'm not so sure I'm an alcoholic."

"C'mon, you know better."

"Whaddya mean?"

"I'm not going to bullshit you, Jon. We've been good friends a long, long time. Both you and I know you're an alcoholic and have struggled with drinking since high school. It's just your bad luck, but you can't deny it."

I sighed and gazed across the harbor at the seagulls darting about the fishing fleet.

"You don't look so good, Jon. I'm just being honest with you. Your face has that puffy look you get when drinking."

"Fuck you."

"Fuck you right back, bub."

"Look, I'm busy now so why don't you just leave me be."

"Busy? Doing what? Gettin' hammered? Drinkin' alone?"

"Fuck off! Mind your own goddamn business."

"I hate to see you like this, friend. How 'bout we make a deal. I'll take you to the next AA meeting. When are they, again?"

"Tuesday evenings at the church."

"And if you quit drinkin', I'll quit with you."

"Right."

"I'm serious."

"Except you're not an alkie so it's not the same."

"Good! You just admitted you're an alcoholic, Jon."

"Shit, I don't know."

"Just come to the next meeting with me. I'll pick you up."

Chapter Thirteen
April 2023

Easter on Archer Island can go either way—cold and damp and miserable, or sunny and pleasant and filled with hope. It's rare the latter happens, but as I now look back over that chaotic year of my father's death, I recall what a beautiful Easter we enjoyed. I'm grateful for those wonderful memories, especially now that I know what happened.

True confession time. I did not stop drinking that spring, despite the concern of so many around me. It would be months before I finally cleaned up for what I hope will be the last time. Freddy Ames did his best to help me but I was in no mood to be helped. If I've learned anything about addiction, it's that the rational mind is supplanted by the addiction's determination to do its thing, resulting in many mistakes and regrets only to be seen in hindsight once breaking free.

We all went to church that Easter, something I rarely did. Ingrid wanted to go, which meant Bobby was going, and I agreed to join them. The church was just up the road from where the Christmas tree lighting takes place, an old brown building with stained glass windows and a small organ and upright piano on the altar. It doesn't look like a church from the outside, and ostensibly serves as much as a community center as a holy space, with

147

frequent bean suppers in the basement activities room, along with craft fairs, memorial celebrations, and graduation parties.

I met my father and Ingrid at the front door of the church and saw they were not alone. Susan, her husband Travis, and her children were there, along with two women I didn't recognize.

"Good morning, Jon," Ingrid gave me an unexpected hug. "I'd like you to meet my daughter Olivia and her wife Naomi, visiting from Boston."

"Nice to meet you," I shook their hands. Olivia and her wife looked very chic in that urban sophisticated sort of way not seen much on this island where flannel shirts and sweatpants rule. I'm not sure why I thought they looked chic, but suppose this had to do mostly with their outfits. (I'm no authority on women's clothing. Surprise.) Olivia's dress was an unusual lemon-lime color, and she wore a string of pearls that looked like the real deal, small and delicate. Naomi looked to be Asian-American, was petite—almost like a child with her pale skin and dark eyes filled with so much light and laughter. She was wearing a blood-orange dress that matched her lipstick color.

Naomi pulled me aside. "Just a heads up, Olivia is concerned your father is trying to take the family compound from Kevin and her."

I sighed. "Great."

"Olivia has hired a lawyer and Kevin is documenting everything in case this heads to court."

"Shit."

"I don't mean to be rude, but I assume you can string together complete sentences?"

"Huh?"

She laughed. "I guess not. Anyway, be forewarned. This could get nasty."

"Figures," I was now intentionally speaking in one-word sentences to get a rise out of her.

She saw this and smiled. "I imagine you don't get many chances at conversation out here over the winter."

"True."

She smiled again. "I guess all I can hope is that I'm not seated next to you at dinner."

I gave in. "Sorry, that was fun for me. I know how people from away tend to think we're all a bit slow out here."

"I hadn't. Until now."

"Just trying to do my part."

"Keep it up. If you can."

Clearly this was a double-entendre concerning my masculinity or lack thereof, odd coming from this tiny lesbian. "You know, I think I'm going to like you."

"Most people do," she laughed. "You know, on second thought, maybe we should sit together at dinner to stay out of the family mess."

"That works for me."

"I think I'm going to like you, too, Jon. Can't be easy having a father like yours, from what Liv tells me."

"Liv?"

"Here we go again."

"Oh, I get it. That's what you call Olivia."

"Wicked shaahp," she did her best to put on a thick accent, which I took to be more Boston than Archer Island.

"May I call you Omi?"

Now she looked confused. "What?"

"Omi. You know, like Liv but for Naomi."

"You had me there for a moment, Jon. I thought I owed you money."

"Maybe you do?"

"Please, just call me Naomi."

"Listen, do you happen to know if Kevin is joining us this morning?"

"I do."

"And . . . might you be so kind as to share with me what you know?" Naomi clearly enjoyed playing games.

She said: "He's with his father for the day, so I think we will be free of him."

"Um . . . so I gather you're not a big Kevin fan either?"

"Correct."

"Why's that?"

"Asshole."

Confused now: "Me?"

"No. Kevin."

"Jesus!"

"Yes, it is HIS day."

"Please. Stop."

She let out a laugh that got the attention of the people gathering around us. "Jon, I can tell you enjoy playing the one-word game. We can practice over dinner. Give us something to do."

"You're a piece of work."

"I'll take that as a compliment."

"So . . . no Kevin for the whole day," I sought confirmation of what had been worrying me all morning.

"Correctamento. He's hanging with his deadbeat father. Come on, we should be heading in," she led the way.

As we hunted for suitable seats (those not being upfront or in too conspicuous a place given we are not church regulars), Ingrid was greeted by friends and acquaintances happy to see her out and about.

"Ingrid, how wonderful to see you," Ethelyn Adair greeted us as Naomi, Olivia, and I hung back. Susan had already found a back pew for herself and Svea and Logan. A back pew in case they needed to make an emergency escape, I presumed.

"Hello, Ethelyn. How have you been?" Ingrid paused to speak with her longtime friend.

"Made it through the winter mostly intact. You?"

"I did, thanks in large part to Robert here. Robert, meet my old friend Ethelyn."

Robert shook her hand and smiled.

Ethelyn continued: "I gather you managed to stay in your home for the winter?"

"We did, thank you," Robert answered for Ingrid, something I had noticed he was doing with increased frequency.

Other women joined them. Gladys Smith who worked the deli counter at the market and another woman I only knew from her many Facebook posts about cats. There were several hyper children running about, undoubtedly all sugared up on chocolate bunnies and Peeps. Most of the children were dressed up—boys fidgeting with neckties that probably struck them as cruel forms of suffocating torture; the girls looking more comfortable in their colorful dresses and Easter bonnets. The girls were much better behaved than the boys, who were chasing each other through the maze of pews.

I could see in the back pew that Logan was pulling on his sister's hair, while his father was talking in the aisle with Cody Wadsworth, who worked the docks at the Fisherman's Co-op.

"Stop that!" Svea punched her little brother in the arm.

He did it again.

"Stop twitching all the time," Svea shot him a look confirming how annoying she found him to be.

Susan regained control, threatening no Easter egg hunt if they didn't behave. I sat towards the middle of the church with Olivia and Naomi, while my father and Ingrid were in the second row. There were yellow daffodils on the altar, along with two clusters of pink tulips with white centers. The service began, the choir singing beautifully as sunlight lit the stained-glass windows. We all were badly in need of some resurrection, and this first day of warm temperatures delivered it for me. The visiting priest from the mainland led the service. Pastor Carroll had taken the first ferry over and had been suitably entertained by the all-female church committee. He reciprocated, taking good care of us, limiting his sermon to just fifteen minutes. My kind of priest.

The first thing I noticed when we arrived at Ingrid's after church was how clean the house was. The rugs had been vacuumed, the end tables dusted, and the outdoor furniture removed from the side of the piano and returned to the porch. The smells of Lemon Pledge and ham cooking in the kitchen mingled in an appealing way. Ingrid had hired Betty Jean from the bar to cater Easter dinner. The dining room table was set with a brightly flowered tablecloth—crystal water glasses and hand-painted plates set out for each guest. A centerpiece of white and pink tulips added cheerfulness to the room.

I turned to my father and asked: "Who'd Ingrid hire to clean this place?"

"No one. Just me."

"Seriously?"

"What . . . you don't think I know how to clean?" he smiled.

I was stunned. "I mean, I've never known you to be one to handle a mop."

He laughed. "You were too young when your mother was off at the sanitarium to see just how much cleaning and cooking I did for us all."

"Mom was in a sanitarium?"

"Yes, when you were around four years old. You don't remember it?"

"Not really. I do have weird dreams where I am searching for her."

"That's probably why. I did the best I could back then, Jon. Your mother was not well and I had to travel for business a good deal. I found a woman to look after you. What was her name? Ah, yes. Dottie." He laughed. "She truly lived up to her name. Strange woman herself. But helpful nonetheless."

This was all a surprise to me. "You know, I do have vague memories of a redhaired woman with bad breath giving us kids our baths."

"Yes, that would be Dottie."

"How long was Mom gone for?"

"About four months, I think it was."

"And how was she when she returned?"

"Better, I suppose. But not great. She had her demons. Probably still does. How do you think she's doing these years?"

"I think mostly well. She's an odd duck for sure."

"That's what drew me to her in the first place. I guess I've always been attracted to unusual women. She was a talented painter. Does she still paint?"

154

"Yes."

"Jon, follow me and come see what we've done in the downstairs study."

We walked across the living room to what had once been the study, but in recent years had served as a storage room for whatever Ingrid decided to toss in there. In the center of the study was a double bed, which two high school boys Ingrid had hired had moved downstairs. Several books were piled on the end table next to the bed, along with what I think was a sleep apnea machine and mask.

"Ingrid has moved into the study. Getting up and down the stairs has become too difficult for her. She truly likes it in here. Reminds her of her grandfather. She's not generating many new memories anymore, so the old ones are what she has left. She is repeating the same stories a great deal, so please be kind to her at dinner and just smile and nod."

"Is there a downstairs shower?" I asked.

"Sadly, not, but I've gotten a quote on one that could be easily hooked up in the laundry room. Just waiting on the plumber to free up."

"Who's the plumber?"

"Billy Wentworth. Do you know him?"

"I do. He's my good friend Walt's brother. We've worked on some projects together. I can give him a call if you'd like and tell him it's an emergency."

"Sure, that would be helpful."

155

Ingrid joined us. "Isn't your father just wonderful?"

"Yes, this is very nice Ingrid. The house is looking great."

"He's been busy cleaning the old place up. Paying my bills, too. I can't keep up with everything around here."

"This study is beautiful," I said.

"Thanks, Jon. My grandfather loved this room. It's nice being here with him now. I would sit on his knee while he read me Nancy Drew books."

"That's nice," I said.

"He would sit in that chair over by the window where the light is good. He'd read me the old Nancy Drew books. Some of those old horse books I loved, too. *Black Beauty*."

"I'm so happy you are allowing me to help you, Ingrid," Bobby smiled, and she gazed at him with a look I can only describe as young love, her eyes widening, her expression warm and tender. He seemed to be returning a similar look. This was all terribly confusing for me. Was it possible my father was not the evil person I had long assumed? Could these two people, now toward the end of their lives, truly be in love? I didn't know what to think.

We returned to the rest of the guests in the living room, and Betty Jean emerged from the kitchen with appetizers: green olives, celery stuffed with cream cheese, mixed nuts, and a large platter of various cheeses and crackers. "These should tide you ovah for a bit," she said.

"Thanks Betty Jean," Susan said. Svea and Logan were

156

running wild on the front lawn that sloped down to the ocean, their father Travis eager to be outside with them.

"What time do you think we'll be eating?" Susan asked.

"I'd say around two."

My father came over and announced: "Let's start the Easter egg hunt for the kids. I know they're eager to get going."

Olivia and Naomi joined us. Olivia was looking at my father with mistrust spread across her face. "I know what you're up to old man."

"Excuse me?"

"Kevin and I are on to you."

"I'm afraid I have no idea what you're talking about."

"Don't play dumb. We hired a private investigator who has told us what you did in Florida."

It was just my father, Olivia, and me huddled off in a corner with Naomi. "Did? In Florida?" Bobby's face scrunched up into a confused look.

"Yes, did. To that Epstein woman at the assisted living place in Sarasota."

"I'm afraid I have no idea what you're talking about," he looked genuinely confused.

I thought Olivia was being inappropriate. "Listen, Olivia, drop this, will you? Let's try and enjoy Easter."

Bobby walked outside to join the children while Olivia hung back with me.

"Are you in on this, too?" she asked.

"In on *what*?"

"Stealing my mother's property, that's *what.*"

"Are you paranoid or something?"

She said: "You're aware that our mother has written Kevin and me out of her will."

"Are you sure about that?"

"Well, not exactly sure because we can't find her latest will. The copy she showed us ten years ago left everything in equal amounts to Kevin and me. But Kevin believes she's changed it with your father's urging."

"I find that difficult to believe."

"Take a look around, Jon. Have you noticed how picked up everything is since your charming father moved in with her?"

"Yes, of course. Is that a problem?"

"And how smitten my mother is with him?"

"I think they are both smitten. Don't you?"

"Do you happen to know if my mother has a new will?"

"No idea. Why would I?"

"Kevin thinks you and your father might be in on this together."

"That's absurd! How dare you—"

Naomi had seen enough and intervened. "Liv, why don't you just drop it. You don't know for certain what's going on here. Let's not ruin the holiday."

Olivia stormed outside, leaving me alone with Naomi.

"Crap," I exclaimed.

158

"Sorry," she touched me on the arm.

"What the fuck?" I looked away, taking this all in. "They've hired a private investigator?"

"Yes, about a month ago. She and Kevin found some guy in Florida who, just between you and me, seems shady. They are paying him a lot for what seems to me to be very little."

"I can't believe this," I gazed out the multi-paned window where I could see my father, Svea, and Logan jumping up and down in excitement. Ingrid was parked in the sunshine in her Adirondack chair on the porch, covered in a woolen blanket.

Naomi asked: "Do you think it's possible your father is stealing their inheritance?"

"No, I don't. I think they're in love. I also happen to think Kevin is a crazy person who steals and cheats and—"

"Well, just so you know, Liv wanted me here today to be a witness to anything I see that looks fishy. She has put me in an uncomfortable position and I'm not happy about it."

"I'm sorry."

"It's not your fault. Will you please sit with me at dinner so I can steer clear of this mess?"

"Sure."

After the Easter egg hunt, we sat down to dinner. Thank goodness for Naomi. She was seated on my left, with Olivia on my right, an intentional split Naomi had made sure happened. Olivia seemed puzzled by this, not at all sure why her wife was having such a good time with this backwoods carpenter from Archer Island. I've never given a second thought to where people are from, being more interested in who they are and what they have to say.

"Hey, Jon. Please pass the wine down this way," Naomi said.

"Red or white?"

"I think I might need both to get through this," she whispered in my ear.

"No shit. Here let's start with the red," I poured her half a glass.

"More," she urged, so I filled it to the top and then filled mine.

"So, tell me, Naomi. What does a wise ass like you do for a living?"

She laughed. "I'm a professor."

"That figures. Teaching what?"

"Creative writing."

"Where?"

"B.U."

"Where?"

She laughed. "We seem to be playing the one-word game again, Jon."

"Damn, sorry."

"Do you know much about complete sentences?" she smiled, popping an olive into her mouth, eyes lit with mischief.

"I do. You might be surprised to learn that I'm an avid

160

reader."

"Of what?"

"Everything, really. History, biography—"

"Fiction?" she asked.

"Sure."

"Thrillers?"

"Not just them. I read a lot of different fiction. Why do you assume I read thrillers?"

"Most men do."

"That's sexist."

"It's also true."

"Where did you say you teach?"

"B.U. Boston University."

"Undergrads?"

"Some, but mostly in the graduate MFA program."

"Do you like it?"

"It pays the bills. My own writing doesn't amount to much financially."

"What have you written?"

"Oh, I doubt you've heard of them."

"Try me."

"I'd rather not say."

"C'mon, I want to know."

She sighed. "*Broken Lands . . . Rivers of Lambs . . .*"

"Yeah, guess not."

"Told you. So . . . what novelists do you like?"

161

"Too many to say, really. Lately, I've been catching up on some of the classics I missed. I'm half way through Tolstoy's *War and Peace.*"

"Excellent choice, Jon."

"I'm enjoying it very much."

"Back when Tolstoy was writing, novelists were the great observers of society. Before the social sciences existed, like sociology and psychology. You can say they were much more important than novelists are in our modern times."

"I hadn't thought of that. But I get it. Tolstoy truly captured what life was like back in his day."

We paused, listening to Olivia raise her voice in conversation with her mother, who sat at the head of the table. Betty Jean had hired a high school girl to be our waitress, a girl I didn't recognize who now brought out the ham, the macaroni and cheese, the rolls, and the asparagus.

"Thank you, dear," Ingrid looked up, eager for a momentary escape from Olivia.

I heard bits of what Olivia was saying. "Just be careful, Mom. Robert Davis has a past you don't know about."

"Such as?"

"He did things to a lady in Florida. Bad things."

"Oh, I don't believe that for one minute."

Olivia cut to the chase, quite possibly the only reason she had come for Easter this year, something she hadn't done in a long time. "Kevin thinks Robert is after this property."

"That's nonsense," Ingrid's face flushed with anger.

"Is it? Why then have you changed your will?"

"What makes you think I've done that?"

"Kevin told me you had."

"Why on earth would he think that?"

"I don't know, he didn't tell me."

Ingrid was visibly angry.

"Listen, Mom. I realize you're not thrilled with either Kevin or me, but we're your blood. We're family."

"I know that."

"Then, may I see your latest will?"

"No, you may not. For one thing, I don't want you assuming you'll get all of this once I'm dead. I don't trust you or Kevin to not stash me away in Eldercare. This gives me some leverage."

Not the response Olivia had hoped for. "At least tell me this. Have you changed your will since this Robert character who is living here with you arrived on the island?"

"None of your business."

Olivia was frustrated but knew better than to press on.

"The ham is wonderful," my father smiled from the end of the table opposite Ingrid. Logan had requested to be seated next to him, having become best buds following the Easter egg hunt. Susan told me later that Robert had hidden all the eggs and come up with clever clues that the children found amusing. Susan was seated between Svea and Logan, doing her best to keep the

163

macaroni and cheese in their mouths and not on the floor. For dessert, we had a trifle that Betty Jean's mother had made.

After dinner, Ingrid excused herself saying she needed a nap. Bobby helped her into her first-floor bedroom and stayed with her, the door shut. I was chatting with Naomi when Olivia joined us in front of the fire. Olivia whispered in my direction: "Can your father be trusted?"

"Honestly, Olivia, I don't know."

"Well, that doesn't inspire great confidence."

"I realize that. But as I watch him caring for your mother, I find myself wondering if we are all jumping to the wrong conclusions. What if they are truly in love?"

"Old people don't fall in love," she galumphed.

Naomi said: "That's a bit harsh, Liv, don't you think?"

"Name one couple you know over the age of eighty that fell in love," Olivia demanded.

"Well . . . let me think . . . how about the book *Falling in Love When You Thought You Were Through* by Jill Robinson and Stuart Shaw?"

"Fiction, no doubt."

"Actually no. It's a true story. I'm sure there are plenty of older people who find love late in life," Naomi shot me a devilish wink.

"Frankly, I find the thought positively disgusting," Olivia gazed down at the floor. Her neck was flushed from the confrontation with her mother, her string of pearls more visible against her skin than before. She looked up. "Are they having sex?"

With hands up in the air like a cornered bank robber I said: "Hell, don't ask me. I doubt it."

Naomi volunteered: "I hope so. And I hope we're still having sex at their age, too, Liv."

Olivia gazed across the room at the study door, which was still closed. It was eerily quiet and Bobby had not returned.

Naomi saw Olivia's disgust and poured gas on the fire. "I think I hear moaning coming from over there right now. Do you, Jon?"

Olivia let out a prolonged sigh and walked away.

Chapter Fourteen
April 2023

Ingrid and Robert listened through their closed door to the muffled conversation in the living room, as they rested in the double bed in the study. Ingrid was upset by her daughter's combative tone, and Robert attempted to calm her so they would be able to return in time to say their goodbyes.

"It's going to be all right, dear," Robert said. "Don't let Olivia upset you so."

They lay side by side on their backs, the laughter of Svea and Logan playing hide-and-seek entering the partially opened window. Sunlight lit a photo of Ingrid's mother and father on the antique bureau across from the bed; it felt as if her ancestors were reaching out in an attempt to help.

"I feel so unattractive," she said.

"Nonsense. You're beautiful, Ingrid."

"And you're blind."

"I mean it, dear. You are beautiful, to me. Granted, neither of us is young anymore, but I think we make a handsome couple, given how old we are. I love getting lost in your dreamy eyes. It feels like I'm swimming back to wherever we came from, some vast unknowable place."

"I love looking into your eyes, too, Robert." She pressed her forehead against his.

"The only thing that matters is how we see each other. And you are a beautiful person, inside and out, Ingrid."

Robert had set up her old record player in the study and got up to put on an album they had been listening to recently. It was a Frank Sinatra recording with the Nelson Riddle Orchestra. The music filled the room and Ingrid began singing along with Robert. *"I've got you, under my skin. I've got you, deep in the heart of me. So deep in my heart that you're really a part of me. I've got you under my skin."*

She pulled him tight against herself, swaying together as they sang. His breath was warm in her ear, his voice low and smooth. He had a good voice. Ingrid's eyes welled with tears as they sang, so many old memories coming to mind: her father's old woody wagon, the family basset hound Louisa drooling in the back seat on long drives; decorating Christmas cookies with her mother in the kitchen and being allowed to lick the fudge bowl; sailing with her father along the shoreline as a little girl, he carefully showing her how to be safe on the high seas.

Her mood changed in an instant and she separated herself from Robert. "My father would be so disappointed in his grandchildren. In me," Ingrid said. "I don't know what I was thinking marrying Kevin's father. I was so naïve."

"We all make mistakes. Don't be so hard on yourself."

She ignored his comment, seemingly sinking into a negative funk. "When I look at Kevin and see how he has lived his life, all the trouble he has gotten into—I am so disappointed.

But why should I be surprised? I didn't give him the best genetic material in marrying his father. And he is just like him. I don't think he has a drop of me inside."

"Don't fret. Try and relax."

She couldn't. "Some people bloom many times over during a lifetime, in so many fascinating and unexpected colors and varieties, while others simply throw up one unimpressive bloom and never change. Never evolve. It's as if they stop growing as teenagers and that's all there will ever be."

"You told me you made a better marriage with Olivia's father, yes?"

"I did. But then he died. Turns out his genes weren't so great either. Damn cancer."

"That's a lovely photo of your mother and father on the bureau," Robert attempted a redirect.

"Would you please bring it to me?" Ingrid rolled onto her side so she was facing him.

Robert swung his legs off the bed and walked to the bureau. He picked up the old black and white photo in its ornate silver frame and brought it to her. He plumped a pillow behind her back so she could sit up comfortably. She patted the bed next to her, urging him to come close.

"This was taken on their honeymoon."

"Where were they?"

"Greece. Mostly on Crete if I remember correctly. Look how young they were."

"Weren't we all," he said.

Ingrid looked contemplative, running her fingers along the cool metal picture frame, lost in the only memories remaining—those from the distant past. Robert was listening to the children outside, their cries mixing with those of the robins, busily building a nest in the rhododendron bush just outside the window. The sound of a small airplane added hope to the spring day, the island once again opening up to the outside world. Sinatra's silky-smooth voice filled the room.

Ingrid set the photo on the bedside table and slid closer to him. "Hold me, Robert. I'm chilly."

Robert got up and closed the window. He grabbed a folded Hudson Bay blanket from the chaise longue in the corner, unfurling it over Ingrid. He climbed back into bed next to her, lying on top of the blanket. They faced each other and he put his left arm over her hip. Her eyes seemed lighter than usual, almost like a robin's egg blue. They rested like this for a few minutes, but then Ingrid's agitation returned and she pulled away and sat up in bed looking angry. It was as if a switch had been flipped.

Robert sat up so they were both upright, side by side.

"Talk to me, Ingrid."

"Turn off the music. It's giving me a headache." He got up and lifted the needle from the album, scratching it as he did so. He came back to bed.

"What am I going to do?" she looked frightened and confused. "I'm losing my mind, Robert."

"I'm here to help you, Ingrid."

She turned to him. "But you cannot be trusted," she looked slightly insane and angry. Robert had noticed the paranoia and anger occurring with more frequency in recent days.

"You can trust me, dear," he reached out to touch her hand, but she pulled it away, knocking the picture frame off the end table and onto the floor.

"Damn it!" she cried out.

"I'll get it, not to worry." Robert got out of bed and returned the picture frame to the bureau. He sat at the foot of the bed.

"Everything is so difficult now," she was sobbing. "What am I going to do about this house?"

"If things reach the point where you need to go into Eldercare, I'm sure it's not as bad as you make it out to be. And I'll come visit you every day."

"That's not what I mean."

"What *do* you mean, then?"

"The house. I can't leave it to my children. They will sell it immediately and throw away all the beloved books and photos and—"

"You don't know that for certain."

"I do! Can you believe the way my own daughter was speaking to me out there?"

"That caught me off guard, too. She and Kevin think I'm out to steal their inheritance. She came right out and said it to me."

170

Ingrid looked puzzled by this as she sat processing what he had said. "I just wish you and I could have enjoyed Easter by ourselves. Family is always so damned complicated."

"Have you given any further thought to the possibility of leaving the house to Susan?"

She sighed. "That's actually what I'm leaning toward doing."

"I think it makes sense. That way, the home would stay in the family and pass down to Svea and Logan."

"Yes, agreed. And I like Susan's husband, Travis. He's an electrician and very handy, so would do a good job keeping this place up and running."

"He strikes me as an honest fellow. Jon likes him . . . I know that much."

"But . . . how do I know Susan won't sell the house? Especially given how she will be pressured by Olivia and Kevin. I'm not convinced she can stand up to that pressure and am not sure it's fair to put her in that awkward position. Her mother will hate her for the rest of her life."

"I believe there are ways your specific wishes can be written into a will. But I also agree it's unfair to Olivia and Kevin. I don't know. It's complicated."

Ingrid rolled onto her side so she could look out the window. "Just listen to Svea and Logan playing out there. How happy they sound. There is no way in the world they would ever be able to enjoy such a beautiful place as this without the home staying in the family. Kevin and Olivia would certainly sell it and Kevin probably would kill himself partying, and Olivia would run through her share on exotic trips and other frivolities."

"Is the house the only asset you have?" Robert asked.

"It's the bulk of it. I have some money in a trust fund."

"Do you know how much?"

"I haven't looked at it in ages. It was a trust my grandfather set up to be accessed only upon dire emergencies that are laid out in the trust. I believe my mother drew monthly interest payments from it after my father died, but I've never needed it as my father left me a trust of my own."

"How much do you have in your trust?"

"Around $400,000, I think."

"Well then, why don't you leave the house to Susan under terms saying she cannot sell it and that it must pass to Svea and Logan upon her death, and then let Olivia and Kevin split the trust? $200,000 each is a nice amount, but not so much as to get them into too much mischief."

In actuality, Robert was thinking about the grandfather's trust and how much that must have grown over the many decades of compounding interest.

"Is it possible to write a will that detailed?" Ingrid asked.

"I think so. Who handled your current will?"

"Sam Loughlin in Portland. He's with one of the big law firms there."

"Why don't you give him a call to discuss?"

"It's all too complicated for me now, Robert. Would you mind doing it?"

"Honestly, I'd rather not get involved."

Ingrid was surprised by this. "Why not?"

"Your children already think I'm a gold digger. No need to provide them with any fuel for their theories."

Ingrid hugged him. "I know you're not after my money, Robert. I love you so much. I wish we had met when we were young."

"Not nearly as much as I do," he said. "We just seem to have some extraordinary chemistry. It's as if we knew each other in a previous life, our souls merged for eternity."

Ingrid was looking and feeling somewhat better now. "At least help me remember what it is I want to ask my lawyer. I've already forgotten."

"Of course. I will write it all down for you so when you call you can ask your questions and get answers. I'm happy to listen in so we can discuss afterwards, but don't want you to mention I'm on the call. It might make sense to use my lawyer friend in Florida."

There was a gentle knocking at the door.

"Come in," Ingrid said.

"Are you decent?" It was Olivia.

"Decent?" Ingrid had no idea what her daughter was talking about.

Robert did. "Yes, come in."

173

The door opened to reveal the wary expressions of Olivia and Naomi. They looked relieved to see Robert and Ingrid fully clothed and sitting on the bed. God only knows what they had imagined.

Olivia spoke: "We need to be on our way. We're going to fly back to Oceanside and then drive to Boston before it gets too late."

Ingrid and Robert walked into the living room where we were all gathered. I thought Ingrid looked upset.

"Good nap?" I asked my father.

"Unable to sleep, as it turned out," he said. "Thank you all for coming."

I stood by the door and whispered to Naomi. "I told you there wouldn't be any elderly hanky-panky going on."

"I cannot begin to tell you how disappointed I am," she shot me that mischievous smile of hers. "I had high hopes for some hanky-panky."

Olivia joined us. "Keep an eye on your old man for me, Jon, will you?"

"I'll do what I can."

"Could you give us a ride to the airfield?"

"Sure."

Ingrid walked over and gave her daughter an awkward hug. It was as if each understood some damage had been done today, damage neither wanted to see happen. But it was too late, and they sensed this as they said their goodbyes. Olivia felt this might be the last time she would see her mother alive, so stopped at the doorway and came back to give her a more enthusiastic embrace.

"I'm sorry we quarreled, Mom. I hope you can forgive me. I just worry about your judgment these days."

Ingrid didn't answer, her expression downcast into a look of anger and disappointment, of regret and confusion.

We heard a truck pull up out front and Kevin came inside to join us. He walked over to Olivia and gave her an awkward hug, towering above her short frame. He pulled away and turned to his mother.

"Happy Easter, Ma," Kevin pecked her on the cheek. "I brought you some daffodils from Dad's garden."

"How is the old man?" Ingrid took the flowers from Kevin and set them on the narrow mail table by the door.

"'Bout the same as always."

"Did you have dinner with him? We've got some leftovers in the kitchen if you're hungry."

"We ate, thanks."

"What did you have?" Olivia asked. Looking at the two of them standing side by side, I was struck by how different they were, Kevin tall and gruff and covered in tattoos, she short and chic and sophisticated.

"Just some beans and franks. It was good. Simple. No big holiday hassles."

"How sad," Ingrid said. "You know you were welcome to join us."

"I didn't want to leave the old man all by himself for Easter."

"That was nice of you," Olivia said.

Kevin turned to his half-sister. "I've got something for you and Jon in my pickup."

"Really?" I looked up in surprise.

"Yeah, follow me."

Olivia and I walked behind Kevin toward his truck while the others chatted at the front door beyond earshot. I could see scabs on the back of Kevin's bald skull; they looked like red eyes, perfectly placed on the scorpion tattoo snaking up from his neck toward the top of his head.

Kevin spoke in a low voice. "So, tell me Olivia, what do you think of Jon's fathah?"

I could tell she felt awkward being asked this in front of me. She paused before saying: "Frankly, I don't think we can trust him."

Kevin turned to me. "Jon, we need you to take care of this. I'm not fuckin' 'round with you, bub. Get your old man away from our muthah or else."

"Or else, what?" I was indignant.

"It ain't gunna be pretty, that's what."

*****

176

At the airstrip, Naomi kissed me on the cheek as she waited to board the Cessna plane.

"I'm happy we met, Jon. Come visit in Boston sometime and I'll show you around."

"I'd like that." I was still visibly shaken by the unexpected encounter with Kevin and she sensed this.

"What's wrong?" she asked.

"That shithead Kevin just threatened me."

"About your father I assume?"

I nodded. "I wish my old man had never shown up out here. He's making my life a living hell."

She touched me on the forearm. "Sorry."

"Thanks."

"You okay?"

"Yup."

Just so you know, I'm still friends with Naomi to this day and have read several new novels she recommended, as well as her most recent one, *Love for the Ages*. I have a feeling the topic came to her over our Easter dinner, as there is a completely inappropriate and explicit ten-page sex scene between an old man and an old woman.

Chapter Fifteen

October 2023

What became of Shane is a whole other story, the incomplete details of which we can piece together now from local and national newspaper accounts. Shane left a trail of evidence, including eyewitness testimony from Miquel who saw him on the mainland. There were rumors flying around the island, and it was impossible to know the full story of how he managed to escape, despite the statewide manhunt, the drug-sniffing dogs, and the air surveillance. That little bastard was slippery. And dangerous.

This is the story I believe to be the closest we can get to the truth. Shane slipped through the woods one October night and hid beneath the boat covering of a summer person's Boston Whaler, which was out of the water for the season. The helicopters with their bright spotlights searched those woods for three nights before moving on, figuring he must have made it across to Dunbar Island. I heard from Timmy Tetreault that he had been put in charge of search and rescue on Dunbar, which was convenient for him since he lived there.

Officer Jackman had participated in a Maine DEA search of Shane's RV, where they found a single boiler setup for cooking meth. They also found lithium, Sudafed, Coleman fuels, and other items used in the manufacture of meth. The DEA and local fire and rescue personnel cordoned off the entire parking lot given the dangers. The townspeople were outraged, realizing Vachon could have blown anyone nearby to smithereens. The RV was taken across on the ferry to the crime lab in Augusta.

Apparently, on the third or fourth night that Shane was holed up under the tarp of that Whaler—and after the chopper spotlights were gone—he broke into a nearby summer person's house (belonging to Phil Brownell, from Hanover, New Hampshire). This part of the story was only pieced together the following May when Phil opened the house for the season and found a mess. The Brownells hadn't left much food in the house, but there were two cans of tuna and a sleeve of Saltine crackers found on the kitchen table. There was also an empty bottle of 40mg OxyContin in the trash. The sliding door from the back deck to the kitchen had been lifted off its rails.

It's because of the events of October 14th that we know for certain Shane was still on the island nearly a week after he first ran from his RV. It was late on the night of the 14th that he broke into the Medical Center and set off the alarm, which brought the doctor, Jeremy Cocroft, down the hill from his rental home. The doctor knew enough to call 911 before he set out, but it would be two hours before Tetreault made it over from Dunbar Island. When the doctor arrived out front of the Medical Center, he saw a light blazing in one of the examination rooms. Who knows? Maybe he paused and thought about heading home and letting the police handle it. Or maybe he thought the last person to leave that evening forgot to turn the light out, and the alarm was simply malfunctioning. The alarm system had recently been updated and had gone off a few times by mistake in the past month.

We will never know for sure what he was thinking, but do know he decided to investigate. The siren was blaring and red lights were flashing in the central hallway, with many neighbors awakened and posting to the local Facebook group complaining about the new alarm system and would someone please shut it the hell off.

Once inside the building, we do know exactly what happened because it was all captured on the security cameras that had been added along with the alarm. The doctor was bathed in red light as he called out. "Hello? Is someone here?"

No reply.

He inched his way toward the lit examination room. "Who's here?"

The doctor paused, seemingly deciding to wait for the police outside. He was turning to leave when Shane jumped out from a dark examination room across from the lit one, grabbing the doctor in a chokehold from behind.

"Open the drug room!" Shane looked to be jonesing big time, shaking and sweating, his eyes with dark rings like a raccoon's.

"Let me go . . ." the doctor struggled to break free.

Shane pulled out a pistol and jammed it into the back of

the doctor's skull. "Open the fuckin' drug storage area, NOW!"

"Okay, calm down. No need for anyone to get hurt. I'll get you what you want and then you can go." The doctor was pushed along the hallway, grasped in Shane's chokehold with the gun pressed against the back of his head. He led Shane into the secured storage room where all controlled substances were kept, punching in the code so the screen door popped open.

"Get me all the Oxy you've got."

The doctor grabbed one pill bottle from the shelf.

"I said *all.*"

"That's what we keep on hand at any given time. I rarely prescribe Oxy."

"Bullshit. Everyone knows you docs are gettin' rich off this stuff. Been on any good drug company cruises lately, doc? Fuck you. Fuck all you all!"

"I swear, this is all there is. Please, just let me go. The police will be here soon."

"Get me whatever else you've got for pain!"

The doctor grabbed a bottle of Percocet. "Here, take these," he dropped them over his shoulder onto the floor, and Shane pulled him down by the neck to grab the bottle.

"Just go. Get out while you can!"

"Get me some Sudafed, too."

The doctor searched on the shelf and found a single box of Sudafed. "Here, take it. Run, quick!"

Shane stuffed the medications into a knapsack he had

taken from the Brownell's house. He ordered the doctor to get down on his knees, facing away.

"Oh, God. Please don't kill me. Please!" Tears were streaming down the doctor's eyes, his entire body shaking uncontrollably.

"Just kneel motherfucker!"

"I have two young kids—"

"Shut the fuck up! Do as I say. NOW!"

The doctor swiveled his neck just enough to see who it was. He probably didn't recognize Shane, given Shane was rarely on the island or seen around town. He was just that mystery loner taking up all the parking spaces in the town lot. Shane, who most likely flashed that yellow-toothed grin of his, had already shot at the police and was a hunted animal on the run. Those who later would watch the camera footage sensed once the doctor looked at Shane, he must have had a sinking feeling. His final expression captured by the cameras was one of resigned fate. Turning to look at Shane had been a mistake and would be the last mistake the doctor would ever make.

The sharp sound of a single gunshot echoed across the neighborhood. Pete Ames, who lived across the street and was up late watching a movie with his wife, heard the shot and ran to the scene. Ames was a big man, one of the most prosperous lobstermen on the island whose family had been fishing for generations, and arrived huffing and puffing just in time to see Shane slip into the woods behind the Medical Center. He followed to the end of the parking lot but felt a twinge in his chest and stopped, gasping for breath.

What Shane did next is subject to some controversy, but I believe the story as told by Mickey O'Donnell, who is a long-timer over on Dunbar Island. Mickey reported hearing a punt motoring across the narrows between Archer and Dunbar islands that night. This was unusual, for why would someone be out on the water after midnight? But he went back to bed assuming there must be a good reason, thinking someone had been over on Archer Island partying late.

Miquel, who was on the mainland the following day, provided the next section of the story. He was waiting with other passengers to board the ferry to Archer Island, when the Dunbar ferry arrived and began unloading. He saw a man who resembled Shane jump from the bed of a gray GMC truck. The man attempted to walk inconspicuously up the hill from the ferry terminal towards the center of Oceanside. But Miquel was convinced this was Shane. He asked the woman behind him in line to watch his carry-on knapsack and jogged up the hill in search of the man. A few blocks into town, he saw Shane jump into the passenger seat of the same pickup truck he had seen him in when taking the stolen job site materials. Miquel couldn't get the license plate number but called 911 to report the sighting of Shane. Within minutes, sirens were blaring in the distance. An alert was posted about a possibly dangerous man on the loose in Oceanside, and later that afternoon the police swarmed a ranch house in Warrenboro where a GMC truck matching the description was parked. Inside the house they arrested Roland Smith, a repeat drug offender, but there was no sign of Shane. Roland told the police he had paid cash for some Oxy that Shane was looking to unload. He didn't know where he was heading.

The trail went cold over the following week and Shane was still on the loose. There were plenty of civilian calls claiming to have seen him, but none of those panned out. Shane was spotted at the Salvation Army store in Portland. A woman at a diner in Biddeford was sure she sat right next to him at the counter. A terrified mother in Freeport swore Shane was the bus driver who dropped off her daughter from school. We only learned about Shane's subsequent adventures when he was on the nightly news and was trending on social media.

A service for Doctor Cocroft was held in the local church, his wife Ellen and two children absent. Ellen blamed the island for her husband's death, an island she hadn't wanted to live on and a place she would never return to. She took her two children and left immediately following the murder, their lives forever changed. Her plan was to have a service at her husband Jeremy's home in Topsfield, Massachusetts, with his parents and family.

The Archer Island church was packed that morning, and I stood toward the back with Walt Wentworth. Timmy Tetreault was there, which was brave on his part as many of the locals blamed him for allowing Shane Vachon to escape that first night when he bolted from his RV. Had Timmy done his job, the doctor would still be alive, was the local line of thought. I saw Timmy standing by himself, awkwardly off to the side, and Walt and I walked over to join him.

"What a tragedy," I said.

He had tears in his eyes. "I can't believe this is actually happening. Two dead bodies on Archer Island in the same year, when there hasn't been a single murder out here in over thirty years."

"Bad timing on your part, I guess," I looked to get a smile, not forthcoming. He was in no mood for levity.

"I'll tell you, Jon and Walt. It's all these people from away with their drugs who are messing up our way of life. I thought when I signed up to be the cop for these islands all I would do is sit in my cruiser and enjoy the scenery. You know, maybe deal with an occasional bar fight. Small stuff. But, hell, not this."

"It's not just here, Timmy. It's across the country. Drugs are making people crazy," Walt tried to console him.

Timmy sighed. "I sure hope someone finds that asshole and he gets the death penalty. I'll go watch it myself."

He wandered off for a pew in the rear of the church, leaving me alone with Walt. "Guess it's going to be tougher than ever to find a doctor willing to relocate out here now," he said.

"Hadn't thought of that."

"I mean, would you want *that* job?" Walt asked as he glanced at Timmy hiding out in the back of the church.

185

"Probably not, although I wouldn't mind the pay. Just not the responsibilities."

Walt asked: "What's going to happen with the Douglas Point project now?"

"Good question. I spoke with Mr. Patel yesterday and he wants me to take over. I told him it's not my decision. It's up to the company."

"Who owns that company, anyway?" Walt asked.

"They're out of Massachusetts. Ciccolini Brothers. I gather Shane had only recently joined them. I imagine they're pissed no end to learn he was stealin' from them, and is now on the loose as a wanted murderer. Not the best PR, if you catch my drift."

Walt nodded. "It would be nice if you ended up in charge, Jon. Maybe you could give Charlie a few hours on the weekends. My son Luke tells me Charlie has been getting into all sorts of trouble at school. Been acting strange, pushing friends away, getting into fights."

"Yeah, I know. Linda worries he might be suicidal. No doubt, that kid has been through a lot. Charlie hasn't seemed to want to work with me this fall."

"I thought he was going to work on weekends?"

"That was the plan, but he's bailed on me."

Walt looked puzzled. "Shit, I thought you bailed on him."

"Please . . . don't get started on that—"

"But, do you seriously think he could harm himself?"

"That's what Linda says. Do me a favor, would you? Ask Luke to keep an eye on him. I know they liked playing baseball last spring. The kid's miserable."

"Sure thing. Geez . . . suicidal? Had no idea things were that bad."

Timmy Tetreault rejoined us.

Walt turned to him: "What's the latest on Jon's father's case? Are you figuring it was Shane now?"

"Don't know yet. The crime lab is getting DNA and prints from the RV. But why would he want to kill Mr. Davis?"

Eager to steer attention away from myself, I offered a theory. "I think Shane and Kevin were hatching a plan to steal from Ingrid. Kevin was pissed when she wrote him out of her will and blamed my father. And, as long as my father was living with her in the house, Kevin couldn't easily steal from her. Getting my father out of the way was important to Kevin."

Chapter Sixteen
June 2023

Once school was out in mid-June, Charlie began working with me every day on the Douglas Point house. He had done a good job and I was enjoying his company. Dale had pleaded with me to take him on for the summer, and I finally agreed. Charlie was making friends, including in our neighborhood, where there were always lots of children out and about. I noticed a change in Charlie that summer. A change for the better, one brought about by what I assume was his first love affair, with a summer girl named Alison Brooks, whose family had been coming to the island for forty years.

The Brooks family lived in an old Cape Cod-style cottage around the bend from where Charlie was living with Dale. The mother, Sarah, had been active in the community for many years, helping to set up bingo in the summer, volunteering for author appearances at the library, and baking pies for the Fourth of July fundraisers supporting extracurricular programs at the school. She was about as local as a summer person can ever get, with many island friends always happy to see her return after the long winter.

I knew that Sarah had a daughter, as I had seen her over the years playing with other children at the scenic overlook. She was one of the carefree kids who wrote graffiti on the granite ledge. The neighborhood always sprang to life once school was out, with kids biking and running around, free at last. There was a small field on the corner where I would see boys playing three-on-three baseball in the evenings. Sarah's daughter, Alison, had blossomed into an attractive sixteen-year-old that year, and she and Charlie met one evening while he and I were walking by their house after work.

Alison was helping her mother weed their small garden bed out front. Everyone greets everyone on the island so as we were walking by Sarah called out to us.

"Hello, Jon," she had dirt smudges on her face. "So good to see you."

"You too, Sarah. Did you have a good winter?"

"If you think you all had a lot of snow out here, you should have seen Vermont. I thought it would never melt."

"Who do we have here?" she saw Charlie.

"This is Charlie Walsh. He's been working on a big project with me out on Douglas Point."

"Hi, Charlie. Nice to meet you."

"Hey," Charlie said and I could see him eyeing Alison as she added compost to the Rosa Rugosa bushes lining the picket fence. They had just popped into bloom and emitted a beautiful fragrance.

"Do you live in the neighborhood?" Sarah asked Charlie.

"Yup. I'm living with Dale up around the corner."

"Oh, how is Dale?"

"He's good. The fishin's not been great, or so he tells me."

"Well, I hope it picks up. I'm sure he's concerned about the warming waters."

Alison got up from the ground and brushed herself off. She had long chestnut brown hair that hung down to the middle of her back, swishing from side to side as she moved. As she approached, Charlie could see her cornflower blue eyes and a splattering of freckles around her nose. She shot Charlie a demure smile. "I'm Alison, nice to meet you."

"Forgive me," her mother said. "I should have introduced you."

"No problem," Charlie did his best to look cool. "Good to meet you, Alison. Are you here for the weekend?"

"It's looking like I'm going to be here for the whole summer."

What a stroke of luck, he thought.

She continued. "I'm usually in Vermont with my dad but he's taking care of his mother in North Carolina, so I'm here with my mom."

"Sweet," he said. "Maybe we can hang sometime?"

"I'd like that. I don't have many friends here and worry it will be boring."

Her mother approached the fence. "Nonsense. You have plenty of friends. You can do your summer reading for school, take sailing lessons, swim in the quarry . . . there's plenty to do."

"Right," Alison emitted that insolent look of teenage ennui I recalled from my youth. What she meant to say was she didn't know any handsome boys her age on the island, and now here comes one prancing up the street one fine summer evening.

Now, despite what you might think, I know quite a bit about teenage romance on this island. There is plenty of it during the school year among the locals, but once the summer girls arrive, the game changes. For the most part, the summer people don't want their precious daughters mixing it up with local boys. And many of the locals don't want their precious daughters mixing it up with the "fancy and fast" summer boys from away. But nature being what it is, this cannot be avoided, and in fact some of my best friends out here are mixed couples; mixed not in a racial sense, but in the islander versus from away sense. In fact, Walt Wentworth's wife came out to the island after college and never left. She fell, as Walt likes to tell it, *wicked hahd* for him after they met at the bar. Walt, being the true gentleman he is, offered to take her out on his lobster boat, and then one thing led to another and now thirty years later they have raised three children here. Kevin used to joke around with Walt that he had diluted his pure gene pool with some "Guido New Jersey blood," and it showed in their swarthy kids. Which, in turn, meant that Walt and his wife Lisa never have anything to do with Kevin.

Now, as I observed Sarah, I got the distinct impression she was not pleased with the look she saw in her daughter's eyes as she gazed at Charlie. Charlie was tall for his age, and his dark hair and dark eyes had a sad, soulful attraction that even I could see. The June sun had dried up his pimples and he was tanned and handsome. Working that spring, as well as playing baseball, had added to his muscles and he looked in great shape wearing his tight-fitting T-shirt.

"Well, we should be on our way," I said.

Alison turned to Charlie: "Maybe we can hang out after dinner?"

"Sure," he replied, looking like he didn't really care.

Sarah sensed what was brewing and did what any wise mother does. "Why don't you come have dessert with us. You, too, Jon."

One has to respect this move on her part. Keeping any teenager action close to home.

"We'd love to," I said. "What time?"

"Come over around seven and we can eat out here on the deck."

"Okay, see you then."

Sarah made strawberry shortcake with fresh strawberries for us as we gathered on her deck, watching the sky off to the west put on its nightly show of swirling cirrus clouds and filtered light in various shades of red and orange. After dessert, Charlie and Alison went for a walk leaving me alone with Sarah. I brought her up to speed on Charlie's unfortunate situation.

"Goodness, that's just awful, Jon. That poor boy."

"I know, and he's a really good kid. Works very hard. Quick learner."

"Must have been difficult for him moving to a strange new school with so few kids."

"Actually, not. Charlie's an excellent athlete so was eagerly accepted out here."

"And Dale. I mean, what a kind man. Taking in a boy that isn't his own like that."

"I know."

"I think I'll invite him over for a cookout some night. You all should come."

"Oh, don't bother. You and Alison can come to my place for a cookout. Let us welcome you back for the summer. You can meet my father. I'll invite Dale and others."

"Your father's here?"

"Yup. Moved in with me in November, but has been living mostly with Ingrid lately."

"How's she?"

"Not too good, actually. Her memory issues have gotten worse."

"How sad. I guess it's nice your father is here, then."

"I suppose. It's been causing problems with her son, Kevin."

"What doesn't," she said.

"I think he's mixed up in some bad stuff. It's with the lead contractor, Shane, on the project Charlie and I are working

193

on. I have a bad feeling about Shane; he's the guy with the RV parked in the town lot."

"I was wondering what that's all about. People are upset, I've noticed."

"Yeah, he's taking up all those parking spaces and doesn't seem to give a shit about what others think. And Kevin . . . what a piece of work he is. He's been after me to keep my father away from his mother, but what the hell am I supposed to do? I think they're truly in love. At first, I had my doubts, but now I'm not so sure."

"How do you and your father get along?"

"So-so. He was absent for good chunks of my childhood."

"Sorry, Jon."

"But now that he's been with me, he's told me things I didn't know."

"Things?"

"Yeah, about my mother. Turns out when I was too young to remember anything, she was admitted to a sanitarium and he took care of us kids. I think he might have been a decent father back then."

"How's your mother nowadays?"

"Okay, I guess. A bit nutty for sure. I worry she's become one of those crazy QAnon people."

"Does she live in the South?"

"I suppose if you consider Southern California to be the South."

She laughed. "Not really. I hadn't realized they had QAnon people there."

"Guess crazy has no political or geographic affiliation."

She smiled.

"Anyway, why don't you come over this Sunday at two and we'll have a cookout. You can meet my father and tell me what you think."

"What should I bring?"

"Nothing, really."

"I have to bring something."

"Well, then, how about some cheese and crackers."

Sunday was a picture-perfect day, with a calm breeze out of the north, which meant the day warmed up nicely with no threat of fog. I had picked up hamburgers and hot dogs from the market, and Dale was bringing over five pounds of halibut he had caught. I had run into Linda at the market that morning and invited her and her two kids to join us as well. She had been doing her laundry at my house on Saturdays and we were becoming friends.

We were gathered on the outside deck when my father arrived with Ingrid. I was happy to see she could make it as I knew she was not getting out much these days. I walked to the driveway to help them as needed.

"Thank you, Jon," I extended an arm for Ingrid to pull herself out of the low passenger seat.

"It's good to see you," I walked with her to the deck. I had prepared a comfortable seat for her, with a soft cushion on the Adirondack chair. My father caught up to us, carrying some potato salad he had bought at the market.

"Thanks Dad. You didn't need to bother with that."

"Not a bother, Jon. Ingrid insisted we not come empty handed."

"Come here, Dad. I want you to meet some people. This is Sarah and her daughter, Alison, who live around the corner. You know Charlie. This is Dale, who is watching out for Charlie. And this is Linda and her children Molly and Connor."

They shook hands and exchanged pleasantries as I headed into the kitchen to grab my beer and fetch the burgers and hot dogs to get started on the outside grill. I hadn't invited Freddy, which I felt guilty about, but didn't want him there judging me about my drinking. I had promised Linda I would have no more than two beers. Dale headed into the kitchen and began preparing the halibut. There were five large pieces, each more than an inch thick.

Dale asked. "You got mayonnaise and buttah I assume?"

"In the fridge. Bottom shelf."

I took my beer and the platter with the burgers and dogs out to the deck and started grilling. Charlie was hanging with Alison on the lawn, and Linda was chatting with Sarah. My father and Ingrid were enjoying the view and watching Linda's children running around. Connor wanted to play with Charlie, and I could sense that Charlie was disappointed he was there, as he had other plans in mind. Linda's daughter Molly was younger than Connor, still in elementary school. I could see some neighborhood children looking at us from across the way and waved to them to join us. They approached cautiously, not sure their parents wanted them over here. I could sense this so called out: "Go check to make sure it's okay. We have plenty of food."

Charlie and Alison came onto the deck and each took a hamburger and hot dog and went inside to watch a Red Sox game on TV.

Alison said: "I'm sorry to hear about your situation, Charlie. My mother told me."

"Thanks. It's been kinda tough."

"Do you know if your mom is going to jail?"

"Not sure. Hope not."

"Did you like school out here?"

"Yeah, it's okay. The kids are friendly and the families have been very nice to me."

"Are you okay living with Dale?"

"I am, but worry he might be leavin' in the fall."

"Why do you say that?"

"He told me. He might have an opportunity to work on an offshore fishing vessel out of New Jersey. Says the money will be too good to pass up."

"Hmm. Where will you live if that happens?"

Charlie sighed. "I don't know."

"God, that's so sad. I'm really sorry," she leaned over and kissed him on the cheek. She smelled of fresh cucumbers. Skin cream, Charlie thought.

"I'll figure it out. I always do."

"I feel like such an idiot," Alison said. "Here I am so fortunate to have my family and to be sent to an expensive boarding school, yet I complain."

"Is a boarding school one of those places where you live there?"

"Yes."

"Where do you go?"

"St. Paul's. It's in New Hampshire."

"I bet it's difficult. Academically."

"The kids are smart, that's for sure."

"Do you play any sports?"

"I love field hockey."

"We don't have anything like that out here. Just soccer in the fall."

"No football?" she looked surprised.

"Nope."

"We have a good football team. I'm friends with the quarterback."

Charlie looked up. "Friends?"

She blushed. "Good friends."

"As in . . . your boyfriend?"

She thought twice before answering. "Yes."

"Lucky guy," Charlie slid away from her.

"He's mostly okay, I guess. Truth be known, he can be a cocky jerk at times."

"Why's that?"

"He's used to getting everything he wants. His father is a senator from New York. The family is powerful. Rich."

"Gee, your mother must be happy about that."

"Excuse me?"

"I mean, don't get me wrong, but I can tell she's not thrilled about you hangin' with the likes of me."

Alison slid closer. "I don't care what she thinks. I like you, Charlie. I'm happy to have met you."

"I like you, too."

"It will be fun to hang out this summer," Alison swished her brown hair from side to side.

Charlie stood up. "C'mon, it's too nice to be stuck inside. Let's go for a swim. But first, I want to show you Dale's mother's garden. I've been helping him get it planted."

"Sure," she followed.

They walked to the right side of the overlook where Dale's mother June had kept a vegetable garden for many years. Dale and Charlie had planted lettuce, beets, cucumbers, tomatoes, and herbs that week and Charlie enjoyed the feel of the rich soil in his hands. The compost they added was dark brown, sitting atop the layers of soil June had lugged over in her yellow wheelbarrow across the many years. It was mostly ledge over here but she had found a ten-foot by four-foot patch she was able to turn into a garden. There was a wire fence surrounding the garden, but one side needed to be repaired, as it had been trampled by deer. Charlie and Dale were planning to do that next week.

"Me and Dale have been keepin' his mother's vegetable garden going. She's moved into a nursing home on the mainland."

"That's sweet of you, Charlie."

"Thanks. It feels good to plant something and watch it grow. Dale says it makes him feel good knowin' we're keepin' her alive through this garden."

"How do you get water over here?" she asked.

"Jon has a couple of connected hoses he's letting us use. See? Back there."

"Nice."

"Although with all the rain we've been gettin' I haven't had to water yet. Just hope everything doesn't wilt. C'mon, let's go to the quarry for a swim."

They had made it back to the deck where everyone was gathered when Charlie turned and saw a deer stepping over the downed section of wire fence surrounding the garden. There was nothing to eat yet, but Charlie knew that other than the weather, deer would be their main obstacles to success. He turned and raced towards the ledge, chasing the deer away.

Chapter Seventeen
September & October 2023

As I recount this story, I am struck by the role happenstance plays in our lives. We do our best to plot a course and stick to it, but then unexpected winds blow in with different plans. I think about Doctor Cocroft and the misfortune that led him to lose his life because he accepted a job on a remote island, a place that up until that time was as peaceful and innocent as any place can be. I think about the long odds that someone like Shane Vachon would be working on Archer Island, and that I would end up working with him. I think about my father and Ingrid, such an unexpected love affair. And I think about Charlie Walsh, just a kid with tough luck putting one foot in front of the other hoping that someday the fates might finally smile on him.

After Shane murdered Doctor Cocroft on October 14th and slipped away to the mainland, many locals were suspicious of Kevin's involvement. It seemed likely he and Shane had been using cash from the stolen building materials to fund their drug dealing and usage. Did Kevin know that Shane was cooking meth in his RV? I find it difficult to believe he didn't, but he did a good job feigning ignorance after the doctor was killed. Most of the townspeople gave him a pass, although not the police and a handful of lobstermen, including Walt Wentworth, who were not buying his story. Kevin and Shane became suspects in my father's murder, which was a welcome relief. That is, until Kevin fabricated a solid alibi, the details of which I only learned about later.

Following my father's death, and just a few days after Labor Day weekend, Kevin and Susan demanded that Ingrid move into the island's Eldercare Center. Ingrid was devastated by Robert's death and became almost comatose, confined to her home, not eating, not wanting visitors. Kevin and Susan moved Ingrid into the Eldercare Center, which fortunately for them had an opening, on a cloudy September day.

"C'mon, Mom. Let me help you up these stairs," Kevin said.

Susan followed behind with a suitcase and a few books and other items from the house. They were greeted by Peggy Mason, the Executive Director. "Welcome, Ingrid," she sounded cheerful. "We're happy to have you with us. Let me show you to your room. It's just down the hallway on the right."

Susan noticed a group of women in the living room having tea. She stopped to chat with Janice Pearson, a friend of Ingrid's who would be happy to have her there. While she was doing this, Kevin helped his mother get her room set up. What he did next cannot be confirmed, but later Susan shared with me her suspicions and explained how it could have happened while she was chatting with Janice.

Ingrid sat on her bed in her new small room looking lost and lonely, as if she wanted to die. She was muttering my father's name, sobbing, grief-stricken. Kevin was hanging her clothes in the small closet, and then placed her large desk calendar on the bureau.

"Mom, there are some things I need you to write in your calendar so you don't forget."

Ingrid looked up puzzled. The calendar—the future for that matter—was the furthest thing from her mind. She was ready to die.

Kevin placed the calendar on her lap and sat next to her on the bed. "Svea's birthday is on September 27th, so let's write that in here." He passed her the pen that he was holding and she wrote what he said in the box for September 27th. He then flipped the calendar pages ahead to December and asked her to write in his birthday on the 9th. She wrote very slowly, absentmindedly. Ingrid was undoubtedly very tired and confused and acting like an automaton. Kevin flipped the calendar back to August and asked her to write in the box for the 28th "Dinner with Kevin, 6 p.m., spending the night." Even though the date was in the past, she couldn't tell one month from the next, nor one day from another, and simply did what he said. Kevin placed the calendar on the bureau just as Susan walked in.

"Ah, you brought the old trusty calendar I see. She won't be needing it now that she has full-time care. What a relief this will be for us to know she's being well taken care of."

"She wanted me to bring the big desk calendar. You know how she likes to gaze at it."

Kevin was standing off to the side and noticed he had left the calendar page turned to August. He walked over and as discretely as possible flipped it back to September. Later, Susan would tell me that struck her as odd, as if he had something to hide, and she left Ingrid that day with a sinking feeling about Kevin.

Now, as I think back about that time, I realize Kevin set up this alibi to be used when he needed it. In September, I had become the prime suspect, so Kevin withheld his ace in the hole alibi until October, when his buddy Shane went on his killing spree. At that time, I pressed Officer Jackman to look more closely into Shane and Kevin as the likely killers of my father. I offered the motive, which was they wanted him out of the picture so they could hatch their plan to steal from Ingrid's house. After Kevin had confirmed over the summer that the house was not being left to him or his half-sister, he declared war on his mother and my father. The police took in what I was saying and went to question Kevin yet again in October, and that was when he suggested they look at his mother's calendar. He was pretty sure he was having dinner with Ingrid the night Robert was killed, and had spent the night at her house. She surely would have written that into her calendar. When the police went to check his alibi, and showed the calendar entry to Ingrid at the Eldercare Center, she simply nodded in the affirmative when asked if this was true. The handwriting was hers. She could see that, so it must have been true.

With Shane now loose on the mainland, the police kept a close eye on Kevin thinking that Shane might reach out to him. The case went cold. This is what we know about where Shane had holed up, recounted from prison by his accomplice, Roy Gastineau.

Shane broke into an elderly man's house in Oceanside that first night in mid-October he was being hunted. An APB had been issued and Shane's phone delivered several public service alerts that a dangerous armed man was in the area and the public should shelter in place until receiving an all-clear notification. The elderly man was found tied up in his bathroom the following evening by his daughter who came to check on him after he had not returned her calls. By the time she arrived and called the police, Shane had driven off in the old man's Chevy Blazer.

According to what Shane later told Gastineau, he headed out that night in the stolen vehicle and drove to Augusta, and then up Route 201 through Skowhegan toward Jackman and the Canadian border. Between the West Forks and Jackman, along the Kennebec River, Shane was stuck behind a logging truck that was barely budging up the hill. Undoubtedly frustrated and eager to pass, Shane had an idea. He seized his opportunity when the trucker unexpectedly pulled into a scenic rest area along the river, high in the mountains outside of Jackman. Shane pulled into the overlook and saw there were no other cars in the small parking lot. He left his stolen car at the far end of the lot, partially concealed behind bushes. Shane walked back to where the truck was parked and saw that the driver was asleep in his cab. He circled the truck, which was carrying long lengths of spruce logs. He had hoped to find a space to squeeze in between two logs but the truck was packed tight. He was about to abandon the idea when he noticed two of the larger logs on the left side of the truck were angled upwards toward the cab, revealing a space he might be able to fit into. Shane hoisted himself up and squeezed his small frame into the space. He was wearing an orange fleece hunting jacket he had quickly removed from a hook in the entryway of the old man's house in Oceanside. He realized this would be far too conspicuous when passing through customs, so he jumped from the truck and tossed the jacket into the woods. He was wearing just a long-sleeved brown cotton shirt underneath, and the temperature up in the mountains was dropping fast. He slid back into the open space, shivering.

Fortunately for Shane, the driver was just taking a short nap, and the big rig's engine soon rumbled back on and the truck edged out onto Route 201. Shane bounced uncomfortably in his log fort as the truck passed through Jackman making the last leg of the journey toward the Canadian border.

He felt the truck slow down and figured they were approaching customs. He could see snow-covered spruce trees lining this stretch of road, the trees frosted and glistening in the low-angled sunshine. They pulled into a special checkpoint for large trucks off to the side. He could hear the customs officer address the driver by his name.

"Bonjour, Claude."

"Good day, Jean. Cold up here."

"Looks like winter's coming in early this year. We already had some snow last week."

This driver was a regular, who probably made this crossing many times a month. Shane heard small talk about the Montreal Canadiens hockey team, and then some laughter. There was just a quick check of the driver's passport and the truck was on its way. Shane stayed as still as possible as the long bed of the truck where he was hiding passed though the checkpoint. The temperature continued dropping as they rode along deserted Canadian roads heading north.

Fifty or so miles later, Shane could see through the logs that they were coming into a town that had a Tim Hortons coffee shop and several car dealerships. The truck slowed along the snow-covered road. While stopped at a traffic light, Shane jumped down and jogged across the way and into the Tim Hortons. Later, the driver would report he thought he saw someone or heard something fall from his truck, but couldn't be certain at the time and was in a hurry to make his delivery. He pulled over into the parking lot of the Metro supermarket to make sure no logs had come loose. Seeing nothing amiss, he continued on his way north.

We know for certain this was Shane because of what happened that evening. He had made it across the border into the first Canadian town of any size after Jackman, Saint-George's. At the Tim Hortons he ran into this Roy Gastineau fellow, another instance of happenstance that would sadly lead to more tragedy. Gastineau was a small-time drug dealer and thief who had moved from Alberta to Quebec Province over the summer.

I realize most people believe the saying that *everything is happening for a reason*, but I'm not buying that for one second. Life seems more like a giant stew of luck—good and bad—as well as some shitty timing. The people with the good luck think they made their luck; those with bad luck know better.

The timing couldn't have been worse for Gaston Devereaux, the pharmacist at the Familprix pharmacy up the road from Tim Hortons, or for Brenda Bourassa and her ten-year-old daughter Pauline. Talk about bad luck. The coincidence that Shane and Gastineau were in the pharmacy at the same time as them was bad enough, but throw in the unlikely arrival of the gun-toting Texan, Hank Abbott—who was on his way to Quebec City for some partying—and one has to ponder what kind of divine force, if any, is driving this crazy bus we call life.

Devereaux was supposed to have the day off but, being a solid sort who was the kind of person who always rose to every need, came in to work after the other pharmacist tested positive for Covid. The security cameras in the pharmacy show two masked armed robbers entering shortly before closing time that night. Gastineau held the Bourassa little girl at gunpoint while the pharmacist, with arms in the air, went to fetch the drugs for Shane.

As Gastineau and Shane were backing out the door to make their escape, the armed Texan, who had been hiding in the makeup aisle, sprang out shooting at Shane. Gastineau jumped him and the gun slid off to the side where Shane retrieved it. Shane's makeshift mask had slipped off and his face was visible. He gazed around like a hunted animal and then shot the Texan once in the head. He paused for a split second, and realizing he could be identified without his mask on, shot the pharmacist and the mother, while the little girl scrambled away behind a Cadbury cardboard display case.

Shane and Gastineau ran off into the night for Gastineau's rusted out Toyota Echo, and drove east towards Nova Scotia, where they would hatch the final scheme that brought them back to Archer Island.

Chapter Eighteen
July 2023

The Fourth of July weekend arrived with many parties and cookouts on the island. After the long hard winter and the spring that refused to come, a switch flipped in late-June and the island transformed from cool and melancholy to sunny and hopeful. I know of no other place where the lows are so low and the highs so high. The island is reborn with the return of the summer people—the parties, the library events, the wine tastings, and the many new romances. There was a good deal of budding love that summer, what with Charlie and Alison, my father and Ingrid, and at long last, yours truly and Linda.

Linda. What to say? The kindest, sweetest, most genuine person you could ever hope to meet. Completely devoid of guile. She and I had been down for so long we had given up hope of ever rising again, but by the Fourth of July weekend we were seeing each other regularly. It all happened so quickly and with such force, I now take back what I've said about happenstance, because this love seemed pre-ordained by some higher power, who most assuredly knows what HE is doing. Or SHE is doing. Or THEY is doing. I don't know . . . you get my drift. I'm working on my pronouns.

Linda had grown up dirt poor, so poor that as a six-year-old most of the food she ate came from school. It wasn't that her parents were absent or lazy, but when her father lost his right hand in a welding accident at the boatyard, and then shortly thereafter her mother was diagnosed with a debilitating multiple sclerosis—requiring mainland medical attention—the sum of the rent and medical bills and making ends meet overwhelmed the family. Her father was denied disability insurance for reasons I still don't understand, and so the family moved to the mainland where Linda's mother went to work at Walmart until her illness progressed to the point where she became eligible for disability insurance. According to Linda, her mother made just enough money to keep the oil tank half full, buy gas to get to work and back, and put some Walmart food on the table.

Linda remembers it being so cold in their rental apartment that a portable heater was always on, and she worried they would burn the place down. Linda ate her free school meals—a kind teacher or two sending her home with leftovers from their lunches—and came right home afterwards to help her parents as needed. Too much to ask of a young child. The weight would be enough to break anyone.

But Linda never broke. They lived poor like that until she was seventeen and married her high school sweetheart. He had dropped out of school, but had a good job working as a fuel delivery truck driver for Otis Brothers. Linda stayed at home with their young children until they started school. She got a job working as a waitress at the local diner, where she made decent tips and was well taken care of by the owners of this longtime family business. The major benefit being she could have a free meal. Life was okay, that is until her husband split on her and relocated to the West Coast. Not sure why, although Linda told me he had some demons he couldn't keep under control. His loss. My gain.

That particular Fourth of July weekend was warm enough to go swimming in the quarries. The roses were out in full force, their beauty enhanced by the pure blue skies behind them. We had a busy day planned for the Fourth, with the morning parade on Main Street and then invitations to two afternoon parties. It was decided that I would drive Bobby, Ingrid, Linda, and Charlie to the first party, which was being hosted by a summer person who lived nearby to Ingrid. Sarah was driving her daughter, Alison, along with some friends visiting for the weekend. Afterwards, we would leave early and go to Walt's for his annual barbeque, always a great time.

The party hosted by the summer person I didn't know was down a private road on the northeastern side of the island. On our way in, I saw two tennis courts painted green and blue, exactly like the US Open courts. A row of yellow day lilies surrounded the court's fencing, their eager blooms reaching upwards toward the sun. The road swerved past two large outbuildings before opening up to reveal a sprawling compound just steps from the ocean. There were roses planted in raised beds, all grouped by color—the pinks, the deep reds, the whites artfully arranged. Pink peonies were supported by wooden frames, their heavy heads bent over. Bearded purple iris looked like Biblical kings. Out on the ocean I saw white sails gliding among the many small islands and outcroppings of granite, navigating between the brightly colored lobster buoys bobbing in cobalt blue waters.

We parked off to the side on a small grass field where others were parked, and followed a procession of people I didn't know toward the large home, people crammed onto second floor decks enjoying the view. My father and I helped Ingrid make her way to the first-floor deck and guided her into a sturdy seat. This was a potluck party, with people carrying plates of food into the well-lit kitchen. A bar was set up on one of the granite countertops next to the refrigerator, and I went in to fetch us drinks. Charlie dashed off to find Alison, who had come with her mother and two friends from prep school.

"Welcome! Welcome!" an elegant woman dressed in a brightly colored caftan greeted us. "So glad you could come."

"I'm Jon and this is Linda. Thank you for hosting us," I said. "And this here is my father, Bobby. I believe you know Ingrid, who is on the porch."

"Oh, that's wonderful to hear. I gather she isn't doing very well," she whispered.

"And you are?" my father asked.

"Forgive me. Lucy von Stade."

"Pleased to meet you," Bobby shook her hand. "Actually, Ingrid is doing quite well today. I've been living with her, helping as needed. She's been bravely soldiering on, one day at a time."

"I don't believe I've seen you around before," she faced my father.

"I just moved here in November, to be with my son, Jon."

"How do you know Ingrid?"

"We met over the winter and have become good friends. If I may ask . . . how do you know her?"

"Oh, God. We go way back. I think I first met her when we were little girls. I spent summers here with my grandparents and we were great friends. We went to sailing school together. Got into some mischief as teenagers. Ingrid was always the girl the summer boys wanted to spend time with."

"She's a beautiful soul," Bobby smiled.

"I couldn't agree more. Please . . . help yourselves to whatever you want. My husband is making cocktails. There's also beer and wine. I'm going to find Ingrid and say hello," she headed off.

"Let me show you where she is," Bobby followed after her.

Linda and I loaded up our plates with fresh crab dip on toast rounds. I was surprised to see Bugles and onion dip, an old favorite I hadn't seen in years. I tried two and they were as salty and addictive as I remembered, so I added a handful to my plate. We strolled out to the lawn where fold-up chairs were set up.

There was a gentle breeze off the water, the temperature not too hot nor too cool, just perfect. Several high-end yachts were moored off Dunbar Island across the way. The ocean waters looked like sparklers, glistening in the sunshine. I saw Charlie off in the distance with Alison. They were laughing, playfully punching each other in the arms, touching one another in that awkward way of teenagers of the opposite sex.

Linda whispered to me: "Do you know any of these people?"

I looked around and said: "Some. Not many."

"I took you for a townie."

I laughed. "Well, I *am* a townie but also have some summer friends. I've met quite a few from doing work at their homes."

"Please don't leave me alone. I feel completely out of place here. Did you see the necklace the hostess is wearing?"

"No, why?"

"I think it's real emeralds and diamonds. Must be worth a small fortune."

I was enjoying my Bugles and onion dip, plus the crab dip, when Alison and Charlie approached.

"Hey, kids," I said. "Get yourselves some food."

"We will," Charlie said. "Right now, we're trying to find Alison's friends. Have you seen them?"

"Not sure I'd recognize them if I had."

"Okay, maybe they're inside," they ran off.

Linda smiled. "Looks like some teenage love is sprouting."

"I know, it's cute, isn't it."

"How is Charlie doing?"

"I think mostly okay. He's a good worker and a quick learner. I can see him running his own little construction business someday with any luck. He has a good head for numbers."

"That's nice to hear. I went to check my school mail yesterday and there was a letter from the case worker in Oceanside."

"What about?"

"They need me to fill out a quarterly form on how he's doing. Where he's living. Not sure if you heard that Dale is considering taking a job in New Jersey this fall and winter."

I didn't reply. I reached down for my beer on the grass and took a long belt.

Linda continued: "I think we tend to forget how difficult those teenage years were despite outward appearances."

"For sure. Kids will go to great lengths to appear normal, as if everything is all right even when it isn't. I was like that."

"You were about Charlie's age when you moved out here, right?"

"Yes."

"I think we had left the island by the time you showed up," she said.

"Yup."

216

"Did you like being here?"

"Not really. Hanging out with Charlie has reminded me how spaced out I was back then. You know, partly hormonal, partly my parents getting divorced and then me being uprooted by my mother. I smoked a lot of weed back then and started stealing liquor from my stepfather's bar. Most of the time I felt like a stranger in my own skin."

"Where does your mother live now?"

"El Segundo, California."

"How come you never talk about her?"

"I don't know. I guess I resent her for divorcing my father—"

"She left him? I assumed it was the other way around based on what a player your old man is."

"Player?"

"Well, you know. He's handsome, even I can see that. A smooth operator. Slick to a point, but in a society sort of way. He'll fit in great among these people at the party."

"I think that slickness is mostly from the years he spent living in Florida. He ran with a fast crowd of socialites. The places we live shape us all."

"When was the last time you saw your mother?"

"Last summer, I visited her. Truth is, she's a bit nutty. Refuses to get vaccinated. Paranoid. I'm starting to understand why my father fooled around on her."

"Really? That's *never* acceptable, Jon."

"Yeah, I know. But I hadn't realized she was sent to a sanitarium when we were kids."

"That must have been tough."

"I have no recollection of it at all."

"Maybe this explains those nightmares you have, Jon. You know, the dreams you told me about after waking up in a sweat."

"You mean the ones where I'm searching for my mother?"

"Yes. It could be those early childhood memories are buried but you need to deal with them."

I laughed. "Have you been re-reading Dr. Ruth or something?"

"Uh . . . that would be sex help, dear."

"You know what I mean. One of those television crackpot psychologists."

"No, but I'm a big believer that our dreams are important."

"I suppose so. I don't know. Much of what I dream strikes me as nonsense. It's like a bad team of writers getting together to throw characters and events together in an absurd jumble. It's like the writers from the Simpson's and South Park decided to get together to create a new show."

She laughed and kissed me on the cheek.

I finished my beer. "We should go mingle. I can probably drum up some business for next winter here."

218

On our way to the porch, we passed Charlie and Alison, who were talking with two boys I didn't recognize.

"Hey, Mr. Davis," Alison greeted me.

"Who do we have here?" I asked.

"These are my friends from St. Paul's. This is Andy Dykstra and Jamie Sprague."

"Hello, boys," I shook their hands.

"Nice to meet you, sir," Andy had long flowing blond hair and a perpetual grin pasted on his face. Jamie's eyes were bloodshot and I smelled weed.

Linda asked: "Have you boys been to the island before?"

Andy answered: "Nah, my folks have a house on the Vineyard. First time here."

"How do you like it?" Linda asked.

"It's okay, I guess. Not much to do from what I've seen so far. I brought my golf clubs hoping there was a course but I guess there isn't."

"Yeah, not that kind of place," I said.

Alison gave Andy a flirtatious pat on the shoulder. This is when it dawned on me that he might be her boyfriend from prep school. I looked at Charlie and he seemed a bit down. I imagine he was not sure where and if he fit into the picture. I had thought Alison and Charlie were more than just friends, but now wasn't so sure. Linda, being more perceptive, saw what was going on and tried to provide Charlie with some ammunition.

"Charlie, congratulations on being named the MVP of the

baseball team. What an amazing accomplishment."

"Thanks," he gazed down at his feet. "They gave me a trophy."

Andy laughed. "You guys actually have a baseball team out here? Who do you play? The girls' team?"

Jamie Sprague high-fived him.

Charlie said: "We travel all over the state to play. It's tough, taking the 7 a.m. ferry and then long bus rides. We play two five-inning games and then have to race back in time for the last boat."

"What was your record?" Andy asked.

"We won four games out of thirteen."

"Shit, man. That's lame."

"Don't be a jerk," Alison looked uncomfortable. "There are only like ten kids in a grade so they are outmanned. His team had two eighth graders playing so they could field a team of nine. It's not like at St. Paul's."

"I'd say," Andy chuckled. "We won the prep championships in football, hockey, and tennis this year. Right, babe?" He reached to high-five her but she wasn't in the mood.

"I'm not your *babe*," Alison looked upset. I imagine at that point she realized mixing her prep school friends with island life had been a mistake. These boys would never understand how it is out here. This was no Martha's Vineyard or Nantucket. Archer Island was far more special to her than any of those other islands she had visited.

Andy realized she was pissed at him and grabbed Jamie and headed off in search of food and drink. Alison and Charlie stood awkwardly in front of us before she said: "C'mon Charlie. Let's go for a walk down along the cove."

Linda and I went to check on Ingrid and Bobby who were in conversation with a small gathering of people I didn't recognize. Standing off to the side by himself was Rohan Patel, who had come to visit for the week to relax and see the progress on his new home. I had met him for the first time yesterday and was struck by what a genuinely nice and thoughtful man he was. He had asked me how I felt the project was coming along, if we needed anything we didn't have, and gave me a free subscription code to use in accessing a new healthcare app he had in development with his newest start-up. He was grateful I had outed Kevin for stealing from the project earlier in June, and I informed him that Kevin was now lobstering.

Seeing him standing by himself, I brought Linda over and introduced her.

"Very nice to meet you, Linda," Rohan spoke in a soothing low voice. "What a gorgeous day."

"Good to meet you, too. How long are you here for?" she asked.

"Just through tomorrow. I need to be in London for meetings later this week."

"London, that sounds nice," she said.

"It's a beautiful city. Have you ever been?"

Linda laughed. "No, I wish. I've been to Boston, though."

"Boston is beautiful, too. A smaller London, I'd say. Maybe someday you and Jon can be my guests in London and I can show you around."

"Are you being serious?" she stood back.

"Of course, it would be my pleasure."

Linda had never met a man of Indian descent and saw in his brown eyes a generous spirit, a kind soul completely at odds with her preconceived notions of what tech billionaires are like. She reached out to touch him on the arm, her eyes welling with tears of gratitude.

"We would love that if you truly mean it."

He smiled. "I mean it. You should come in April when the tulips are out. Come for Easter. I'm sure escaping the chilly dampness here at that time of year would be a welcome break for you."

Jon said: "That's very kind of you, Rohan."

"Please, call me Row. Might you know how I can go about getting lobster on the island?"

"Of course, I'd be happy to get you some from one of my friends. How many do you want?"

"How many do you suggest I get?"

"Is it just for you?"

"Yes."

"Do you have plans for later this afternoon?"

"No, just here at the party and then back to the Airbnb in

town. I have a car rental."

"How about you come with us to a real island party at my friend Walt's? There will be lobster there."

"I'd love that, Jon. Frankly, I feel quite awkward here with these people I don't know."

"You're not alone," Linda touched him on the elbow.

"I can leave our truck with my father and then you can give us a lift back to town, okay?"

"Be delighted," he said.

"We should mingle some," I turned to Linda. "Rohan, we'll come find you when we're ready to leave."

"Sounds like a plan, Jon. And please, call me Row. As in a boat," he smiled.

Linda didn't want to mingle. "Why don't you go secure yourself some future billings, Jon, and I'll stay here with Mr. Row Your Boat."

We all laughed.

I walked along the porch where Ingrid was in her seat deep in conversation with a couple I didn't recognize. Bobby was off somewhere else.

"Can I get you something to eat or drink, Ingrid?" I offered.

"Thank you, but I'm fine." She nodded her head toward the man and woman near her, flashing me an eye roll that made me think she was eager to get away from these people. They seemed to have her cornered as they hovered above her in her seat.

"Hello, I'm Jon," I introduced myself to the couple, who had that out-of-place look of someone's weekend guests. The balding middle-aged man was wearing a flowered blue and white wide-collared shirt, unbuttoned one button too many revealing a clump of chest hair. His white jeans matched his white Oxford shoes. He was short and stocky, with bushy brown eyebrows that made me think of the former Soviet Union General Secretary, Leonid Brezhnev. The left side of his mouth was lower than the right. Standing next to him was a young woman, who looked to be in her early twenties.

"I'm Penny," she smiled.

"And I'm Harrison," the man said.

"Nice to meet you both."

"So . . . as I was saying . . ." (apparently, I had interrupted him) "I worked for many years as an editor at *Travel & Leisure* magazine, but once I saw the possibilities of heading out on my own as a social media influencer, I left and started my own brand. Penny and I have been exploring Maine's islands posting about food and culture. We're in the process of pitching a travel book in New York."

"Influencers?" Ingrid looked up in confusion.

"Yes. Magazines, newspapers, and books are all a thing of the past. Nowadays, the real action is on social media. We're content creators building up large followings, which in turn allows us to be paid by advertisers hoping we will shine our spotlight on them."

"What in God's name are you talking about?" Ingrid's expression was turning hostile, a look I had seen occurring with more frequency in recent weeks, which I attributed to her dementia.

"Penny, fetch me a gin and tonic," his tone was peremptory.

Penny disappeared into the kitchen.

"Is she your girlfriend?" I asked.

"My assistant."

"Oh . . . and she travels with you?"

"Lately, yes. I'm teaching her to understand what makes for good content that can translate into ad sales."

"You don't say."

"Tell me, Jon. What do *you do*?"

"Excuse me? What do *you do*?"

"I just told you."

"That's a full-time job?"

"You'd be surprised how lucrative this line of work can be."

Penny returned with his drink and I did my best to extricate myself to rejoin Linda, but this man liked to hear himself pontificate.

"I also dabble as a filmmaker."

"One can dabble in filmmaking?" Ingrid gazed up from her seat.

"It's a new venture. Content is content, so why not start

225

with social media, and then move into other forms of expression?"

"Harrison is going to cast me in a film after he lands his book deal," Penny looked like a lamb heading for a surprise slaughter. Her hair was pulled up into a bun and she was chewing bubble gum, which rested between her lips before she sucked it back in.

"You don't say."

Harrison spoke in a low bombastic voice. "One important thing I've learned is that people have very short attention spans. We only have a split second as they scroll through their feeds to arrest attention. You can see this trend carried over to many of the new novels being published. Novels like *Summer Party*, set on Cape Cod, by Alexandra Frothingham. Take a guess what that story is about? You got it. A summer party. Another new novel Penny read recently is *Summer Love*. You get my drift. Men don't read anymore, so these are both clearly written for women to bring to the beach. Escapism reads. Both authors began by building huge followings on social media and then got six-figure book deals."

"That's quite the sweeping generalization. I read and I'm a man," I was growing to deeply dislike this pretentious man.

"Fiction?"

"Yes, fiction."

"Mysteries, I suppose?"

"Actually, I don't like most mysteries, other than the British ones."

"What then?"

"John Irving, Jane Smiley, Elizabeth Strout—"

He shot me a skeptical look. "Well, you're the exception. Almost all consumers of media these years are women. True for social media influencers. True for books. Anyway, my earlier question was to find out what you do for work."

"I'm a carpenter."

"Where do you live?"

"In town."

"No, I mean where do you live when you're not on Archer Island."

"I live here year-round."

"Really?"

"Yes."

"My goodness, that must be god-awful."

"No, it's very beautiful. Unpretentious. So . . . help me out here. I'm trying to understand how you get paid for being an influencer."

"It's no different than anything else. Advertisers will spend if you can deliver them a targeted audience that will buy their products. And the great thing about being a travel influencer is fine hotels and restaurants give us freebies in exchange for posting about them. They like the authenticity of the content we produce."

"We're taking over an art gallery on Dunbar Island next week to showcase a food and wine tasting," Penny said. "I'll be doing the styling."

"How authentic," I heard Ingrid mutter.

The sarcasm was missed. "Thanks. Harrison says I'm a natural at this."

I was about to break free when Ingrid came out of the blue with: "I cannot begin to fathom what you're talking about. This all strikes me as pointless fluff. Serious journalism is in decline because of these vapid new ways of making money. Our world is degenerating into an endless pile of *look at me* vanity. If I were you, young lady, I'd put as much distance as possible between this odious man and yourself. Quickly."

Harrison and Peggy stood back, not accustomed to being insulted like this.

Harrison said: "One needn't get all worked up. We're talking about social media, not exactly essential items."

"Essential?" I asked.

"The pandemic showed us how non-essential much of what we do is. Who the truly essential workers are."

"Ah, I hear you, there. I agree that doctors and nurses and school teachers and delivery drivers are far more essential than, say . . . *influencers.*"

"And carpenters," he chortled.

"At least carpenters produce something of value with their own two hands," Ingrid's face flushed with hostility. "Unlike you, who goes about panhandling off desperate fools seeking attention, while doing God knows what with young girls like this one here, who can't be half your age. Maybe you could learn how to do something essential. Or at least not be a pompous ass! Jon, where *is* your father? I want to go home. Now."

I found Bobby in the kitchen fixing a plate for Ingrid, but he had been intercepted so many times he was having difficulty making his way back to her. "Dad, there you are. No need to bring Ingrid any food. She wants to go home."

"Already?" he looked surprised. "We just got here."

"Yes, now. She's surrounded by some real pieces of work. She's not feeling well. Linda and I are going to head over to Walt's so we'll catch up with you this evening. You can take my truck, here are the keys. Mr. Patel will drive us to Walt's."

Linda laughed as we dashed off for Row's rental car.

"What's so funny?" I asked.

"The bumper stickers."

"What about them?"

"Look at this one: *Biden/Harris; Black Lives Matter; Sierra Club; Save the Whales; LGBTQ Rights . . .*"

"So?"

"This is how I always know summer has returned."

When we arrived at Walt's, Linda brought my attention to an old pickup truck parked in the driveway. "See?" she laughed.

"See what?"

"Look at the bumper stickers: *Go Brandon; Fish for Life;*

Trump 2024: The Revenge Tour; Defund NOAA; Proud NRA Supporter . . ."

"All right, already. Point made."

A rock band was playing Steely Dan down along the waterfront where Walt's lobster boat was moored in the cove. I knew the guys in the band, all locals. Two kegs were set up on the porch. A long table covered in a checkered tablecloth was loaded with food: lobster rolls, pasta salads, grilled hot dogs and hamburgers, cookies, and cakes.

"Walt, I'd like you to meet Rohan Patel. He's the owner of the house I've been building."

"Nice to meet you. I'm sorry, I'm bad with names. What did you say your name was again?"

"Rohan," he answered. "Friends call me Row."

"Welcome to the party, Row. Please help yourself to whatever you want."

"I think we could all use a beer," I said. "Just came from a party up island that was a bit tough to take."

"We've got kegs, but if you prefer a mixed drink or wine, those are in the kitchen."

"Beautiful place you have here," Row said. Walt's split-level ranch sat on five acres along a cove.

"Thanks. Been in the family for four generations I believe it is."

"Are you a lobsterman?"

"I am."

"He's also an EMT and volunteer fireman."

"That must keep you busy," Row said.

"It does."

"Can you recommend a restaurant in town where I can get a boiled lobster dinner?"

Walt laughed. "Believe it or not, there are none left. We always had at least one but with the rising rents, brought about by people who don't actually live here buying up the main drag, the locals can't afford to operate restaurants despite the demand. You can imagine the looks on the day-trippahs who come out thinkin' they'll get a lobster lunch. It's truly sad and downright bizarre."

"I don't understand," Row looked confused. "Why would someone buy up commercial property here if they didn't plan to live here and use it?"

"You and me, buddy. What I've heard is that it's some sort of tax write-off for now, and an investment when property values rise."

"But why not lease the property at reasonable prices?"

"Beats me," Walt said. "All I can guess is that he'd rather not have the wear and tear on his property and doesn't need the rental money. Who knows? Could be some guy came out here for the day and made an impulsive purchase. People visit in July and fall in love, not understanding how hard it is during the offseason."

Row said. "I'm sorry to hear the locals are being priced out. It's happening everywhere now and is especially bad in San

Francisco."

"You from there?"

"I am."

"Row is a tech entrepreneur," I said.

Row lowered his voice. "If you don't mind, I prefer not to be identified as some wealthy tech asshole."

"Shit, gotta be better than being some poor fisherman asshole," Walt laughed.

"I'm sorry, I didn't mean to insult you, Walt. It's just this isn't a great time to be a tech entrepreneur in terms of public image."

"None taken. Truth be told, it's not a great time to be identified as a lobsterman."

"Why's that?"

Walt exhaled deeply. "Haven't you read the latest five-part series in the national newspapers?"

"No, guess I missed it."

"We let some award-seeking journalists come out here to tag along with us. Thought they were going to write a nice story about our tight little community, how hard we all work doing what we love. How our livelihoods are under attack by people who don't know the first thing."

"And?" he asked.

"The story ended up being about how we're resistant to change, unwilling to try the new ropeless fishing methods. You know, don't believe in global warming. Made us look kind of greedy and dumb all at once. This, after we let them stay with us and fed them and thought we were friends. Go figure."

"Ah, yes. The media writes what they want. I could have forewarned you."

"Live and learn," Walt said.

Row's expression changed to one of serious introspection. "My intentions have always been to help society, to solve problems that will allow people to live better lives. I've been lucky to have my dreams turn into success. I have a foundation that does good work helping the less fortunate. We currently are focusing on lowering health care costs using smarter tech tools."

"Good to hear," Walt smiled. "Maybe you can throw some of that money at the island. We have a lot of need out here."

"I'd like that. In fact, I have already asked the head of my charitable foundation to contact you, Jon. I'm thinking you would be an ideal point person on the island to help identify the best uses."

Walt laughed. "Be careful. Jon is likely to ask you to fund a brewery and pizza joint."

"Stop it, Walt," I slugged him playfully in the arm. "C'mon, Row, I'll introduce you to some locals you should know."

"Before you disappear, I can boil you up a couple of lobsters if you'd like," Walt offered. "The soft shells are coming in now. And there are fresh lobster rolls on the table if you prefer to not deal with crackin' lobsters."

"I don't want to be a bother," Row said.

"No bother, a-TALL. Go get yourself some drinks and I'll bring them out in fifteen minutes or so. Meet me at the picnic table out back."

Miriam Mishkin came over to say hello. "Hi there, Jon. How was your winter?"

"Stormy. I picked up some of the downed tree limbs at your house and took them to the dump. We had some wicked storms."

"Thank you, Jon. I appreciate that very much. Looks like the squirrels set up house inside from what I see."

"Miriam, this is Row Patel. I've been helping build him a home up at Douglas Point."

"Hello, Miriam."

"Nice to meet you, Mr. Patel. What brings you to our lovely island?"

I came here three years ago with a friend. We were on vacation exploring the state. My friend had been here before and I immediately fell in love with the island. Do you live here, Miriam?"

"Yes, my mother and father bought a summer house out here back in the early 1960s. Now it's just me and my ten children."

"Ten children?"

"Well, not all here at the same time!" she laughed. Miriam was dressed in a gray skirt and blouse, traditional Hasidic garb.

234

She had cheerful brown eyes and short brown hair.

"Where do you live when not here?" he asked.

"Borough Park. Brooklyn."

"You must be happy to escape the city heat."

"Yes, I try to get here at least twice a summer. Sometimes I make it in October for the house to be closed up, the water turned off. The rest of the time my children and grandchildren come. Anyway, great to see you, Jon. And nice to meet you, Row." She headed down the hill to where the band was playing.

Row turned to me. "Must admit, I'm surprised to see a Hasidic Jewish family way out here. For one thing, I thought they only lived within kosher communities."

"I believe they made an exception in this case. I'm surprised to see her at this party, as they mostly keep to themselves. Very nice family."

"I wonder how they found this remote island?"

"Same as most people. A friend of a friend invites them out and they immediately fall in love with the place."

"What an interesting story."

"Yes, what a story it is. Her grandmother managed to escape to London during World War Two. And then when the war was over, she went back to Germany to teach English as a second language to the Germans. Can you imagine?"

"Wow."

"There's more. She then moved to Brooklyn where she married one of the leading Jewish intellectuals of the time, a professor and civil rights activist. They participated in many civil rights marches; I believe occasionally risking their lives. Together they worked tirelessly to promote peace around the world. Clearly, she had a remarkable capacity for forgiveness. And, as was true for many Jews after the war, she faithfully did her part in rebuilding the Jewish population, having twelve children, Miriam being the youngest. Miriam, in turn, now has ten children of her own."

"They must have a large house!" Row said.

"Quite the opposite. Theirs is a small home around the bend from mine. They are never all here at the same time. Some of the kids come from Brooklyn, others in Pennsylvania. All living in Hasidic orthodox communities. I worry that sometimes they drive all that way and only stay for two or three nights."

"That's quite something," Row stared off into the distance. "People are remarkably resilient."

"We have no choice."

"I suppose."

Kevin's father came over and joined us. It was rare to see him out and about as he typically stayed to himself, "Hello, Jon. Helluva summah, huh?"

"I know, the weather has been awful."

"Ain't just the weathah. It's all the fuckin' people in town. No place to park in the town lot. I hear that fella takin' up all those spots is your boss at that construction project you and Kevin are workin' at."

"He is. Shane Vachon."

"Can't you tell him to find another place to park that ugly tin can he calls a home?"

I had to chuckle at this description of Shane's old RV. It was beige, red, and white and rusted out along the bottom.

"I've brought it up several times but he doesn't seem to care."

"You know, I was driving through town yesterday needin' to get to the dump, and these day-trippahs on their fancy electric bikes were stopped in the middle of the road, like they owned it. The way the pah-tridges and turkeys do! Just waddlin' there, not movin'. What the hell is wrong with these people? Can't they see we have work to do? That it ain't all fun and games?"

"Well, it's that time of year again."

Row stood there quietly listening and I decided not to introduce him.

"Anyways, do us all a favor, wudya Jon? Talk some sense into that boss of yours. Get that RV outta the lot before someone does it on their own. People are pissed." He headed off and got into the pickup truck with the bumper stickers Linda had noticed on the way in.

"Let's see if the lobsters are ready," we walked toward Walt's house. On the way into the kitchen, Row pulled up abruptly. "Is that you, Amari?" He addressed a dark-skinned man I didn't know standing next to Betty Jean.

"Row Patel!" the man exclaimed. "What in the world are

you doing out here?"

Row laughed. "That's what I was going to ask you."

"I live in town. My wife and I bought a home five years ago. And you?"

"I'm building a place out on Douglas Point."

Betty Jean smiled. "Welcome to Archer Island, where the world is just six degrees of separation. Never ceases to amaze. I'm Betty Jean," she shook Row's hand.

"And I'm Rohan . . . but please just call me Row."

"How do you two know each other?" she asked.

Amari said: "We went to medical school together in Boston. I headed off to work at the National Institutes of Health and Row left to make his fortune on the West Coast. Or so I read in the *Wall Street Journal*."

"I didn't know you were a doctor," Betty Jean said to Amari.

Row said: "He's a bigwig at the NIH. He tries to keep that quiet. Always been the most modest person I know. What are you working on these years?"

"Immunotherapy for cancer treatment."

"Good for you. My new start-up is working on a new healthcare app to remove much of the redundancies in healthcare."

"It's so good to see you, Rohan. What a small world it truly is."

Betty Jean said: "I was on a Princess cruise two years ago

and ran into a couple that used to summer on Archer Island for many, many years. It's just one of those strange things that seems to happen all too often."

"What do you do to keep yourself entertained?" Row asked Betty Jean.

"You mean other than work three jobs?" she stood with hands on hips.

"So . . . no time for any fun?"

"Are you hittin' on me?" she pushed her body close to his and then pulled away, laughing. "I own the bar in town. Plus clean a few summer homes and volunteer at the second-hand bookstore. You should stop in at the bar for a drink this evening. What with all the summer folks here now, it will be packed."

I walked with Row and Amari to the picnic table behind the house, where we sat enjoying our beers beneath the shade of a large chestnut tree. We were joined by Brooklin Morton, who I had known since high school. Brooklin had fallen on hard times, but I didn't know the full extent until she sat with us.

"Hey, Jon," she said as Amari and Row talked with each other on the other side of the table.

"Happy Fourth, Brooklin."

"Not so happy for us. Looks like we might lose our house."

"How's that?"

"Jonny went and took out a second mortgage so we could buy a new boat. We've been missing some house payments."

239

"I'm sorry to hear that. Won't the bank give you a break?"

"Yeah, you're a funny one, Jon."

"Have you asked?"

"We've asked, but they don't give a shit. Everything is about money. Those who have it and those who don't. It never ends, I tell you."

"Have you let anyone know?"

"Nah. It's embarrassing. I hate that we're such losers."

"You're not losers, Brooklin. I know how hard you and Jonny work."

"Maybe we can live on the boat through the summer and then find a rental. I'm going to miss our home so much," her blue eye shadow ran down her left cheek. She looked at me through teary eyes, her face contorted into a painful grin in resigned acceptance of yet another setback.

"How much money do you need?"

"The two mortgages total $2,500 a month. The boat, at least, is paid for."

"Do you know how far behind you are with your payments?"

"I think Jonny said six months. That's more than we can come up with. The fishin' has gotten off to a slow start. Jonny's thinkin' of sellin' the boat and payin' off the mortgages and we'll move someplace with more job opportunities. Make a fresh start."

"I can't imagine Jonny not fishing. What else could he do?"

"Maybe get a job at a marine supplies store? I don't know. This sucks. We had been hopin' to send our daughter Jenny to culinary school."

"You should let people know you're at risk of losing everything. I bet an online fund would be set up, and with the summer people here now, who knows? Maybe you could get a good amount."

"I hate to take money from others. Just not the way I was raised."

Walt came out with a steaming platter of lobsters and set them in front of Row and Amari. "There you go, guys. Eat up."

Row and Amari began pulling off the legs and sucking the meat out. Then they broke off the claws and the tail.

Brooklin said: "Here, let me show you the easiest way to get that tail meat out." She leaned over and took one of the tails on Row's plate. "These are easy. Soft shells, just push the tail meat out, like this. Are you goin' to eat that tamale? If not, I'll take it."

"Thanks," Row smiled at her. "Here, it's all yours."

"Hell, I've been around lobster for so long to me it's the last thing I want to eat. I do like the tamale, though. I'll take a good burger over lobster any day."

"Funny how that is," Row said. "It's true everywhere that people take for granted what they have. One man's delicacy is another man's ordinary dish."

We ate and drank and laughed the afternoon away and even Brooklin eventually managed a smile. When Row dropped us back at my house that evening, I told him her story. He was genuinely moved and shared with me how he grew up middle class in Ohio, his parents were recent immigrants to the United States who struggled to find jobs. His father had opened a laundromat that grew into a chain of four. His mother stayed home with the children, three in total. His siblings had done very well for themselves and once Rohan made his first fortune, he bought his parents a new home in Half Moon Bay, California so they would be near him. Row was under considerable pressure to start a family of his own, in particular from his mother.

The town came together to hold an online fundraiser for Jonny and Brooklin. I saw the total had reached $15,000 by early August. And then one day I saw it had jumped to $100,000 and everyone thought there had been a mistake. But the money was there. I had my suspicions this was Row's doing, but he never said so. The family was saved and it was Jonny who saw the last Facebook post my father would ever make on that sunny late-August morning, as he and his daughter happily set out to go haul.

Chapter Nineteen
July 2023

Alison and Charlie had wandered off from the first party, walking the trails meandering along the cove. Alison was feeling embarrassed by her prep school friends and could see how they had wounded Charlie, who already looked plenty wounded without any additional attacks. She was drawn to his vulnerability, his good lucks, and the fact he was unlike anyone she had known. He was like a hurt animal, a wounded bird, that she sought to comfort. The trail they took passed through low deep forest, with spruce and birch and light green mosses covering granite boulders. The trail rose up a hill leading to an old farmhouse with a red barn. There didn't seem to be anyone there, probably an absent summer person's home. They walked into the barn and sat on some hay, talking.

"I'm sorry about Andy."

"That's okay."

"No, it's not. He can be such a jerk at times. The way he enjoys finding someone's weak spots and poking his finger in their wounds, like life isn't hard enough."

The sun was filtered through wisps of low-floating fog advancing ashore, its rays entering through gaps in the barn's siding lighting Charlie's face in a way that reminded Alison of a

Dutch Old Masters painting. She was drawn to his sad eyes and could tell he was feeling out of place, out of sorts, outside himself. She knew that remote feeling. She leaned in close and kissed him on the lips. She put her tongue in his mouth and they kissed more deeply, holding each other tight as they lowered themselves to the soft ground. They kissed passionately for nearly a half hour. Each time Charlie tried putting his hand under her shirt, she pushed it away, so Charlie was content to just kiss and hold her, to inhale her fresh smells, to bury his face in her long hair. Her cheeks were pink and he did what he could to disguise the bulge in his cargo shorts. Things were going too far, too fast, and Alison pulled away. Charlie was the second boy she had kissed, Andy the other.

"You're so pretty," Charlie gazed into her eyes.

She blushed.

"You should probably text your mother and let her know where we are."

Alison had completely forgotten about her mom. Charlie heard her phone pinging as she and her mother exchanged texts.

"Everything okay?" he asked.

"Yeah, we're good. She's having a great time and doesn't want to leave the party yet. I told her we'd be back in about an hour." Alison was standing and reached down to help Charlie to his feet. "I have an idea, follow me."

They continued along the path away from the farmhouse and through the woods until they came upon the waterfront. There was a long dock with an old wooden boathouse perched at the end.

It looked like some recent work had been done to the boathouse, new wooden shingles evident along two sides. A fog bank was pushing ashore.

"Follow me," she took him by the hand. They walked to the end of the dock where several day-sailing boats were tied up. They couldn't have been longer than 12-feet, Charlie figured.

"Let's go for a sail!" Alison was animated.

Charlie gazed down at his sneakers. "I don't know how to sail."

"That's okay, I do, and you can simply come along for the ride. Help me push this boat here away from the others."

She sat in the stern and extended her hand for Charlie to jump in from the dock. "Just sit up on the right side there while I hoist the main."

"What can I do?"

"Grab those life jackets and pass one back to me and put one on yourself." Charlie did as instructed, feeling dorky in his bulky orange life jacket. It took him a few minutes to finally get the snaps fastened. Alison pulled up the mainsail and the boat began to glide away from the dock in a fresh southeasterly breeze. The fog was thickening and creeping ashore, the visibility lowering as they set off.

Charlie looked uncomfortable and concerned as the sailboat picked up speed. They were running ahead of the wind and the bay was choppy. Alison sensed this and pulled the sail tighter so it caught less wind and they slowed down. "Charlie, when I shout come about, that means we're going to tack into the wind. We'll just putter around here and stay near the docks. You'll need to duck down low so the boom doesn't hit you when it swings across. Then switch to the other side of the boat. Ready? Come about!" she shouted.

Charlie slouched down as the boom swung across with considerable force, catching him off guard. He stumbled on his knees awkwardly for the other side of the boat. He had the boom held in one hand, not allowing it to come completely across.

Alison called out: "Just guide it past you until the sail fills with wind on that side."

Charlie managed to swing the boom all the way across and they raced off in a different direction toward Dunbar Island. He relaxed a bit, enjoying the feel of the wind and misty fog against his face, powered solely by nature, unlike the motor boats he had been on. They tacked a few more times and he was getting the hang of it with each pass. Alison looked to be in her element at the tiller, commandeering this boat across the open waters, the breeze blowing her long hair. Charlie, now feeling less nervous, stood up to stretch his legs and missed hearing Alison call come about. The boom swung across and knocked him directly on the head, sending them both overboard, capsizing the boat.

"Help!" she called out from the water. "Charlie, where are you?"

She swam to the other side of the capsized boat where Charlie was hanging onto the keel. She paddled closer and saw blood trickling from his forehead. "Are you okay?"

"Where are we?" he asked. His face looked ashen gray as seen through the low-floating fog.

"Between Dunbar and Archer."

"I don't feel so good," he slumped into the water as if he might pass out. Alison pushed him up on the hull and looked around hoping a lobster boat would see them. But it was the Fourth of July and most lobstermen were not out to haul today. The fog would make it difficult for them to be spotted by pleasure craft.

"Talk to me, Charlie."

"What?"

"Let's talk until someone comes along."

"I don't feel like talking. I'm dizzy. Everything is swirling around. Where are we?"

"Close your eyes," she said.

"Doesn't help, my head is spinning."

She was concerned he had a concussion so asked: "Where do you live, Charlie?"

"I . . . I . . . don't know."

"You live with Dale Hildings, right?"

He looked at her with a blank stare.

After being in the water for around ten minutes, Alison saw what looked to be a skiff approaching from Dunbar Island. She waved and, at first, they didn't see her though the fog, but then they switched course, speeding up to come help.

"Are you okay?" a boy with black hair called out from the skiff.

"Charlie here has a concussion. We need to get him to the Island Medical Center."

There were two boys in the skiff, probably not older than twelve. They had been out fishing for halibut, hoping to make an easy $100 selling fillets to summer people eager for fresh fish. The other boy in the boat jumped into the water and tried to help Alison right the capsized sailboat, but they were not strong enough to flip it. Unsure of what to suggest, he took a breather perched next to Alison on the hull as they bobbed in the swells of the bay.

Alison said: "Do you think we can get Charlie into your boat? You could take him ashore and call an ambulance, then come back for me later. I'm good here for a bit."

The boy got back in the skiff and he and his buddy reached over and hoisted Charlie onboard. Charlie lay sprawled out on his back, pupils dilated. The other boy in the boat hollered: "What's your name?"

"Alison Brooks!"

"Okay, Alison. We'll be back as soon as possible," he called out as they raced for the dock nearest them along the foggy shoreline.

Walt Wentworth was having a good time at his party when his phone rang. It was a 911 call to head up island. He called Doctor

Cocroft who sounded a bit tipsy but said he'd meet him there. Walt realized as they drove up the long road they were heading for Ingrid's address. They pulled in and found Ingrid and Bobby standing over Charlie Walsh, who was on his back on the grass down by the waterfront.

"I think he has a concussion," Bobby said.

"Stand back, we've got him," the doctor leaned over.

"What's your name, son." Walt asked.

Charlie's eyes were still dilated and he struggled to answer. He looked frightened. "I don't know!"

"Listen. You have a concussion but you'll be fine. Just do your best to relax."

They loaded him into the ambulance and sped off for the Medical Center. After the rescue boys had dropped Charlie at Ingrid's dock, they went back to get Alison. It's good they got there as quickly as they did as Alison was shivering badly when they arrived. She had been in the water for over an hour and her lips were turning blue.

Alison and Charlie were fine by the next day. Just shaken up by the experience. Charlie had a headache for a few days, but that cleared up and life returned to normal. Alison's mother, Sarah, placed an ad in the local newspaper thanking the boys who rescued them and asking them to please give her a call so she could thank them in person. No one ever came forward. Just two little local heroes doing what any good seamen would do.

Chapter Twenty
July 2023

At the end of July, I went with Charlie up to Ingrid's to help install a ramp. My father had ordered one from a supplier in Oceanside, and I went to the mainland on a Wednesday thinking the ferry lines wouldn't be too bad coming back to the island that afternoon. I was mistaken. I pulled forward in the line for nearly four hours as the boats came and went. I was the last car on the last boat at 4:30.

My father greeted Charlie and me when we arrived at Ingrid's that Sunday morning. We were not working at the job site, awaiting a shipment of cedar shingle siding. "Thanks, guys. I hope this won't be too difficult to put together. I figured over here at the front door would be the shortest and easiest access."

"How's she doing?" I asked.

"She's taken a turn for the worse."

"Oh, sorry to hear that."

"She had a mini-stroke last week and Doctor Cocroft wanted to send her to the hospital but she didn't want to go. It's left some new damage. She's not talking much. I'm hoping with this ramp I can at least drive her around so she can get out."

"Charlie, help me unload these two boxes."

"Should we get the ramp bottom out first?" he asked.

250

"I don't think it will matter. Let's just get everything out of the truck and then we can spread it all out and see what we're looking at."

We unboxed the parts needing to be assembled and were able to get the ramp in place over the next three hours. It had been well designed and constructed and the instructions were clear. My father invited us inside for some iced tea. We removed our muddy boots (it had rained for six of the last eight days) and walked into the living room where I saw Ingrid slumped in her favorite chair by the hearth. She was looking very thin and sad, the light disappearing from her beautiful eyes. It was as if the person was being scoured out by the illness, death surely not far off. Ashes to ashes, dust to dust. She didn't speak when I went to hug her, but just nodded in a forced grimace. The right side of her mouth was sagging, and she was wearing a nightgown and bathrobe.

"Let me get us some iced tea," my father headed off for the kitchen.

I could tell Charlie was uncomfortable being around someone as old as Ingrid. Young people like Charlie were invincible and would live forever. Death was not in the plans. There was a slight smell of urine in the house. My father had brought in some daisies and geraniums from her garden and arranged them on the end table next to her in a vase.

My father returned with the iced teas and we sat in silence with Ingrid. An ethereal fog was rolling in once again, and Bobby got up to turn on the heat, even though it was July.

"Would you like me to read to you, dear?" he sat next to her. She nodded yes.

He reached for a copy of a novel by Jane Smiley he had been reading to her. It had a horse as the lead character, and Ingrid was enjoying being read to very much. I could see the bookmark was near the end of the novel. Bobby began reading and some light returned to her expression. She nodded in approval at some of the humor in the novel. They sat like this for several minutes while Charlie and I finished our iced teas.

"Charlie, let me show you around this grand old home. They don't build them like this anymore." He followed me to the central staircase.

"Look at these newel posts. Do you see the intricate design work on each of them?"

"Yes," he said. "How did they get them shaped like that?"

"With hand tools we don't use anymore. Everything is powered now and high-speed. There isn't time for craftsmanship. Follow me up the stairs."

We ascended the long staircase and Charlie leaned over the balustrade gazing down into the open space below where my father was reading to Ingrid.

"Isn't this cool?" I said.

"I've never seen anything like it," Charlie said. "Imagine having all this space. And it's just the two of them. When was this built?"

"Would have been late-nineteenth century. A heyday for

fine summer cottages like this."

"Cottages?"

"That's what they were called. I realize they are huge by our standards today."

"How did they get all these materials out here back then?"

"Good question. From what I've read in books about the islands, the Boston and Portland architects who designed many of these old homes brought their own work crews with them. The materials were transported by barge from Dunbar Island, given it is just a short way across from here."

"Were there no builders living out here?"

"I think there were, but none who had been trained in the ways that the Boston builders were. But with time, they trained a local by the name of Cliff Littlefield, who they came to trust with other projects. He made a small fortune as their preferred builder out here."

"Is Jaxon Littlefield, who played baseball with me, related?"

"Most likely. You should ask him."

"Come take a look at the finished detail beneath these built-in window seats. See the ornate carvings? They are tiny little books being carried off by angels. See the wings? How delicate they are? Yet carved out of wood."

"Amazing."

"And you see the bookshelves all around the perimeter up here. Can you imagine someone going to that level of detail nowadays?"

"No. Geez."

"It's kind of a shame, because I was trained in fine woodworking, but rarely get to use those skills. No one wants to pay for them anymore. How I would love to get a job someday doing work like this."

"How about at Mr. Patel's?"

"The architect doesn't have it in the plans."

"Maybe if you mentioned it to Mr. Patel, he'd ask for something special. You know, so you could leave a unique signature."

"Like what?"

"I don't know. Maybe he'd like to have a game room? Or a bar?"

"Yeah, I don't know. I might bring it up to him after we get the house built. As it is, we're running behind and I doubt he wants any changes that would further delay the schedule."

"I like Mr. Patel. He's cool."

"I agree. Not only is he cool, as you say, but he's a builder of sorts himself. A modern-era builder. But instead of using wood and nails he builds using ones and zeros."

"Huh?"

"The building blocks of today are all about software code. That's where the big money is."

"There's a math teacher at school, Mrs. Williamson, who wants to offer a class on software coding."

"You should take it if she does. I'm told you have a good head for numbers. Who knows, Charlie. Maybe you could design computer games some day."

This got his attention. "Really? That would be totally awesome."

We walked back downstairs where Ingrid had fallen asleep in her seat. My father covered her in a blanket and walked us out front.

"Thanks again for installing the ramp. I've got a wheelchair coming from the Medical Center next week, so should be able to take her out for long car rides. Seeing her old haunts is about the only thing that cheers her up these days, so this will be good."

"Have you looked into getting a full-time nurse?"

"I have, but it's difficult being out here on an island. Maybe in time, but for now I think we're good. Susan has been a huge help. She spent the night before last out here so I could get a good night's sleep."

"Have you spoken with Olivia? Does she know that her mother is getting worse?"

"I asked Susan to call her and she did. I gather Olivia plans to come visit again at the end of August."

"How about Kevin, has he been coming around?"

"Yes, although he's being very rude to me. I will not kid you, he scares me."

"You're not alone there, Dad. Did I tell you I caught him

255

stealing from the job site?"

"No, I didn't know that."

"He's been fired but got his boat back so is going out to haul."

"Didn't he get in trouble with the law for that?"

"He did, but is only on probation. Row Patel didn't want to cause trouble out here so didn't press any charges."

"Do you think he's doing drugs?"

"I do."

"What kind of drugs?"

"Word around town is Oxy."

"What do people do with that drug, anyway?"

"They grind up the pills and snort the powder."

"You mean like cocaine?"

"Yeah, but it's far more addictive than coke. Sometimes they mix other drugs in with it."

"You mean, like the fentanyl I keep reading about?"

"Yes."

"What a shame."

"Do you think Ingrid knows about Kevin's drug usage?" I asked.

"I'm not sure. I tend to think she assumes he just smokes a lot of marijuana. I don't want to upset her any more than she already is."

"Sounds good, Dad. Can I do anything to help you up here?"

"No, Jon. Installing this ramp is a godsend. You know, I couldn't find anyone willing to do it."

"I'm sure some of the guys in town would have helped if you asked."

"I know, but they're all busy fishing now."

"Okay, we're heading back to town. Call if you need anything. And let me know if Kevin hassles you."

Three days later, Row Patel was back on the island and came to check on his house. Shane had added three new day workers to the crew. We had just installed the last of the windows and were getting ready to start the electrical and plumbing work. The plans called for a top-of-the-line sound and alarm system beyond my pay grade, and Row let us know he had some people coming from California who would oversee that work. They would need our help, but we should let them take the lead.

I pulled Row aside that afternoon and told him that Charlie was showing interest in the computer sciences and it would be nice if the guys he was bringing over would mentor him on the specialized work they would be doing.

Row waved Charlie over.

"Hello, Mr. Patel. It's good to see you, again, sir."

"Hi, Charlie. You, too. How have you been?"

"Not bad. Jon has been teaching me a lot. I was able to help install the windows."

"Good for you. Jon tells me you're interested in learning

257

about computer science?"

"I guess. I'm good with numbers, or so the math teacher has said."

"Would you be interested in tagging along with the sound engineers I have coming out? I'm putting them up for two weeks in an Airbnb in town, and am sure they'd be happy to spend some time with you."

"Really? That'd be awesome."

"Great, I'll ask the head engineer to show you around as he does his thing here."

"Thanks so much, sir."

"My pleasure."

Chapter Twenty-One
November & December 2023

Ingrid died in early December. It was the day of the tree lighting in town, just a year from when my father and I had spent the evening with her at Susan's. The night nurse at the Eldercare Center told me Ingrid went to sleep that night with the Mary Oliver book Bobby had gifted her by her side, having said goodbye instead of goodnight with a finality that led the nurse to believe Ingrid would be gone by morning. And she was.

Ingrid had asked to have her ashes scattered on the waters out front of her beloved home. My father's ashes had been sitting on my mantle while I considered where to spread them. When Ingrid died, I knew the answer. Her ashes were mingled with those of my father, and we flung them into the wind, watching them carried out into the cove on a gray December day. Ingrid had wanted to keep her ceremony small so it was just Olivia, Naomi, Susan, Travis, Kevin, and me. Susan thought it best not to have her children attend, and Kevin and Olivia concurred.

Kevin had settled into his mother's home after she moved into Eldercare in September. Now, with her death, the will was read and Ingrid's lawyer, who was not local but from Florida, informed them that the house was being left to Susan, with the

259

understanding she would pass it along to Svea and Logan. Kevin and Olivia would each receive $200,000 from her trust. The grandfather's trust, which turned out to be worth over two million dollars, was left to Svea and Logan to access for educational needs and emergences when they turned eighteen. There was no mention of Robert Davis anywhere in the will, not that it would have mattered too much to Kevin and Olivia, as he was dead. But it mattered a great deal to me.

I learned about the will from Naomi, who called me knowing I would want to hear that my father was not named. I had been struggling to comprehend what kind of man Bobby had been, contemplating whether I had completely misjudged him. Now that I know what happened, I'm increasingly certain he changed in his final months with Ingrid, and that even when I was young, he was not as bad as I had made him out to be. Yes, he was a philanderer. But he was not a thief. As is true for us all, he did his best but was not without shortcomings. The way my father looked after Ingrid in that final year confirmed they were very much in love—that she had been the love of his life, as he had told me previously when I wasn't in the mood to listen.

Naomi informed me that the private investigator Olivia and Kevin had hired found no wrongdoing on Bobby's part with the Epstein woman in Florida. My father had been under suspicion because he was so charming, but in the final analysis, he had done nothing unethical or illegal. Quite to the contrary, the investigator reported that the Epstein woman's daughter had wanted to locate Bobby so she could thank him for being so kind to her mother at the Florida assisted living facility.

He had fallen in love with Ingrid and she with him, and that thought gives me great comfort to this day, knowing they spent their final months together in happiness. And, had Ingrid lived to hear what Kevin did, well, that would have been cruel. Sometimes it's best not to know everything. She went to her grave spared the details.

After Shane and Roy Gastineau robbed the Familprix drugstore in Saint-Georges, leaving behind three dead bodies, they took the backroads up and over the crown of Maine heading for Nova Scotia. They stopped just once to gas up, and then drove through the night to the small fishing village of Meteghan, where Gastineau was renting a ranch house on the outskirts. They arrived at sunrise, the temperature below freezing with a new dusting of snow on the lawn. Shane slept in the basement while Gastineau went to see if he could find work in town. Security footage had captured Shane when his mask came off at the drugstore, and was now playing across Canada on television and social media. But Gastineau's mask had not come off so he was free to move around town without being spotted.

Gastineau came back that first day with a job on an offshore scallop boat. He napped most of that day and then headed out to sea the following morning eager to earn some badly needed money. The good thing about the scallop boat he would be working on was that he would be paid in cash at the end of each week.

While Gastineau fished, Shane was bored to tears cooped up in the basement. After two weeks of hiding out, he was going stir crazy. One afternoon in mid-November, he saw his cell phone ring with a number he didn't recognize. He had been letting all previous calls go to voicemail, ignoring Roy's demand that he discard his phone. Roy was still unaware he had it, a dumb move on Shane's part, one of many he had made and would still make. He decided to answer this call.

"Shane, this is Kevin."

"Shit, Kevin, what are you doing calling me?"

"I'm using the pay phone down by the ferry terminal. I'm surprised you still have your phone."

"I shouldn't but I'm going nuts hiding out."

"You've been all over the news, man. Are you in Canada?"

"I've got a TV where I'm staying. I've been watching. What a shitshow. I never wanted to kill anyone. It was an accident."

"Don't look like no accident from what I've seen. Are you living with the other guy captured in the security footage?"

"What if I am?"

"How'd you meet him?"

"Just a random thing. He was having coffee at the Tim Hortons I went to and we started talking. He's a dealer here."

"Why's he helping you?"

"Good question. Honestly, he's a bit out of his mind. Got a worse Oxy habit than I do. Can't get a great read on him but he's keeping me hidden and fed."

"Hmm."

"What do you want, Kevin. I shouldn't be on the phone."

"My mother is now in Eldercare so I have her house to myself. She's very close to death, it seems. I think she's written me out of her will and put that fucker Bobby Davis in instead."

"Are you sure?"

"Not exactly, because I can't find what lawyer they hired. But I think that sleazy fucker found someone he knows in Florida to redo her will and I've been cut out."

"That sucks, man."

"No shit. Listen, now that I have the house to myself, I have access to her safe. There are valuable necklaces and rings that belonged to my grandmuthah inside. We could hock them for good money."

"Oh, yeah?"

"Yeah."

"So . . . why tell *me* this?"

"I'm thinkin' we can team up again. You know, start cookin' again. Buy a new RV and head out west somewhere."

"You think we could get enough for the jewelry to buy an RV?"

"For fuck's sake, Shane. I don't know for sure, but I think

263

so. I'm not completely off the hook in Bobby's murder case, and am being watched closely by the cops and townspeople. It would be best if you could break in with my help."

"Do you have the safe's combination?"

"Not yet, but I think I know where she hid it. In one of her old poetry books. I just need to find which one. Then you could pawn the shit."

"How could I pawn anything given my face is everywhere? There's no way I can be seen out in public after what I've done."

"We'd wait. I was thinkin' we could drive to Florida or Nevada and hide out for a bit. Then once things die down, pawn them there."

"Kevin, how the hell am I gunna get back to Maine? And how would I avoid getting caught at the border?"

"Will you tell me where you are?"

"I'm in a fishing village in Nova Scotia."

"Yarmouth?"

"I prefer not to say."

"Can you get a job on a boat and cross into Maine waters? I doubt you'd be stopped on a commercial fishing vessel."

"I dunno."

"Can't you disguise yourself? Change your appearance somehow?"

"I've already grown a beard and am wearing eyeglasses."

"Won't that work?"

"Too risky. Plus, let's talk after you find the combination and confirm what's inside the safe."

"All right. I'll keep lookin' for the combination."

"What's the number at that pay phone?"

Kevin read it to Shane who wrote it on a slip of paper he tucked into his wallet.

"Listen Kevin, I'm going to ditch this phone and call you back next Thursday around midnight, okay? Just be there. Be sure to pick up."

Another week passed with Gastineau fishing and Shane holed up in the basement. Gastineau was pissed Shane still had the phone, and he took it with him one morning and chucked it overboard while fishing. He bought Shane a burner phone, which Shane used to call Kevin at the phone booth the following Thursday. Kevin picked up after the first ring.

"Shit, Shane. Talk fast, it's fuckin freezin' out he-ah tonight."

"Did you find the combination?"

"I did and you wouldn't believe how much is in the safe. There are diamonds and rubies and other stones I don't recognize. Could be worth more than half a million bucks or more, for all I know. Shit, Shane, it's our ticket outta he-ah."

"Here's the thing, Kevin. I've got this guy, Roy Gastineau, with me and would need to cut him in. He's my only hope for safe passage."

There was a lengthy silence on the phone. "Can he be

265

trusted?"

"I think so. He's been working on a scallop boat."

"Do you know where they fish?"

"I don't but can ask. But before I open that can of worms, I need to know if you would cut him in. I think we'd have to."

"Why don't you find out more about where his boat has been fishing. It could be if they're close enough to Jonesport we could sabotage the engine and get them into that marina for repairs. You'd be back in Maine waters and it would take some seriously shitty luck for you to get caught by the marine patrol."

"Yeah, but . . . how would we sabotage the engine?"

"Feel this Gastineau guy out first, and if it sounds like they're fishing near Maine waters, I can tell you how to do it. And if they are, tell him there is around $100,000 of jewelry in the safe and we will split it three ways."

"Okay."

"Chuck this phone and get a new one. Call me here in two days, same time."

Shane asked Gastineau where they were fishing and he told him offshore, but would likely fish closer to the coasts of Canada and Maine later in December. Shane told him about the jewelry and he was interested. Shane relayed this news to Kevin, who sent instructions on how to sabotage a boat engine. They would need to order from Amazon a pound of fine-grained carborundum, which he said could be put into the fuel line using the deck fill when no one was watching. This should make it

266

through the engine's filters. Within a few hours the engine should begin to sputter and they would need to take it into a marina. The engine wouldn't die, just run bad. They'd make it to port.

Kevin said Gastineau could bring Shane along just for that day as a potential new hire. The boat owner should be okay with that, given the labor shortage.

Gastineau would let Shane know when they would be fishing near Maine, so he could let Kevin know when to bring his lobster boat up to Jonesport at the marina.

Gastineau ordered the carborundum from Amazon Canada and they had it within a few days. Shane had never heard of it but saw it was an additive used as an abrasive for cutting and polishing purposes.

"Hope this shit will do the trick," Gastineau said after reading the label. "Has your bud done this before? Know what he's doing?"

"He told me he has. Did it years ago to get back at a lobsterman who stole two of his traps."

"Nice fella, this friend of yours. How'd you say you know him?"

"We worked on a construction project on Archer Island. Did drugs together."

"Speaking of which, look what I got today." Gastineau chopped up two 80mg Oxys on the coffee table and they snorted several lines.

*****

267

Three days before Christmas they put their plan in motion. Shane had spoken with Kevin who sounded down. His mother had died and he had learned he was not inheriting the house. They talked about the marine forecast, which was favorable for the crossing from Jonesport to Archer Island, with light northerly breezes and no storms in sight. It was going to be very cold, though, so Gastineau gave Shane one of his flannel shirts that morning as they set off. Shane must have been happy to get out of that basement, his beard now longer and hair cut into a buzzcut. With his eyeglasses, he looked different enough from the photos that had been circulating, so they were hopeful he would avoid being identified.

Gastineau introduced Shane as Luke James to the boat captain, Guy Desjardins.

"Welcome aboard, Luke. Have you fished before?"

"Not in a long time," he said.

"Well, we can teach you. Not much to it, just could use some extra muscle onboard."

The scallop boat pulled out into the harbor and set off on a southwesterly course. There were two other deckhands and Shane observed them getting the lines for the gear set up. Gastineau was up in the cabin talking with Desjardins as the boat powered out into the frosty sunrise. They spent the morning trawling, pulling up large loads of scallops onto the deck. The catch improved as they left the coast of Nova Scotia moving closer to Maine waters. Gastineau had told Shane to create a disturbance by getting his foot caught in one of the boat lines, and he would put the carborundum into the fuel line when no one was watching.

According to Gastineau's later account, the boat's engine began sputtering that afternoon two to three hours away from the Maine coast. Desjardins was going to put out a distress call, but Shane did as Gastineau had instructed, pleading with the boat captain not to, as he had mistakenly brought some cocaine onboard with him. One can only imagine the look Desjardins must have given him.

Shane said he knew of a good marina in Jonesport. The engine was still running, just poorly, so they should be able to make it there. He claimed to have a friend who lived in Jonesport who would put them up while they waited for the engine to be repaired. Desjardins had no choice but to agree, so they made their way slowly toward Jonesport. Shane must have been nervous that they would be pulled over while crossing the international line, but they made it easily.

The boat pulled into Jonesport around sundown and Shane and Gastineau went to use the bathroom in the marina. While Desjardins spoke with the mechanic on the docks, they slipped away to the shoreline where Kevin had told them he'd be waiting in his skiff. From there they made it to Kevin's moored lobster boat and headed off for Archer Island, two hours south. Kevin had forgotten to get fuel and they were concerned they wouldn't have enough for the nighttime journey, but they made it running on fumes. It was dark and cold when they arrived at

Kevin's mooring off Ingrid's dock. The three of them rode in the skiff across to the dock, and walked up the sloping lawn to the house. They were tired and slept for a few hours, until around 4 a.m.

What happened next is known from the accounts of Timmy Tetreault and from Gastineau's confession given in prison. Tetreault had been asked to spend the night on the island, as it was Christmas break and a lot of people were expected to be at the bar. Sure enough, he had to break up a domestic dispute, and then after the bar closed, he returned to the room in town provided at Jake Swenson's house. But he couldn't sleep and finally gave up trying. He got up to go drive around and then head for the Dunbar Island ferry lot to wait for the first boat. When on his way up island, he noticed a light on at Ingrid's. Now that Susan had legally inherited the house, Kevin had been forced to move out, and as far as Tetreault knew, Susan had not yet moved her family out to Ingrid's. Susan had struggled to get the irate Kevin to vacate the premises, and rumor around town was that he still had a key and was staying there on occasion.

Tetreault pulled into the dirt driveway, turning off his headlights. As he rolled closer to the house, he heard four rapid-fire gunshots. He phoned Oceanside for backup, which he knew would take at least an hour to arrive. He got out of his cruiser and moved stealthily alongside the driveway until he was behind the house. He crept onto the porch to gaze inside. There were no sounds. The sliding French doors were unlocked and he tiptoed inside. He had his gun pulled as he checked each room, the way he had been trained at the police academy. He opened the door to the study and saw two bodies face up on the floor, blood spilling from their heads. He saw they were Kevin and Shane. When he leaned over to check if they were alive, he heard a car start up outside and drive off. Kevin and Shane were dead. He raced outside to pursue the car.

Gastineau later told the police the plan had been for the three of them to split the money, but that Kevin had come up with a revised plan to make it look like Gastineau broke in on his own. After Kevin opened the safe, Shane clubbed Gastineau over the head with a poker from the fireplace, but without sufficient force to knock him unconscious. Now that the safe was open, Gastineau didn't need them and shot them both with Kevin's pistol, which Kevin had placed on the end table when opening the safe.

Donna Littlejohn had just arrived at the Archer Island ferry terminal, which she did every weekday morning exactly at 5:20. She would take calls starting at 5:30 from islanders looking to get line numbers for the next day's ferries to Oceanside. Tomorrow was Christmas Eve day, so the call volumes would be unusually high for this time of year, with many families heading to the mainland. She picked up the first few calls, munching on her breakfast sandwich, looking forward to Christmas Day. She wouldn't have to work on Christmas and was going to church with her husband and children.

She had strung Christmas lights around the inside of the small ferry terminal and was listening to "Charlie Brown's Christmas" playing on the portable CD player. She was on the phone assigning a line number when she heard a car come skidding into the parking lot. It was too early for anyone to be showing up yet for the first ferry. She looked out her window and saw it was Ingrid's Volvo SUV. How odd, she thought.

She finished her call, and with one eye on the Volvo, picked up the next call. She noticed the Volvo was not parked correctly, but was straddling the reservation and line number lanes. She wanted to go check but knew if she didn't pick up the calls, people would be angry. There were already over forty calls waiting in the queue.

Sometime around 5:50, Roy Gastineau climbed in through the ferry terminal's unlocked bathroom window. Normally the window would have been locked, but someone had been smoking in there the previous evening and Donna had opened it slightly first thing that morning so the room could air out. She got up to see what the noise was, and Gastineau jumped out and held her at gunpoint.

"Please . . ." she pleaded. "We keep no cash here. Don't kill me."

"How the fuck can I get over to the mainland?" he pressed the gun against her skull.

"I can print you a ferry ticket. Just let me go, you're hurting my shoulder."

"I ain't going on the ferry, you dumb bitch. You think I'm stupid? I need a boat I can steal from the harbor."

Just then she heard another car pull into the lot. Gastineau, who was dripping blood from his right leg, turned to gaze outside, and in that moment, Donna kneed him in the balls and broke free. "Asshole, I'm no one's bitch!" she ran out into the cold screaming for help. Gastineau limped outside toward the ferry ramp, where the boat was waiting to board and leave at 7 a.m. He raised his gun to shoot at her back, but decided otherwise, realizing he was running low on bullets.

The car was Tetreault's. He helped Donna into his cruiser and told her to post on the public Facebook group advising people not to come to the ferry, that the first boat was cancelled. He told her he had already called over to the Oceanside police. Donna did as he asked, but also sent a message to Walt Wentworth and her husband, telling them that a crazy man was on the loose at the ferry.

Timmy ran down toward the boat in search of Gastineau. The ramp was lit, as was the ferry, but no crew had arrived yet. Timmy followed a trail of blood down along the metal ramp. As he stepped onto the boat, the trail disappeared. He stopped and looked back, trying to figure out where Gastineau had gone. He walked as silently as possible back along the ramp. He stopped to listen. He thought he heard breathing below him. He called out: "Guess he's gone, nothing here. All clear!" He then walked back to the terminal and circled down to the waterfront so he could see beneath the ramp. It was still pitch dark. The tide was low so he was able to walk across some of the large rocks between the shoreline and the boat ramp's underbelly. He stepped quietly toward the ramp, and then a single gunshot rang out and a bullet whizzed by his left ear. His ear was ringing as he checked for blood but saw he had not been hit. Tetreault fired back, his bullet pinging off the metal substructure of the ramp.

He saw Gastineau emerge from the end of the ramp and limp off onto the boat deck. Tetreault raced after him. Just then, several pickup trucks pulled into the lot and Walt Wentworth, Donna's husband Phil, and Freddy Ames all ran toward the boat with their hunting rifles.

"Stay back!" Tetreault called out.

"Is it Shane?" Walt asked.

"No, it's some other guy I don't recognize. Just stay the hell back so no one gets hurt. I don't want you fucking this up!"

The men stopped in their tracks, debating what to do, their confidence in Tetreault as low as ever. They hung back watching as he boarded the ferry.

Tetreault followed the trail of blood, which lead to the right inside cabin of the ferry. He crept down the narrow aisle between the metal benches, one careful step at a time. When he arrived at the bench farthest forward, Gastineau jumped out of the bathroom behind him and fired a single shot. Tetreault should have been killed, but Gastineau's gun had no more bullets. Tetreault clubbed him over the head with the butt of his gun and

Gastineau fell to the ground. He kneeled on Gastineau's back and cuffed his hands behind his back. The marine coast guard cruiser arrived and two men boarded. Walt Wentworth and the other local men entered the cabin. The marine patrol took Gastineau away.

"Look at you, Timmy," Walt came over and patted him on the back. "A real cop after all. I'll be damned."

Tetreault managed a smile, even though his arms were shaking uncontrollably. "I got him good, didn't I?"

"Who the heck is that guy?" Walt asked.

"Not sure, but whoever he is, he killed Kevin and Shane up at Ingrid's place."

"Shit, man!"

Tetreault went to check on Donna who was standing out front of the terminal.

"You're my hero, Timmy!" she hugged him.

"Thanks, Mrs. Littlejohn. Just doing my job."

"Nobody, I mean nobody, calls me a bitch!"

Tetreault nodded in the affirmative.

Donna, who was not one to be upset by much of anything, went back inside and continued taking calls for the next day's boats.

Chapter Twenty-Two
August 2023

Linda and I were lounging in bed listening to the seagulls, lobster boats heading out to sea on the morning of that late-August day when my father was killed. Her children had spent the night with friends, so we took advantage of the opportunity to enjoy a night alone together.

"Look at this," Linda rolled over to show me her iPhone.

"What is it? I can't see at that angle."

"Take my phone. See for yourself."

"It's a beautiful day to be alive," I read my father's Facebook post. "Shit, he's here already?" I jumped out of bed and threw on the same shorts and T-shirt I had worn yesterday. We had invited Bobby and Ingrid for breakfast but weren't expecting them until eight o'clock. I looked at my phone and saw it was not yet seven-thirty.

"I'll get the coffee started," I said.

"Do you want me to go get scones and muffins from the bakery?" she offered.

"Sure, that would be good."

We walked to the kitchen and I put on a pot of coffee. Linda grabbed the keys to her car and headed down the hill to the bakery. I walked outside toward the ledge, where my father was standing stoically. He had been looking much older to me lately, the toll of caring for Ingrid evident. Oftentimes it is the caretaker who suffers most, and Bobby was too old to be changing bed pans and sponge bathing Ingrid. But he insisted I shouldn't worry about him, that he could handle it.

"Hey, Dad," I approached.

"Good morning, Jon," he was startled to see me. He looked distant and sad as our eyes met. "Isn't this simply spectacular? Look at the orange sunlight reflecting off your windows."

"I'm happy the fog finally burned off for one morning. It's been so wet this summer. Not normal."

"Supposed to warm up to eighty I saw on the morning news," he said.

"Where's Ingrid?"

He turned to face me and we started walking back for my house. "She's not feeling well this morning. Sends her apologies but won't be joining us for breakfast."

"Sorry to hear that."

"She's having difficulty initiating anything these days. I think if I were not with her, she wouldn't eat or get dressed or leave her bed."

"Who's looking after her while you're here?"

"Susan kindly agreed to give me a break this morning."

"That's nice of her."

"She's a kind soul. I think her love of Ingrid is stronger

than either Kevin's or Olivia's."

"I can see that. She seems more like Ingrid than either of them."

"And Kevin is applying pressure on us both to leave the house. He has found a memory care center on the mainland with an opening. Ingrid is incapable of making decisions for herself at this point. Maybe I'm being selfish. Possibly she'd be happier and safer not at home. Maybe Kevin is right."

We walked into my kitchen and I poured him a cup of coffee. "Have a seat on the deck, Dad. You look exhausted. I'll join you in a moment."

"Thanks," he took the mug I handed him and headed outside.

I heard Linda's car in the driveway and she came in with a bag of ginger scones and blueberry muffins. We cut them into small sections and put them on a plate for sharing. She grabbed a cup of coffee and we joined my father out on the deck. The rising sun cast long shadows through the trees, the dark figures of dancing maple leaves visible on the deck flooring.

"Good morning, Linda," Bobby started to get up to greet her, but his legs had grown weaker in recent weeks and she stopped him.

"Don't get up, please. I've brought us some muffins and scones."

"Those look good. From Becky's?"

"Yup," she said.

"How that woman can bake! You know, when I first moved out here, I remember when I met Ingrid at the market I was wondering whether I could handle being without my mainland delicacies. Turns out the food is better out here than over there!"

We laughed.

"Have you given further thought to the Charlie situation?" he asked.

"Linda has come up with an idea, but I'm not quite ready to say yes."

Linda was irritated that I was being so stubborn. "It's a good plan, Jon. Not just for Charlie, but for you. You need to stop with all the drinking and take on some responsibilities. To grow up and be a man."

That hurt.

"What plan?" Bobby asked.

"That Charlie move in with Jon when Dale moves to New Jersey," she said.

"I like Charlie, I really do. But I also like my peace and quiet."

I saw the look of disappointment on Linda's face. She faced away gazing out at the harbor, before turning back to me.

"Great, so you're just going to let the state take him. Send him to some foster home. Nice. Really nice."

"Is the problem money?" Bobby asked.

"Partly," I said. "The kid eats like a horse based on what I've seen."

Linda said: "Wouldn't you get state assistance if you took him in? You know they don't want him. Placing teenagers is always difficult."

"I don't know, everything is happening so fast, give me a chance to think on it."

In hindsight, the truth was I was too in love with drinking to make sacrifices for others. This was a pattern I couldn't break, one that had led to the loss of two previous girlfriends, as well as my good friend Freddy Ames, who had given up on me and was no longer coming around to visit. Instead of missing him, as any good friend would, I was relieved not to have him bugging me to go to AA meetings. The booze was my one and only true love. The booze was driving all decisions and behaviors.

Linda looked annoyed and got up to leave. "I should be getting my kids. They'll want to go swimming at the quarry. It was good seeing you, Mr. Davis."

After she was beyond earshot Bobby said: "She's upset with you."

"No shit."

"If I were you, I wouldn't let her go. She's a good one. I can see that clearly."

"I just wish Dale wasn't leaving. I like Charlie, but not enough to adopt him. Don't you think that's asking a lot?"

"Well, you're too old to have any children of your own. I'm surprised you never wanted them."

"I'm surprised to hear you say that, Dad."

280

"Why?"

"I mean, do you ever wish you hadn't had kids? Considering one of them died in a freak car crash and the other killed himself?"

He hesitated before replying. "I feel my life would have been completely meaningless without you children. I always wanted kids. I have no regrets there."

"Not even with me?"

"Of course not, Jon. Why would you say that?"

"Even though I'm an alcoholic who can't stay in a relationship and refuses to help a teenager in need?"

"I'm sorry you're an alcoholic, Jon. I can only imagine how difficult that must be, especially living out here."

"Was Grandpa an alcoholic?"

"You mean my father?"

"Yes."

"No. Your drinking problems come from your mother's side, I'm sorry to say."

"Hmm."

"Let me tell you something important, Jon. Something I learned when your older sister was born. The responsibilities of caring for someone are in fact acts of selfishness."

"Excuse me?"

"You heard me. For most people, anyway, taking care of others makes them feel good. It's like caring for a dog, or a garden, or anything really. It provides us with a sense of purpose, of progress that we can see daily. The baby that learns to walk and speak and play. The garden that sprouts new hope each spring and blossoms into astounding beauty. Much of this is about exerting control over a life that is horribly messy. Do you know that I think about your siblings every day?"

"No, I guess not."

"Do you think of them?"

"Of course, but not every day. But I miss them."

"Me too. Your brother was such a delightful little boy. Loved playing with his trucks, playing practical jokes on me when he was old enough to start controlling his environment. And your sister . . . well that hurts too much to talk about." His eyes were tearing up as he composed himself. "Sure, I have regrets, but it's the memories we accumulate that are what we're left with. Even the false ones are important. We should strive to build as many happy memories as we can while we're still above ground. Spending these months with Ingrid has made this very clear to me. All she has left are her old memories, which are a source of joy for her. Probably her only joy."

"So . . . you think I should adopt Charlie."

"No one can make that decision for you, Jon. It's a very important one. Personally, I like the boy very much. I think with a stable loving home he could grow up to do good things."

"That's good to hear, Dad. He's been down lately, now that Alison is about to head back to school. I'm thinking we'll go for a quarry swim later."

"Sounds good. Do you mind if I just sit here on your deck until midday?"

"Of course, take a break."

"I want to think about what to do with Ingrid. Plus, Olivia is coming to visit this afternoon so I'd like to rest up before then."

"Help yourself to anything you want."

"Thanks."

I took Charlie and Alison to the quarry at noon. The quarry was packed with parents and kids, many of the older children diving from high cliffs into the deep waters. The day had warmed up nicely and it struck me as somewhat cruel that after a long summer of fog and rain, summer decided to arrive just a few days before the kids and teachers were returning to school. It had been many years since I remembered us being cheated out of summer the way we had this year.

We set out our towels on a long smooth section of granite. There were several rounded large stones along the ledge, looking as if an artist had carefully arranged them in an exhibition. A few of the birch trees visible at the far end of the quarry had leaves already turning yellow. Charlie and Alison walked through the adjacent woods to the back end of the quarry, and I watched them jump feet first into the water.

Shouts of laughter echoed around the quarry as residents and their guests enjoyed this last weekend before Labor Day. I walked down the stone steps leading to the bottom rock and lowered myself into the water, not being one of the thrill-seeking youngsters leaping from the heights. The water was clean and cool as I swam toward the center, passing three people on their blow-up floats. I paddled away from the others and floated on my back, gazing up at the blue sky. A majestic eagle circled effortlessly above, carried by the breeze, rarely needing to flap its wings. Seagulls scattered, evidently concerned about this larger bird.

I swam ashore and climbed the stone steps and toweled off. I sat on my towel and watched Charlie and Alison across the way splashing water at each other in the quarry. My father's words of that morning echoed in my head. Could it be true that caring for others was in fact an act of selfishness? I supposed it could be possible. I messaged Linda who had not responded to my two previous messages. I knew she was pissed off at me, that she wanted me to stop drinking and to act like an adult. To volunteer to let Charlie live with me; if not adopt him, at least provide him with a home and shelter in the near term. It all seemed like too much for me. It was becoming clear that my father would likely outlive Ingrid, who was fading quickly. He would move back in with me and I would need to care for him as he declined. That would be difficult enough but was something I was preparing myself to handle. Throwing Charlie into that mix was simply asking too much.

An hour or so later, Charlie and Alison swam to where I was sitting and climbed the rocks to join me.

"Good swim?" I asked.

"Yeah, the water is perfect," Charlie hopped on one leg attempting to dislodge trapped water from his ear.

"I'm so sad I have to go back to school," Alison dried sections of her long hair with her towel, ringing out each section of hair so the water fell at her feet. "It finally warms up and now I'll be stuck in a hot classroom dozing off to Algebra equations."

"At least you'll have field hockey," Charlie said.

"True. And our team is going to be good this season."

"Do you think you'll go out for soccer, Charlie?" I asked.

"It kind of depends if I'm still here or not."

"Dale isn't leaving until mid-September," I said. "You could at least start the season with your friends."

"Yeah, but I'm not sure I want to commit to a team and then bail on them."

His words *bail on them* cut deep into my conscience. Here was this teenager concerned about disappointing others while I was in fact the one doing the bailing. On him.

"What ferry are you catching?" I asked Alison.

"The 4:30. If you don't mind, Mr. Davis, we'd like it if we could spend our last hours together at your house."

"Sure, come for lunch."

There was a prolonged silence and then Charlie said: "Actually, no offense, but we were hoping you might let us have the house to ourselves for a couple of hours."

"Ah, I see."

"You know, just to talk and hang out," Alison added.

"Sure, why not?" I said. "I've got some errands to do."

"We should get going," Charlie took Alison by the hand and we headed for the dirt parking lot where my truck was parked. We dropped Alison off at her house so she could shower and change. I went inside and told her mother I was going to fix them lunch, but didn't tell her I would be leaving them alone. Would she have objected? Probably. But I remembered being young and wanting to make out and having no place to go.

At my house, I pulled Charlie aside while Alison was out on the deck.

"You okay?"

"Yeah, I'm good."

"You won't do anything stupid, right?"

"Nah."

I turned to leave but then came back and whispered into his ear: "I'm not sure if you're planning to have sex, but if you are, make sure you use a condom."

He blushed and I headed off for the lumber yard to pick up some supplies for the construction project.

Chapter Twenty-Three
August 2023

Charlie walked out onto the deck where Alison was watching the fog bank lurking in the distance.

"Looks like we might have caught the only sunny morning of the week," she said.

"Dale told me it's supposed to roll back in later today. You're lucky to be gettin' outta here," Charlie said.

"I don't feel lucky," she turned to face him. "I'm going to miss you, Charlie. You have to promise you'll come visit at St. Paul's."

"I'd like to. But how would I get there?"

"You can catch a bus right at the ferry terminal in Oceanside. If you can make it to Concord, I'm sure I can find a day student with a car who will pick you up."

"I don't know, Alison. We're from different worlds. Maybe it's not such a good idea."

She pulled him against her body. "That's not true, Charlie. I love you. Don't you love me?"

He paused, looked away, and then looking at her again whispered: "I think I do."

She rubbed her hand through his unruly hair. "Then we need to figure out how to stay together."

287

"I dunno. We'll hardly ever see each other and you'll be back with Andy and Tad and Ladd and all the other rich preppy boys. Somehow, I can't see you still lovin' me for long."

"That's not true," she gazed into his sad brown eyes. "Just promise me you'll stay in touch. I can visit you here on school breaks and you can come stay with me. I can sneak you into my dorm room."

"Except when you say *visit here,* I'm not sure where *here* will be. What if I have to go into a foster home on the mainland? What if I drop out of school and run off again to fend for myself, as I've been doin' since I was eight years old?"

Alison didn't know this about him. "Is that true?"

"Of course, it's true. Why would I make up some bullshit story about bein' on the streets, havin' cigarette butts put out on my arm by my mother's latest junkie boyfriend, eager to take the state's money but not spendin' any on me. Why would I lie about stealin' from the supermarket so I could eat?"

"Oh, Charlie, I'm sorry," she went to embrace him but he pulled away, his eyes filling with tears.

"Just leave me alone, Alison."

"What's wrong, Charlie?"

"You should go now. You deserve better than me. Trust me, you don't want me messin' up your life, too."

She looked away, hurt. The plan had been for them each to lose their virginity, but this was now not going to happen.

"Stop pushing me away, Charlie!" she was crying. "Let

me help you. Let me love you!"

They stood in silence. Charlie felt awful for upsetting her, but was relieved that he had done the right thing. They didn't belong together. She was a beautiful girl from a wealthy family with all kinds of opportunities ahead of her, while he was about to return to the streets, a future of crime and drugs likely his lot in life. He came close to her and they hugged. He whispered into her ear: "This is for the best, and I think you know it, too."

She was sobbing, her warm eyes now cold. "How can you be so heartless? Were you just using me this summer?"

"No. But we must be realistic. We're from two completely different worlds. I want to be your friend, Alison, I really do. But the emotions you've stirred up in me have me all confused. Right now, as we had planned, I want nothing more than to have sex with you. But that would be a mistake. I can see it now. And it would be unfair to you, where I'm in no position to commit to you. You don't want your first experience to be with someone you never see again. You deserve better."

She stood back, letting his words soak in. She ran her hand through her long hair, attempting to compose herself. "Truth is, I've been nervous about having sex for the first time."

"Me too. Maybe we're too young. Let's just be friends, okay? If I'm still here next summer, we can hang when you come. I promise I'll stay in touch. Will you do the same?"

She kissed him. "Life is not fair, Charlie. I wish there was something I could do for you. Why won't Mr. Davis take you in?"

"I dunno. I think he has his hands full with his father. It's asking a lot of someone to look after a teenager, I get it."

"Let's just sit here and enjoy our final hours together." Alison dried her eyes.

They sat quietly until they were interrupted by a crashing sound in the kitchen. They got up to see what had happened and saw the large pane glass window was smashed. Charlie ran outside and saw Kevin's pickup truck speeding away. He ran down the dirt road trying to catch up to Kevin, but his truck raced off toward town. Back at the house, Charlie called Jon who answered on the first ring.

"What is it? Everything okay, Charlie?"

"Kevin just threw a rock through your kitchen window and sped off."

"That fucker! Sit tight, I'll be right there."

Chapter Twenty-Four
August 2023

When I got home there was broken glass all over the kitchen floor. I was fuming mad and called my father to warn him that Kevin might be heading up that way.

"Alison, you should probably go home," Charlie said. "I'll come see you off at the ferry after we clean up this mess."

"I'm happy to help," she said.

"No, Charlie is right," I said. "Go home and then we'll be over to drive with you and your mother to the boat so you can say your goodbyes."

She walked away and Charlie and I swept up the broken glass, placing it carefully into two cardboard boxes I used for recycling.

"Why is Kevin always such a prick to you, Jon?" Charlie asked. "Is it because you turned him in for the stolen job site stuff?"

"Partly, but it's mainly because he wants my father out of the house with Ingrid so he can get her to move into Eldercare."

"That sucks," he said.

I turned to him. "Did you and Alison—"

"Nah."

"Sorry."

"It's okay. We're not ready."

"Good for you, Charlie. I was thinking you're too young."

"I guess."

"You don't need to help me clean up. We're almost done here. Why don't you go spend your final hours with Alison and then I'll come get you around 3:45 and we can head down to the ferry to see her off."

"Nah. Let me stay and help you pick up this mess."

"Okay, but you really don't need to."

An hour later we had the place picked up. I walked outside with Charlie and tossed the rock Kevin had thrown through the window off to the side of the dirt road.

"Charlie, go to Alison's and I'll come get you in a bit."

"Okay. Thanks, Jon."

I walked around to the storage shed and found a plastic drop cloth. I cut it down to size to fit over the broken window, duct taping it into place. I phoned my father to make sure Kevin had not gone up there looking for him. He told me there was no sign of him. I suggested he spend the night in town with me since Olivia could look after Ingrid.

Over at Sarah's, Charlie came outside and got into the truck looking very sad. We followed behind Sarah and Alison as they drove through town on the way to the ferry terminal. Several passengers that had disembarked from the last boat pulled their suitcases on rollers along the uneven sidewalk. Sarah had booked a reservation and pulled into the red reservation line. I went to talk with her while Charlie and Alison sat on the bench overlooking the small rocky beach. The fog was starting to roll back in, wisps of cool mixing with the warmth from the sun now fading in and out behind the mist.

Sarah and I sat outside the terminal office chatting.

"Alison seemed upset this afternoon," she said.

"Charlie, too."

"Did they have a fight?"

"Not sure, but knowing Charlie as I do, I wouldn't be surprised if he broke things off."

"Honestly, that would be a huge relief. Do you think he did?"

"Here's the thing that's hard for others to understand about Charlie. He can't trust anyone to get close to him, because they have always let him down. I have a feeling they fell in love this summer and he's pushed her away."

"Love? Really?"

"Well, you know. Teenage love."

"God, I had no idea. Do you think they had . . . you know, sex?"

"No, they didn't."

"How can you be so sure?"

"I asked Charlie and he said they're too young."

"He did?"

"Yes."

"Good grief, maybe I've completely misjudged him and

all the other boys."

"You might have misjudged Charlie, but not so much the other boys," I smiled.

"What's going to happen to him when Dale leaves?"

"I don't know."

"I don't want to interfere, Jon, but Linda and I are friends, as I think you know. She seems to believe you should adopt Charlie."

"Yes, I know. We argued about it this morning."

"It's none of my business, and I realize that's asking an awful lot of you. Of anyone."

"It's nice to have someone on my side for a change."

"I don't envy you one bit. His is a very difficult situation."

"The thing is, I might do it, except with my father in the mix, it's just too much."

"Yes, I can see that."

"But . . . here's the thing. Spending these months with my father has showed me we all have our failings. I resented him for not being a good father, when in fact it turns out he was not at as bad as I had thought. He had his reasons, just like I have my reasons now for not looking after Charlie."

"God doesn't throw anything at us that we cannot handle," she said.

"That's a nice thought, but I have my doubts."

"Here's a thought for you, Jon. What if God sent Charlie and your father to you this year as sort of a test."

"What?"

"A test . . . to see if you can forgive your own father and, in the process, become a good father to a boy in need."

"Wow. That's a lot to take in, Sarah. I hadn't realized you were so religious."

"I was raised a good Protestant girl," she smiled.

"I wish I had your faith."

"Give it some thought. Even if you don't believe in a knowable god, life has a peculiar way of presenting us with the challenges we need to move on in our personal development."

The ferry was ready to begin loading vehicles so I walked Sarah to her car and she handed her ticket to Donna, the attendant.

"Off for the year?" Donna asked.

"Afraid so. How was your summer?"

"Honestly, the usual mess. Boats with mechanical issues, crew shortages, and people getting angry at me. Nothing I can do about any of that."

"I understand."

"Plus, can't believe how disrespectful some of these people from away can be. I had a man last week insist I get him on the next boat even though he didn't have a reservation or line number. Talked to me like I was his servant. Anyway, I said if you're having a medical emergency, I can get you on. Are you having one? I think that finally shut him up."

"Well, things will be slowing down now. Have a good winter."

"You, too. Drive safe."

Charlie and Alison were talking to summer people I didn't recognize. They looked to be college kids on their way back to school. Charlie stood uncomfortably off to the side, nodding his head, looking like he didn't belong. Here were rich kids heading back to Bowdoin and Wesleyan, enjoying a never-ending party. College boys and girls kissing goodbye. Yellow labs, noses sucking air through cracked windows of electric Volvo SUVs, inhaling the seaweed-laden air before returning to New Jersey.

And there was Charlie, future unknown.

He hugged Alison who jumped into the passenger seat next to her mother, blowing him kisses. Charlie waved as their car headed down for the boat ramp. These island farewells were always emotionally fraught. Charlie and I waited for the ferry to load and then watched it pull away into the harbor, Alison now on the top deck waving, tears streaming down her cheeks.

Chapter Twenty-Five
August 2023

I could tell Charlie wanted to be alone so I dropped him at Dale's. My father was back at the house when I returned. I grabbed a beer and headed onto the deck where he was sitting, deep in thought.

"How'd the sendoff go?" he asked.

"As well as can be expected. It's always sad to see summer friends go, even though it's nice to return to a slower pace out here."

"Now that I've been here for almost a full year, I can see what an unusual life this is. I've been trying to think of other places where there is a swarm of people who show up for a few months and then are gone just like that, with the flip of a switch."

"Like mosquitoes," I smiled.

"Funny, Jon."

"After a few years, you get accustomed to the unique clock out here . . . the comings and goings of people and the changing of the seasons. It all seems to spin faster and faster the older I get."

"You might find when you're closer to the grave that things slow down a good bit."

"Well, then, I have something to look forward to."

He smiled.

"Have you noticed the Canadian geese starting to show up?" I asked.

"I have. They're beautiful. And the cormorants."

"Shags, as they're known."

"I hadn't known that," he said.

"Soon the geese will be making their annual trip south. They leave shortly after the summer residents do. Then, in September, the crowds of summer people will continue thinning out through early October, and then a steep plunge occurs, when suddenly there will be days with only one or two cars on Main Street. By January, as you saw for yourself, there will be times when not a single car is on the main drag. A ghost town."

"I never thought I'd like that, but after this summer of so much activity, I'm looking forward to the quiet again."

"Me, too. The fall is my favorite time of year."

"I picked up Olivia at the ferry and drove her up to Ingrid's. I told her what Kevin did to your window. She didn't seem to care."

"He's such an asshole."

"I hope you'll let me pay for the damages."

"Why would I do that?"

"I doubt any of this would have happened if I weren't around. Kevin attacked you to get back at me. He wouldn't come after an old man, but you're fair game."

"I see."

"After I left this morning—and thanks again for the breakfast—I went to Ingrid's and Kevin was there. He and I got into one helluva shouting match, which only stopped when Ingrid threw a plate at my head. I think she was aiming for him. At least I hope so."

"Not sure if you've noticed, but Kevin is getting deep into drugs. His behavior at the job site has become very erratic."

Bobby shifted uncomfortably in his seat. "Hmm, that's what I was afraid of. Anyway, Kevin is convinced I'm stealing from his mother when in fact he's been stealing from her. I confronted him about it. She always hides some cash in a cookie jar in the kitchen, something she told me her grandmother did because *you never know when the world will be ending.* I had noticed the cash was missing on more than one occasion, so when she hid $100 there this week, I moved it into a different canister. I'm pretty sure Kevin was looking for it when he came up this morning."

"Well, we know he's a crook."

"He was screaming at his mother to get rid of me once and for all. That he was sending her to a memory care facility he's found on the mainland. She got upset, I got upset, and Kevin stormed off, apparently to come here and throw a rock through your window."

"Listen Dad, stay here with me tonight."

"Maybe I should. Poor Ingrid."

"Is she really that bad now?"

"It's complicated."

"What isn't?"

"It's just with her mind the way it is, she's becoming a different person. I've seen it before in others. I guess we're just a bunch of chemicals and as those brain chemicals are altered, our personalities change. She's not the Ingrid I knew back in January."

"It's good of you to look after her the way you have."

"I love her, Jon. She's the true love of my life. I only wish we had met sooner. Despite her dementia, we've had a lot of laughs and good times this year."

"My friend Sarah was just telling me that God doesn't send us anything we can't handle."

"I hope I can handle this. If you don't mind, I'm very tired and would like to take a nap."

"Of course. I need to go into town to get some food for tonight. I'll be back shortly and we can have dinner."

"Sounds good. Thanks, son."

It was thickafog as I drove down the hill for the market. I narrowly avoided hitting a deer that jumped out in front of my pickup as I turned to head down the hill for town. I was only able to see a few car lengths ahead of me, the fog becoming thicker as I got closer to the working waterfront. I parked on the street and walked into the market, where I ran into Jake Martin, an old friend from high school who had moved off island years ago.

300

"Hey, bud," he approached.

"Jake, what are you doing out here? Good to see you, man."

"You, too, Jon. My daughter is getting married on Saturday."

"Where are you living these years?"

"Point Judith, Rhode Island."

"What took you there?"

"My wife grew up there. And the fishing's good and there's less fog than out here. Can you believe how thick it is right now?"

"It's been like this for much of the summer. Where's your daughter getting married?"

"Out at Joe Hamilton's place. Joe's letting us use the barn. We've got the Lion's Club doing a lobster bake for us. I hope it clears up by Saturday. Tawny has a lot of friends coming up for the wedding. Kind of a pain in the ass getting out here so I'm sure they'd rather not be stuck in the rain and fog."

"Tawny would be your daughter?"

"Yes."

"Do you have any other kids?"

"Just the one. Tell you what, Jon. Let's go to the bar and we can catch up."

"Sure, but just for a bit as I've got my father up at the house and need to get back and make supper. Let me grab a few things here and take them home to put in the fridge, then I'll meet you at the bar for a drink."

"See you there, Jon."

The bar was packed when I arrived. I found Jake and we stood behind a group of regulars seated at the bar who were watching a Red Sox game. There were a lot of young people I didn't recognize, probably here for the wedding. Jake was talking to a young man when I walked in, possibly the groom. He had bought me a Budweiser, and we stood there catching up until two guys at the far end of the bar got up to leave. We pressed through the crowd to get their seats before anyone else could. I looked at the clock on the wall and saw it was six. I also saw my name on the Walkout Board, which was a list of those who owed the bar for unpaid tabs. I saw Betty Jean pouring drinks and we made eye contact..

"Betty Jean, I need to settle my tab. Here's my card."

She came over and took it. "Was wonderin' when you were gunna settle up. Not like you to stiff me, Jon."

"I'm sorry, just a lot going on these days."

"I heard you was goin' to adopt that boy you've been mentoring."

"You did?"

"Yeah, people are sayin' what a kind soul you are."

"Well, that's not true, Betty Jean. I'm not sure what's going to happen with Charlie. My father is enough to worry about."

She was bent over, working the ice bin. "I like Bobby a lot. He can take a good ribbin' as well as anyone. I won't lie to you, though. I was worried when I first met him that he might be after Ingrid's money. But now that I've seen how he's taking care of her, I realize I was wrong."

"Understood."

"Let me get you fellas a round on the house," she poured us each a large glass of Seagrams and 7.

"Thanks, Betty Jean."

"Are these youngsters here for your daughter's wedding?" I turned back to Jake.

"Yup. She's got friends coming in from all around the country."

"How many at the wedding in total?"

"We're figuring around a hundred and fifty."

"Shit, that must be setting you back a bit."

"She's my one and only, Jon. Can't tell you how happy seeing her happy like this makes me. Took a while for her to meet a good guy. Do you have any kids?"

"Nope. Never married."

"Full-time bachelor, huh?"

"Not by design. Things just haven't worked out for me."

"Sorry about that, bub."

Kevin walked into the bar with Shane. They pushed their way through the mass of flesh and parked themselves right behind us.

"What's doing, Jon," Shane looked to be in a bad way. His sallow complexion was now complemented by a series of cuts on his cheeks, possibly boils. He was wasting away with that gaunt look of drug addicts. I hadn't seen him at the job site in three weeks and, from what I could tell, he was either holed up in his RV or on the mainland. For the most part, I could supervise the work crew without him, but needed Shane to order materials for the job, as he had the purchasing authorization. We were now behind schedule because he had not ordered the lumber for the interior trim work, which I was looking forward to getting started.

"Hey, Shane," I said.

"Look at all these young fillies," Shane was surveying the scene. His mouth was hanging open revealing several missing teeth, just black holes set against his yellow skin.

I stood up to confront Kevin. "What the fuck do you think you're doing throwing a rock through my window? Asshole."

"Fuck you, Jon. And fuck your father."

Jake stood up between us. "Whoa, chill out guys."

"You're a piece of shit, Kevin. You're going to pay for a new window or I'm reporting you to Tetreault."

"You can't prove it was me."

"Don't be so sure about that. I've got an eyewitness who saw you do it."

"Doubt that."

I sat down and turned to Shane. "Did you get the trim boards ordered?"

"Shit, I forgot."

"What the fuck is wrong with you, Shane? We stand to make good bonus money if we get the job done on time."

"Chill out, Jon. I'll get it done." Shane was twitching and scratching his left arm. He was wearing a black hoodie and reeked of cigarettes.

A young woman approached. "Hey, Dad."

"Hi, Tawny," Jake turned to his daughter.

"Could you set up a tab for me and my friends?"

"Sure thing, honey. Betty Jean, start a tab for the kids' drinks, will you?"

She nodded and walked to the cash register.

Kevin and Shane found seats at the other end of the bar while I caught up with Jake. Jake bought us each two, perhaps three, more drinks and before I knew it, I saw it was eight o'clock. The bar was as loud as it ever gets, bodies pressed together, youngsters squished together dancing to the jukebox. Every now and again a roar would roll through the bar as one of the youngsters downed a shot.

The front door to the bar opened and Dawn Philbrook pushed toward where Kevin and Shane were seated. She was active with many local causes, including a drug and alcohol rehabilitation program she had recently established at the Baptist church on the far end of the island. Kevin saw her approaching and turned to face her.

She pressed her face close to his, screwing her head up

like a corkscrew, jabbing him in the chest with her forefinger. Dawn was a big woman who still held the high school girls' softball record for most home runs in a season. "Don't you *evah, evah,* fuckin' wave at me again!"

She turned and left, just like that.

"What was that all about?" Jake asked.

"I think Kevin got her son Adam hooked on drugs back when they were in high school."

"Shit."

"And, as you may recall, there is no slight worse on this island than not being allowed to wave as you drive by someone."

He laughed. The entire bar was laughing at the bizarre scene they had just witnessed.

I don't remember much of anything after Dawn left the bar. I know Walt showed up after Betty Jean phoned him. And now that my head is clear, I know that Freddy showed up, too. Trying to help. What I've been told is that I did some Jello shots with the youngsters at the bar. At around ten o'clock I smashed a chair over Kevin's head and a bar brawl broke out. Walt reached into my sweatshirt pocket and pulled out the keys. He and Freddy put their arms around me and guided me to the door. I knocked over a chair on my way out.

Chapter Twenty-Six
September 2023

In the weeks following my father's death, I found some solace in the work up at Douglas Point. Losing a parent, no matter how complicated that relationship might have been, is certainly one of the most numbing experiences of life. One moment a mother, a father, is in your life, still walking the planet, among the living, and then in an unexpected missed heartbeat, they are gone. Just like that. Gone. The emptiness that ensues is unlike any I have felt.

Every nail I hammered up at Douglas Point felt like a nail in the coffin of my confused relationship with Bobby, the closing of a lid on any possibilities of building upon the progress we had made in recent months. The hardness of my hammer's sound reverberating throughout that huge empty space, a space not yet a home, just a hollowed-out shell. Tears fogged my vision as I methodically pounded one nail after another, as if securing some elusive logic into place, a solidity and reliability not to be found outside these newly constructed walls.

Walls. Walls between my father and me. Walls between Linda and me. Walls between Charlie and me. There would be no way to get to the other side of the wall between my father and me now that he was dead. But might I be able to break through to the other side of the wall between Linda and me?

And it was not just that I missed my father, which was a truth I had not anticipated, but that I was becoming increasingly concerned that Tetreault and Jackman would show up any day and haul my ass off to jail. Kevin had his fabricated alibi via his mother's calendar entry for the night of the murder. Shane was missing and although I did what I could to push him forward as the prime suspect, my fingerprints were on that damn stone. I was feeling time was running out for me. Tetreault had swung by the job site three days ago and there was something about the way he was questioning me, looking at me, hanging around longer than necessary, that made me think they were getting close to bringing me in. Had they found new evidence? Would I be able to make bail? I wasn't sure how much that might come to. I had managed to squirrel away five grand over the summer, but would that be enough? I felt those walls closing in on me, too.

And Linda. Lovely kindhearted Linda. Linda—who had been abandoned by her husband and deserved so much better— was applying pressure for me to take custody of Charlie, to clean up my act, to go into rehab. The thought of going into rehab again, knowing from my previous times just how difficult it is, was more than I could contemplate. I wanted to take care of Linda. I wanted to help Charlie, but first needed to help myself, and that healing was not going well. Further complicating the situation was my concern that the last thing Charlie needed was for me to take him under my wing and then have me sent away to jail. Enduring that with his mother seemed like cruelty enough.

My cell phone rang on a chilly mid-September day as I was working on the interior trim. The day was heavy with the feel of sudden seasonal decline, the grayness settling upon us with swift and determined force. There was no doubt we were now circling back down, summer over—and not even a good weather summer at that. The easy days of shorts and sneakers soon to be replaced by jeans and boots.

"Hey, Linda. What's up?"

"Can you break away to come to the school? Charlie got into a fight."

"Shit, did anyone get hurt?"

"No, it was just more of his acting-out behavior. Something is going on with him that I can't get a handle on. Anyway, he and Sam Warren got into a shoving match during history class."

"I thought he and Sam were friends?"

"They are. But you know how these things go. Sometimes it's those nearest us we fight with the most."

"Hmm, are you trying to tell me something?"

"Maybe. Have you noticed a change in Charlie lately?"

"I suppose so. But I assume he's just bummed about splitting up with Alison."

"I thought that too, but I'm not so sure anymore. He is pushing everyone away at school. He's become an odd combination of combative and numb. I'm afraid he might need therapy before he does something extreme to himself."

"Seriously? You think it's that bad?"

"I do. I see it a lot with kids like him, the ones who have been cast off so many times they naturally feel something is wrong with them, that they deserve the abandonment."

"Shit. I hadn't thought of that."

"The other concern I have is the state is asking me if he has a stable home out here what with Dale leaving. I've been delaying that the best I can. But I had a call from them this morning so can't delay any longer."

"What a mess."

"I know. Anyway, I need you to come get him."

"Sure. Be there in twenty."

The old school smelled like floor wax and cafeteria food as I walked down the long hallway toward Linda's office. I recalled the many times I had been sent to that same office for detention back in the day. I couldn't remember exactly what I did to get into trouble, but think it was mostly frustration with some of my new schoolmates who were not thrilled to have me there, and my own confusion at being resettled to this strange new island, living with my mother and stepfather.

"Hey, Linda," I leaned in to kiss her, but seeing the principal seated behind his desk, pulled away, maintaining professional decorum.

"Thanks for coming, Jon," Principal Holmgren gestured to a seat next to Linda. Charlie was seated in the corner, looking contrite, tears streaming from his eyes. His right eye was black and blue. I took a seat and exhaled deeply, thinking about how complicated my life had become. Charlie raised his head just enough to make eye contact with me, his expression making me think of a sad hippo, those dark brown eyes weighted down by life's many burdens. I smiled at him and immediately saw this was not what Linda or the principal were looking for. I was taking the wrong side in this matter, so did my best to put on a stern expression.

The principal spoke. "Charlie got into a fist fight in history class this morning. My first inclination is to suspend him for a week, but Linda has persuaded me to just suspend him from soccer practice and games for two weeks. I'm not sure the parents of the student he hit will be okay with that, but I'll do what I can."

I got the feeling I was supposed to thank him for this great kindness. His High Principal Excellency. God, how I had hated the power tripping of certain teachers and school administrators back in my day. I had felt completely powerless. The adults were setting the rules, meting out the punishments. At times, being inside the school building on a sunny early-June day had me daydreaming about running away. Far away. Someplace no one would ever find me.

I turned back to the principal, a man looking to be in his late-thirties, a youngster handed great power as he ascended the

311

administrative ladder within the public school system, teeming with confidence.

I said: "Thank you for your understanding. I'm sure Charlie will miss soccer very much." In fact, I knew he had been thinking of quitting, so this punishment would not mean much to him. He had not wanted to play in the first place, assuming he was about to leave the island so should not commit. In fact, Charlie had seemed eager to want to leave the island behind, a change in behavior that surprised me.

"He can't stay in school for the rest of the day, Jon," Linda said. "Could you take him with you to the job site?"

"Sure."

Charlie sat there looking very uncomfortable. "You don't need to take me to the job site. I should go help Dale pack."

"No, that's okay, Charlie. I could use your help with the flooring that was just delivered."

Linda stood up and walked over to Charlie, who was sitting with head bowed, unable to make eye contact with anyone in the room. "Promise me this will not happen again, Charlie."

"Sure. Whatever," he mumbled.

"C'mon, Charlie. Let's get outta here," I nudged him towards the door and down the long hallway into the fresh air.

On the ride to the job site, I tried to draw Charlie out. He sat facing away, gazing out the window.

"You going to be okay?"

He was sniffling and wiping his eyes with his shirt sleeve. "Yeah."

"What happened?"

"Sam was teasing me about being homeless. How I would soon be over in Warrenboro and how he'd be glad to see me go. I told him I'd be glad to get away from this stupid island. He got pissed at me for making fun of the island and the people here."

"That jerk. He's just jealous of how good an athlete you are."

"Yeah. Sure. Whatever."

"Anyone can see it. The way he tripped you on the soccer field last week. Your own teammate. What a little shit."

Charlie let out a prolonged sigh. "I wish I could drop out of school and just work. Other than the computer science class, I don't understand why I need to learn any of this stuff. Who cares about all the stupid wars people fight over and over again, anyway? All of history class is just one fucked-up war after another. Why don't we remember the good things people do?"

I smiled. "I hear you, bud. But you need to complete high school, at a minimum."

We rode in silence, the sunlight lighting the side of Charlie's face, which looked to be split right down the middle as I gazed at him.

"Do you miss your father?" Charlie asked out of the blue.

"Of course. Very much."

"I'm sorry about that."

"Thanks, Charlie. It's been such a strange year with him living with me and then moving in with Ingrid, and then being murdered. I feel like I missed some opportunities to better express myself to him."

"Like how?"

"I guess I came to realize this year that life is far more complicated beneath the surface than we know. People post all these happy pictures of themselves on social media, pretending all is good when in fact they're dying inside."

"Tell me about it. Some are actually dying on the outside, too."

"One thing's for certain. We're all flawed. We all make mistakes."

He refused to make eye contact with me as he gazed out the side window. I could see his reflection in the window flying by, superimposed against the backdrop of a long stretch of birch trees. I slowed down a bit.

"And it's important to forgive others for their mistakes. I've never been good at forgiveness, but I'm working on it. I want to be able to forgive my father."

Charlie sat quietly watching the trees whiz by as we drove along the winding roads to the northern side of the island. I saw an occasional tear roll down his left cheek.

"It's okay, Charlie. Everyone gets in trouble at school. I'm just relieved you didn't get suspended."

"Maybe I deserve to be suspended?"

"Why do you say that?"

"I dunno. I did something bad and there should be consequences, right? How come some people get away with stuff while others don't?"

"I think the principal, being aware of your tough situation, was just showing you some deserved leniency."

"Right. Deserved."

"Try and cheer up, bud."

"I hate most of the kids at school and don't want to live here anymore." Where this was coming from, I had no idea, but in weakness I saw this as an opportunity to be free from the pressure to take him in with me. Charlie seemed to be offering me a way out.

"Maybe you'll be happier over there?" I couldn't believe how hollow those words sounded as soon as they escaped my lips. I wanted Charlie to find happiness. I just wasn't prepared to provide it myself.

At the job site, I led Charlie over to a pile of wide pine flooring that had been special ordered from central Maine, one of the few remaining places on the planet where one can find first-rate wide pine boards. Much of this lumber is exported to Asia, where it is highly prized. I checked the boards, noting how few knots there were.

"Charlie, help me bring these floor planks inside the house. Just grab a few and pass them to me through this unfinished doorway."

He passed me three long boards and then several others until I asked him to come inside and help me lay them out to measure for the cuts I would need to make. We set the ten-foot-long boards side by side in the living room, Charlie standing off to the side gazing out though the doorway.

"Are these going to be used upstairs, too?" he turned to face me.

"Yes, throughout most of the house."

"Cool. Imagine being so rich that you can live in a place like this?"

"I know. It would be nice. I'm sure Row will have a house opening party once we're done. That should be fun, right?"

"I don't think I'll be here then."

"Well, you can always come over for the night."

"I don't ever want to come here again. I hate this fuckin' place!"

This sudden outburst caught me off guard. Charlie's face was flushed with a mixture of anger and resentment.

"You don't mean that. You're just getting over Alison. I know how that can hurt."

"Nah. It's not her. It's just I'm such a pain in the ass to everyone. I feel like such a loser."

I didn't know how to respond to this. "Pass me my hammer, will you?"

Charlie slid my hammer over to where I was kneeling on the floor boards. I drove two nails into the end of one of the boards

316

to fix it in place so I could set up more to get a sense of how many would be needed and where the gaps would best be situated.

"Why do you use a hammer and not a nail gun?" Charlie asked.

"I use a nail gun on the framing and other work that isn't visible, but not for these wide pine boards. The nails must be set very carefully."

"Oh."

"Plus, I prefer using a hammer most of the time. It feels more like fine craftsmanship than simply firing off a bunch of nails like I'm holding some automatic weapon."

We worked in silence for ten minutes and then I stood up and walked to the far end of the room to get a sense of how the flooring would look once all nailed into place. "Looks great, right Charlie?"

"Sure. Whatevah. You know, I really should be headin' back to Dale's to help him pack. I need to pack up my stuff, too."

"Okay, I think I'm at a good place to stop for the day."

Chapter Twenty-Seven
September 2023

I met Linda at the bar for dinner that evening. Charlie was helping Dale pack up before that kind man headed down to New Jersey. Dale had rented a U-Haul van, now parked out front of his mother's house, and as I passed by on my way to the bar, it served as a sad reminder of all of life's comings and goings. Our time here seems so insignificant across the grand sweep, as though we're just stones on some random beach, rolling back and forth with the tides until we're sand beneath some stranger's feet.

Linda had already arrived and was seated at the bar next to Freddy Ames, who I hadn't seen since the night he drove me back from this same bar. Linda had saved a seat next to her.

"Hi Jon," Freddy said.

"Hey, bub. How've you been?" I pulled up a stool at the bar.

"Not too bad."

"You look good. Have you lost weight?"

"I have. Stopped drinkin'."

"Well, good for you. I'm happy for you."

"Thanks, Jon."

Betty Jean walked over and tossed menus at us. I sensed she was pissed at me for the damage I had caused the last time I

318

was here, not that I could remember much of it. "Want a Coke, Jon?" she asked with a knowing look.

I turned to Linda who shot me one of those signature looks of hers, the one saying *don't be an idiot.* "Sure, a Coke sounds good."

I could tell Freddy was uncomfortable being in the bar, and probably being with me, undoubtedly assuming I was a lost cause. Word had spread around town that I was not taking Charlie in to live with me, and many of the leading citizens of the island were ignoring me these days. I was being quietly expelled from the community, what with no more car waving and no more friendly glances in the market. I had noticed some of the #JusticeforJon signs around town had been removed. So, at least that was something good that came from my new pariah status.

"I'll leave you two alone," Freddy got up to go. "Nice catching up with you, Linda. I meant what I said. Don't hesitate to contact me."

I sensed I had interrupted something.

"See you, Jon."

"Take care, Freddy," she said.

After he was beyond earshot, I asked Linda: "What were you two talking about?"

"Believe it or not, not you."

"What a relief."

"Molly needs braces and Freddy's brother is a dentist on the mainland. He offered to connect me."

"Ah, that's nice of him."

"Yes, he's the kindest man."

I was hungry after missing lunch due to the Charlie school incident, and ordered the fried shrimp platter. Linda ordered a cheeseburger and fries. We sat quietly together, the bar mostly empty as it was only five o'clock. Linda had come straight from school and looked frazzled.

"Tough day?" I asked.

"The school is out of control right now."

"What's going on, other than with Charlie?"

"We've got a couple of new teachers who are struggling to fit in out here."

"Where from?"

"One from Idaho, one from New Hampshire."

"Wow. Idaho? Really?"

"Yup. A young woman in her first teaching job out of college. She's a bit green."

"I'm sure that's tough."

"And there are a couple of parents unhappy with her."

"Ah, the parents. Either too involved or not involved at all."

"Exactly."

"How'd you get into the guidance counselor racket, anyway?"

She smiled. "It's not a racket. I like helping the students. The parents can be a bit much at times, though."

"I won't kid you, being at the school today sent me back to those old days. I hated it. All the noise and chaos. I used to stare at the big clock on the wall and wonder why it was stuck."

She sighed. "It's not a good sign I'm already this stressed out and the school year is still so young."

"You sure you don't want a glass of wine or a beer?"

"I won't kid you. I *would* like one."

"Well, don't deny yourself on account of me. I can stick with my soda, but you don't need to be deprived."

"No, it's okay, Jon. I want to set a good example for you. Honestly, drinking just makes me feel worse most of the time so it's no big deal."

Betty Jean brought our meals over from the back kitchen and lingered. I felt like she was watching me eat, just hovering there, refusing to move on.

"Shit, Betty Jean. I'm trying to eat, here."

"I'm disappointed in you, Jon. Thought I knew you."

"That could well be true, but would you mind just backing up a little bit? I feel like you're about to spit on my food."

"What makes you think I haven't already?" That devilish smile of hers crept across her face as she stood there with hands on hips.

"You wouldn't. Right?"

She ignored me. "How've you been, Linda?"

"Hangin' in."

"Ain't we all. How's this drunk fool been treatin' you?"

"Betty Jean! Shit, cut me some slack already, will ya? I told you, I'm sorry I damaged the bar and will fix anything needing to be fixed for no charge."

Linda smiled, enjoying her burger and amused to see someone else take me on.

Betty Jean was locked and loaded. "So, tell me Jon. You just gunna let that poor boy go off to some random foster home?"

"Why the hell can't everyone just leave me alone!"

"Whoa, calm down there big fella," Betty Jean stood with arms folded across her chest.

"Let me ask you something, Betty Jean. Why don't *you* take the boy in? How about Walt or Freddy or Donna or—"

Betty Jean knew enough to head away at that point. I felt anger rising in my belly, compounded by my bewilderment at the loss of my father. Everything seemed to be completely out of control. The police were closing in. Linda was on my case nonstop about Charlie, whose recent behavior was puzzling, and the Douglas Point project was all-consuming with the bonus deadline now just a few months off. I really wanted a drink at that moment, and Linda sensed this, so backed down.

We sat in silence eating until she said: "I don't want to fight with you, Jon."

"Good, I don't want to fight with you either."

"It's just I thought I knew you. I thought you were a kindhearted man. The fact that you're refusing to take Charlie in, if only until he can be placed in a good home, is just beyond me."

"Haven't you noticed how he actually doesn't want to live with me?"

"I have, but I think that's due to his feelings of self-loathing brought about by all the rejection he's faced. It's not uncommon for teenagers to lash out and make rash decisions. Their brains are not yet fully formed. I would not expect a child of his age to know what's in his best interests."

"But what's going on with him? He was acting so strange at the job site today. Refused to look me in the eye."

"I've been trying to draw him out at school, but he's locked up and refusing to talk to me. At first, I assumed it was heartbreak over Alison and his concern about where he'd be living next, but now I'm not sure it's that simple."

"He actually came out and told me he's looking forward to living on the mainland. He hates it here."

"Well, he doesn't mean that. Going into foster care will truly suck."

"But it's like even that doesn't bother him. He just seems to want to get away and close out this chapter in his life."

"I know. It's puzzling. Dealing with these teenagers every day is exhausting. I still think you need to step up and do the right thing and take him in with you. That's undoubtedly want he wants but he's just lashing out due to hormonal changes. Can't you do that for him? For me?"

"Look, I'm sad. I'm sad about my father. I'm sad about Ingrid slipping away over at Eldercare. I'm sad about Charlie. I'm sad that I crave drinking so much that it's always at the forefront of my mind. I'm sad that I live on a fuckin' island where the only place to eat out is a goddamned bar!"

"Language, Jon. Maybe it was a mistake meeting here," Linda said.

"I'm sorry. I can handle it."

"Have you given further thought to going into rehab?" she asked.

"C'mon, Linda. Can't we just eat in peace and quiet? I'm so tired of everyone being on my case. People with all their problems are just too much to take. You would think on a tiny island like this there wouldn't be so much drama."

"We're on your case, as you say, because we care about you. Trust me when I tell you it would be a helluva lot easier on us all to not constantly have to be on your case."

She got my attention with that. Linda had become very important to me and I didn't want to lose her the way I had lost my last girlfriend. Buried somewhere within I knew she was good for me, that I was lucky to have her in my life. I could see she was upset, that her attempt to leave her stress at work behind was not going to happen with me in this foul mood.

"Let's start over," I suggested.

She managed a smile. "Hi there, Jon. Did you have a lovely day?"

"Why thank you, Linda. I did. So very kind of you to ask. And you?"

324

"I feel so fortunate to have this *amazing* job at the school, where every day I make a difference in a child's life. And the pay and the benefits. Ooh, the pay! So much better than Walmart."

"That does sound amazing. They're lucky to have you."

"You got that right. And how about your day, dear?"

"Terrific. A whole lot of hammerin'."

"That must feel good."

"It does. You're welcome to join me this weekend if you'd like to work out some of that stress from your delightful job launching our youth into their bright new futures."

"I just might do that, Jon."

Chapter Twenty-Eight
December 2023

I learned on the very last day of that year who killed my father. It is because of that story that I now have landed on happenstance as the main driver of life's events, with apologies to those of you who believe in a guiding, all-knowing, divine force. But possibly I've been too rash in coming to this conclusion because I must admit there was plenty of good that came from my father's death. I think about that every day. The good that comes from the bad. The yin and the yang. The two sides of every coin. How the way we perceive life's events has as much to do with us as the events themselves. One thing is for certain. Getting sober again has cleared my head and improved my life dramatically. It hasn't been easy—now just seventy-six days out from my last drink—but with each passing day I feel a gradual freedom from my addiction. But let's be honest. I have replaced one addiction with another. I traded in booze for love and if this love were to leave me, who knows what I might do? The fear of losing love has become my main motivating factor.

Linda and her kids moved in with me back in early-November, but not until we made our collective way through some troubled seas that September. The fog had become thicker inside my head than outside. Linda and I had been stuck in a hot and cold relationship, the cold due to my inability to stop drinking or deal with the Charlie Walsh situation. Dale had left for New Jersey in mid-September and Charlie had been placed in a foster home in Warrenboro. Linda was furious with me but I was preoccupied with defending myself against the likely charges in the death of Bobby, plus taking over as the lead on the Douglas Point project. And I reminded Linda over and over that Charlie had made it clear he didn't want to live with me or be on the island.

What I didn't know was that Linda had gone to the DHHS office in Augusta and brought Charlie back to the island under her care. This after his first week in the new foster home, which was run by a serial-case foster home woman, who did it for the money to fuel her meth addiction. Linda told me there were five teenagers living with her in filth inside a doublewide. How the woman managed to conceal this abuse from the state is beyond me, but I gather this is not all that uncommon.

Charlie and Connor shared a room in Linda's apartment and she drove them, along with Molly, to school every day. It's fair to say this was when Linda went completely cold on me. That hurt. I was a mess, drinking heavily, drowning my sorrows in my pitiful lonely life, with fewer and fewer friends coming to check on me. I was surprised how much I missed my father. We tend to miss the people and things in our lives more once they are unavailable to us. In hindsight, I wish I had spent more time with him in those final months he was on the island.

I was at home one evening in early October when Linda

and Charlie came to visit. I hadn't known Charlie was back on the island.

"Hey, Jon," Charlie greeted me, his head bowed.

I pulled myself up from the sofa where I had fallen asleep. "Hi, Charlie. What are you doing out here?"

"I've taken him in with us," Linda began picking up the empty beer cans on the rug.

"How's the project coming along?" Charlie asked.

"Good. I've been working with the electrician in getting the last light fixtures in place." I hesitated and then smiled. "Want to know something funny, Charlie?"

"Sure."

"I took your advice and asked Row if I could leave a woodworking signature there. You know, do something handcrafted along the lines of what we saw at Ingrid's."

"Sweet."

"He didn't want me having anything to do with a bar, so asked me to build a newel post staircase. I've got most of the posts made. Just need to put them in place."

"Maybe you could help Jon with that?" Linda suggested.

"Nah, I'm good."

Linda sat down next to me. "Jon, I'm worried about you. You look like shit."

"Geez, thanks."

"Your face is all puffy and you smell terrible. Have you showered lately?"

"Not sure."

"Is this really how you want to live? In a pigsty? All alone?"

"Maybe. Not sure."

"Let me help you."

"How?"

"You know how. You need to go dry out."

"Shit, I don't want to go back to rehab."

"It's your only hope. It's *our* only hope. I miss you. I need you. I love you. But not like this."

So, with her insistence, off to rehab I went.

Now, on the last day of the year, a year unlike any other in the memory of the islanders, what with the multiple murders and the death of the Island Queen, I reflect on how fortunate I am to have Linda in my life. I'm changed, but so is the island. The loss of Ingrid, in particular, has weighed heavily on these sacred grounds. One of the true greats gone. She and Old Weezy and others I barely knew, now gone. More connections to the island's past severed. The future for an old way of life threatened by the changing climate and the influx of people from away settling here year-round. I jokingly call them year-round jerks. In tribute to Kevin.

Linda, Charlie, Connor, and Molly now all live with me. Charlie had not been happy about this but Linda was legally in charge of him and insisted. After I returned from rehab, Linda was hinting not too subtly about all the space I had. Her lease was coming up for renewal and the rent kept going up. It seemed like the right thing to do and even though I'm still getting used to having so many people underfoot, I know being with others is my best bet to staying sober. My father had been right. Looking after other people would take my mind off myself, and I was finding it easier with each passing day, what with the love and support of Linda and the responsibilities of raising three children. Our plan was to have a low-key New Year's Eve, but as I've said before, plans are almost always overrun by happenstance, and this would be the perfect ending to an imperfect year.

It was a mild December 31st and we were at home enjoying pizza that Linda and I had made. Connor and Molly had adjusted well to living with us. Charlie, on the other hand, was still having a rough go of it at school. He was doing poorly in his classes and had been depressed and anxious for much of the fall. Linda was concerned he might be suicidal and asked me to keep a close eye on him. The main activity that seemed to cheer him up were the software programming classes after school, as part of a new program funded by Row Patel. There were three kids in the class, two girls and Charlie. His teacher told me Charlie was a natural. But he was still acting out at school and being disruptive in most of his classes.

"Help yourself to more pizza, Charlie," Linda stood by the stove, sipping a ginger ale.

"I'm good. Thanks."

"Connor, Molly . . . do you want more?"

"I do," Molly grabbed a slice of pepperoni.

Charlie had just returned from visiting Alison at her home in Vermont. He didn't seem to want to talk about it, but I got the sense the visit hadn't gone well. I had arranged the trip after speaking with Alison's mother, Sarah, who had phoned to say that Alison was missing Charlie. That Sarah didn't much like the boys Alison was hanging with at prep school. So, I bought him a bus ticket and he had been gone for three days after Christmas. He had been very eager to get away.

I went over to talk with him.

"Anything I can do to cheer you up? Want to rent a movie?"

"Nah, that's okay," he stared at his feet.

"There are some good new ones."

"I watched *The Holdovers* with Alison's mother."

"I've read good things about that. Did you like it?"

"Yeah, pretty much. It's set at a prep school a lot like where Alison goes. This teacher takes the rap for something one of his students did. Not sure that would happen in real life, though."

"Good to know."

"I'm going to my room to lie down," he said.

"C'mon, let's go outside and get some fresh air. Look at the stars."

"Nah, I'm not feelin' great."

331

"There's something I want to tell you. I've got some good news for you. Follow me."

It was cold outside but not as cold as it should be that time of year. The wet summer turned into a wet fall and there had been no snow at all out here, which was highly unusual. Charlie sat next to me, each of us in our fleece jackets and winter hats. I could see that Charlie had tears in his eyes.

"What is it, Charlie? Did something happen at Alison's?"

"She's back and forth with her prep school boyfriend. I thought she was goin' to dump him, but I guess not."

"I thought you told her you didn't want to be her boyfriend when she left to go back to school?"

"Yeah. But I didn't really mean it. It sucked seein' her and that asshole boyfriend of hers, me there as some sort of curiosity. I spent more time with her mother than I did with her."

"Sorry. I'm sure that was tough."

"You've been so good to me, Jon. Not sure why, but thanks anyway."

"You know why. I like being with you. Hang in there, bud. It's always tough over the holidays."

"I wonder if I'll ever see my mother again?"

His mother had been sentenced to five years and was serving her term now. "We can visit her."

"I'd like that. She's not a bad person. She's just a drug addict. I wish I could live with her."

"I've seen all those photos she posted of you on her

Facebook feed. Nothing but photos of you. I like the cute baby shots."

"She tried her best. Always promised the next time would be different. But then—"

"I can tell you from my many attempts at stopping drinking, that these addictions are incredibly difficult to kick. Booze is one thing, but the opioids are an entirely worse place in hell."

"Yeah. Whatevah."

"Promise me, Charlie, that you'll never start drinking or doing drugs."

"I've seen what they do to people. I would never want to be like that. I'm hopin' I can get a college scholarship to study computer science. Mr. Patel said I should consider going to college out in California. That's where the action is."

"I'm sure he's right. But, that's a long way from home."

"That's partly the point. To get as far away from all this shit as possible."

"I'm sorry you feel that way."

"I hate this weather. I hate the school. I hate Alison."

"There are plenty of other girls out there for you."

"You and Linda seem to be doin' well."

"We are. I'm lucky to have her in my life."

"She's nice, no doubt. She's been very kind to me. So has Mr. Patel. You, too."

"You've been good for me, Charlie. I don't recall a time

when I've felt happier."

"Really?"

"Yes."

"That's nice to know. So, what's this good news you dragged me out here all about?"

"While you were at Alison's, we got our bonus checks from Mr. Patel. I've got yours inside. $1,000."

"Damn, that's generous of him. Keep it and use it towards my food."

"Absolutely not. You earned it. Buy yourself something fun."

"Are you sure?"

"Yes."

We sat in silence for nearly five minutes and then Charlie came out of the blue with: "I feel badly you didn't get your father's life insurance money."

"It's okay. As long as the case remains unsolved, and I'm the only suspect, there's no way they're going to pay out."

"How much was it for?"

"$250,000."

"Shit."

"I know. A nice chunk of change."

Charlie got up and walked to the far end of the deck. He let out a heavy sigh. "There's something I need to tell you, Jon. Please don't be mad."

"Of course."

"On the night your father died, you may recall it was very foggy." Charlie's lower lip was trembling, his eyes welling with tears.

"Thickafog," I smiled.

Charlie took a few steps away from me so that his back was pressed tightly against the deck's far railing. He continued: "I was upset about the way Alison and I ended things. You know, the way I had hurt her. She was crying as the ferry pulled away, and I felt bad. I came over here around eight o'clock to talk to you, but you weren't home."

I shook my head from side to side. "Yup. Should have been but was off drinking at the bar."

"When I arrived, there was a woman I'd never seen before goin' through your desk drawers."

"What?"

"Yeah, she was kinda fancy lookin', wearing a dress and all. Told me she was Ingrid's daughter and had come to pick up some papers Ingrid had forgotten."

"That's bullshit. There are no papers here."

"Anyway, I got a bad vibe from her. She hurried off after I interrupted whatever she was doing."

I ran my left hand through my hair, puzzled by this news about Olivia.

He continued: "I sat and waited for a half hour after she left, but gave up on you coming home. I walked outside to head back to Dale's and could only see a few feet in front of me in the

335

darkness and fog. I heard a noise over on the ledge and thought it might be Kevin who had come back lookin' to hurt you. Or a deer goin' after our garden. I picked up the stone you had tossed aside when we were cleanin' up the glass from the busted window, and stepped quietly toward the ledge."

I sat up in my seat with a sinking feeling about where this was heading.

Charlie was struggling to complete the story, his body shaking, his voice barely audible. "As I approached the ledge, a deer startled me from behind, running up the dirt road. Scared the bejesus out of me. I assumed the sound I had heard on the ledge was another deer munchin' on our vegetables. You know how they travel in packs and have been after our garden all summer. So . . . I chucked the rock as hard as I could at the ledge. I heard a thud and then somethin' large go tumbling down the cliff, amazed that I had actually hit the deer. But then the next day I learned the truth. I'm sorry," he started crying uncontrollably. "I should have told you sooner but was afraid I'd be sent to jail, lose my job, that you would hate me."

I was momentarily unable to process what he was saying. "Wait . . . are you telling me it was *you* who killed my father?"

"I didn't mean to."

"Shit, Charlie. I thought for sure either Kevin or Shane killed my father. Or even Olivia after what you just told me. And now you're telling me it was just an accident? A freakin' accident? Fuck!" For some reason I began laughing, at first slowly and then uncontrollably. After this year, how perfect was this. Just another case of shit luck and being in the wrong place at the wrong time for my father. How must he have felt when the rock struck his head and he went tumbling down the cliff? Was he thinking about Ingrid, most likely? And Charlie, too, who was also in the wrong place at the wrong time, simply trying to be helpful. Because I was off drinking and not home when he came seeking solace. Shit. Figures.

Charlie started walking off into the night. "Anyway, I'll leave now. Please don't hate me, but I've been needin' to get this off my chest."

I tilted my head back and gazed up at the stars above. Was my father one of those stars? Sometimes I thought so. There were two stars close together, shining brightly, and I wondered if they might be Bobby and Ingrid, unburdened at last. I stood up and grabbed Charlie by his fleece before he could escape.

"I'm sorry, Jon. It was just a freak accident," he was still shaking violently.

"It's okay, Charlie. Try and collect yourself. I'm not going to abandon you. I don't hate you. But we need to go to the police and you need to tell them this story."

"I don't want to go to jail," he sobbed.

"You're not going to jail."

"How can you be sure?"

"Because I'm the only one who would press charges and I'm not about to do that. It was an accident. Not your fault you have that amazing pitching arm of yours."

Charlie managed a smile through his tears. "I know. I can't believe I actually hit him."

"Shit happens. And, as much as I hate Kevin and Shane, I think now that they're both dead we should clear their names in my father's death."

I could see his burden emptying away as his breath steamed into the night air. In that moment he looked like a young boy. Just a kid trying to survive. Like us all, but with the odds stacked high against him. I wanted to help him make his way. I wanted him to have the chance to reach his dreams. I wanted him to be loved. Charlie was now my most important project.

"Are you sure you're okay with this, Jon?" he wiped his sleeve across his dripping nose.

"Yes, I am. Pull yourself together and then let's go inside in a few minutes and make some root beer floats."

"Thanks."

"You know, Charlie, it took a lot of courage to come clean and I appreciate that. I can't begin to tell you what a relief it is to know the truth at long last. This entire situation has been bothering me ever since Shane and Kevin were murdered. I had begun to think there would never be any closure. This closure you have now offered is a gift in its own odd way."

Charlie walked to the edge of the railing gazing out at the few lights of the town burning across the way. The ferry was parked at the terminal ready for the morning run. The wind was stirring in the branches above, our first snowstorm forecast to arrive the next day. I was looking forward to taking the family cross-country skiing up island after the storm. Linda and I had bought us all skis, boots, and poles for our big Christmas presents.

Charlie turned to face me. "Does this mean you might get the insurance money?"

"Come to think of it, I don't see why not."

Chapter Twenty-Nine
Today and Every Day

The other night I was on Facebook and saw my father's final post still there, living on even though he is gone. How odd the way social media keeps dead people alive, a blessing and a curse. The tech world's glimpse of a future immortality? I suppose in some ways it already is immortality.

Bobby took many excellent photos while on the island. He made a Facebook album titled "Ingrid," in which he captured the many expressions of the Island Queen: her laughter, her wisdom, her intelligence, her sadness, her resigned fate, her anger, her confusion, her love. There is a photo of her I especially like. She is sitting on her porch with freshly cut peonies and roses arranged in a vase on the wicker end table next to her. Bobby must have surprised her, as her tongue is stuck out and her eyes are filled with playful mirth, like a little girl teasing a mischievous boy. This is how I will remember her.

First thing every morning I open Facebook to my father's page and read his last post: "It's a great day to be alive." I plan to have the beautiful sunrise photo he took framed with those words printed below.

About

Caleb Mason is the author of *The Isles of Shoals Remembered: A Legacy from America's First Artists and Musicians Colony* (1992), about which Allen Lacy of *The New York Times* wrote: "Provides a fascinating look at an important time period in the American arts." Caleb has authored four previous novels under the pen name Don Trowden: *Normal Family* (2012); *No One Ran to the Altar* (2016); *All the Lies We Live* (2017), and *Young Again* (2022), co-authored with Valerie McKee. Caleb welcomes reviews on Amazon and Goodreads, as well as constructive comments on his social media outlets, where he is mostly to be found under the pen name Don Trowden.

Acknowledgments

Writing a novel is a solitary undertaking where one vacillates in a maddening manner between confidence and doubt across an arduous and, at times, exhilarating journey. For *Thickafog,* I relied upon many early readers to help me make this as good as I could manage, all the time clinging to my core objectives of shining light on our shared humanity, despite our differing political beliefs and personal ideology. People are fundamentally good and despite the low times when our faith is challenged, it's important to not forget that we all struggle and need the love and encouragement of others.

One sees our shared humanity especially well in island communities, where the citizens look out for each other in ways that truly stand out compared to the mainland. I am most grateful for the caring citizens of Vinalhaven island, who inspired some of the content within this novel. In each of my novels, the characters are amalgamations of people I have observed, and there are so many outstanding people living year-round on Vinalhaven. I'm aware of several novels describing island life, but most of those works do not capture the off-season, which is where I spent the bulk of my focus when drafting this novel. This is a work of fiction and my imagination ran off into places I felt were entertaining, places I hope will stimulate thought. As has been noted by many novelists, I drove into the fog and managed to make the full journey by just looking directly in front of me. This is a good philosophy for our lives, too. I have been particularly struck living here by the many kindnesses of strangers, and aimed to capture that through the character of Dale Hildings, a kind man who takes in a boy facing long odds, even though they are not blood relatives.

Many of the locations described within the novel are actual places on Vinalhaven island, and it was those locations that set my novel in motion. I post on Facebook photographs taken from a ledge near my house, and it was after taking a photo there in August that the first line of this novel sprang to mind. Sometimes a novel starts with a title, other times with a germ of an idea, and in this case the place itself was the engine powering my imagination. Of possible interest is the fact that the children's book classic *Goodnight Moon* was written on Vinalhaven, which has a long history of inspiring artists and writers.

During a period of doubt, after I had completed my first draft, I received helpful encouragement and feedback from two authors I greatly admire: Joyce Kornblatt and Jane Smiley. Their encouragement gave me the confidence to believe in the novel, and they also offered suggestions that made their way into this final version. Many people, including you now reading this, have opinions on art, but there are not many with the experience and skill who can identify what is working well and what needs attention. Joyce and Jane made the time in their busy lives to help me make this better than it would have otherwise been relying solely on my questionable aptitude. (I am reminded of a high school report card where the wise-ass, but perceptive, teacher wrote: "Mr. Mason is skating by on his aptitude alone, very thin ice indeed.")

Others who read early drafts and provided feedback and knowledge are Paul Barclay de Tolly, Anna Blauveldt, Adam Chromy, Wayne Karlin, Holly Taylor Young, and Nico Walsh. I sincerely thank you all.

One final note. It's possible some readers were confused by my use of time and the shifting point-of-view within this novel. Many probably didn't notice but for those who did, I used a combination of first-person narrative told from Jon's perspective, and then employed an omniscient narrator who sees everything. I was careful to start a new chapter when the point-of-view shifted, or add extra lines to indicate a voice shift within a chapter. My reasons for doing this had to do with my goal of presenting Jon through his own voice as a possible unreliable narrator, and contrast his scenes with those of his father and Ingrid so the reader can form their own opinions of the father and son. To do this, I could not have Jon be our eyes and ears for every scene. The time-puzzle structure felt appropriate for a mystery, allowing me to jump back and forth while building out the plot threads and adding new suspects as we move along. I think of this structural choice as being like a thumb puzzle, where we move the pieces around until we have solved the puzzle.

I hope if you are reading this far into my novel you found the time getting here worthwhile. And I thank you very much for joining me on this journey. I hope to have another novel set on Archer Island coming out after this one.

Book Group Suggested Questions

1) Who are the sympathetic characters in the novel? Why do you think so?

2) Do you believe that Bobby and Ingrid were genuinely in love? If so, why?

3) What examples of good coming from bad can you recall within the novel?

4) What examples of bad coming from good can you recall within the novel?

5) How might Jon's life have turned out otherwise had he not mentored the abandoned boy Charlie Walsh?

6) Do you think Jon will stay sober? Why?

7) Even though *Thickafog* is a mystery, what parts of the novel did you find humorous, if any?

8) Do you think Charlie will lead a happy life?

9) What juxtapositions of year-round residents and summer residents did you find interesting?

10) What threats do you see to the old ways of life on Archer Island?

11) What, if anything, helps make Kevin, Ingrid's son, a somewhat sympathetic character?

12) What role does opioid addiction play in the novel?